Hazard of the Pursuit

A SPENCER & REID MYSTERY
BOOK SIX

CARA DEVLIN

First Cup Press

Any references to historical events, real people, or real places are used fictitiously. Names and characters are products of the author's imagination.

Edited by Jennifer Wargula

ISBN paperback: 979-8-9923057-5-3

Chapter One

December 1884

The cluster of traffic along James Street broke apart, giving Leonora Spencer an opening. She darted off the pavement and across the narrow lane, careful to avoid a few puddles of icy slush. The first flakes of winter snow had fallen two days ago, followed by a sleeting rain that had coated cobblestones and wood paving blocks around the city in an icy crust.

Once across the street, Leo returned to the raised pavement and readjusted the basket in the crook of her arm. The sign for Tate's Funeral Service was just ahead, and for once, she looked forward to stepping inside. While she detested the scent of lilies that so often permeated the air inside an undertaker's premises, where the flowers were arranged and ready for funeral processions and graveside burials, her numbed toes would appreciate the warmth of the building's interior. In truth, she'd been cold all morning while working at the Spring Street Morgue.

This time of year, the stone blocks that made up the old vestry-turned-morgue absorbed the frigid air and held onto it throughout the day. Despite needing to wear a jacket indoors, and sometimes gloves, Leo vastly preferred the cold to the summer months, when the day's heat increased the decay of corpses and filled the air with all the unsavory accompanying odors of decomposition. She never flinched at dead bodies, but in the winter, she could at least breathe more easily around them.

The bell above the door to Tate's chimed her entrance, and as Leo stepped inside, warm air wrapped around her. So did the rotting scent of floral sprays.

"Ah, Miss Spencer," greeted the funeral director, Mr. Otto Tate. In his early fifties, he possessed a rotund middle and a swirl of thin, copper hair neatly combed around his bald pate.

"Good afternoon, Mr. Tate." She closed the door behind her, shutting out the clatter of traffic along the street. "Is my uncle out back?"

Once the assistant coroner at the Spring Street Morgue, Leo's uncle, Claude Feldman, had now been working at Tate's for a handful of months. He went in a few days each week to manage the process of embalming, a skilled task that took a steel-like constitution—something Mr. Tate had confessed to Leo he did not possess. Thankfully, the tremors afflicting Claude's hands, which had ended his career performing postmortem examinations at the morgue, did not matter so much when preparing the dead for viewing at a funeral service.

"I do wish you would not join him, Miss Spencer. I am

more than happy for you to use my office to take your tea together," Mr. Tate offered, a pleading squint to his eyes, set behind a pair of wire-rimmed spectacles.

Leo brought her uncle his midday meal at least once a week, and so she'd become a familiar face to Mr. Tate. Even so, he had yet to accept that the sight of her uncle's work would not spoil her appetite.

"I thank you for your concern, Mr. Tate, but it truly does not disturb me," she replied, once again. Surely, he thought her hardiness strange. Most people did.

Leo could only imagine his reaction if he ever learned that at one time, she'd even been helping her uncle to make neat incisions and place closing sutures when his shaking hands could not manage those tasks. The new assistant coroner at the morgue, Connor Quinn, would never have allowed her to do such things, nor would she attempt them. Noting the coroner's findings, typing post-mortem reports and death certificates, attending to family members, and seeing to the official registry of personal items that arrived with each corpse were the duties she much preferred.

Leo took herself through the front parlor to a door leading to a collection of rooms in the back. Customers were not permitted here, where a sharp, overly sweet odor of formaldehyde took over. Leo preferred the smell of the embalming fluid to that of the sickly lilies, which had always reminded her of her family's funeral.

After seventeen years, the memory of that day was still vivid in her mind, though she didn't think it was just due to her photographic memory, which captured everything she saw as images, then stored them in the endless depths of her mind for later perusal. No, Leo believed any person who'd been made to walk behind the caskets bearing their parents and siblings to their graves would likely recall the memory clearly.

Leo didn't understand how or why her peculiar memory functioned the way it did, and for the most part, she wished it didn't. There were things she yearned to forget, painful memories that would never soften with the passage of time. And yet, there were benefits to having a mind that clung to details like ivy to brick.

Recently, she had been using it to assist Detective Inspector Jasper Reid in several of his inquiries. While the Criminal Investigation Department at Scotland Yard hadn't been keen on her assistance, helping Jasper had been natural for her. Most of the time, she'd been involved in his cases one way or another anyhow.

A smile touched her mouth as she thought about the serious, handsome detective inspector. Since his return from Liverpool, where he'd spent four months working to topple a large counterfeiting operation, she and Jasper had been courting. He was busier than ever at the Yard, with a sergeant and three constables at his command and, as usual, stacks of paperwork to be completed for the housebreakings, missing persons, and murders that kept him occupied. So occupied, in fact, that often Leo only saw him once or twice a week, in passing. It wasn't nearly enough.

She longed for more time with him. Thankfully, they were dining at Roy Lewis's home that evening. The newly promoted Detective Inspector Lewis had invited them last week, and Leo was looking forward not only to meeting Mrs. Lewis and their two sons, but also to spending more time with Jasper.

Leo rapped her knuckles against the door to the funeral service's embalming room.

"Enter," came her uncle's voice from within.

She pushed open the door and found him standing over a corpse lying on a metal table. Claude's pale blue eyes, set behind the thick glass of his spectacles, lit with pleasure when he saw her. "Ah! Is it already time for tea?" He checked the clock on a wall and chuckled to himself. "I suppose it is. This is my second one this morning, you know. Poor fellow. Tuberculosis. Give me a few moments."

Leo joined her uncle at the table. The dead man looked to be in his thirties and showed the usual emaciated chest and limbs, and pale skin of a person afflicted by consumption.

Postmortem examinations were invasive and messy, and they required a lot of physical effort on the part of the coroner. By comparison, the technique of embalming was quite simple. Claude would make incisions in the external carotid artery in the neck and in the femoral artery in the leg, and would insert tubing in each vessel. He'd then inject formalin, a solution of liquid formaldehyde, into the carotid, flushing the blood and gases remaining in the corpse's vasculature toward the answering incision in the leg. Tubing placed at that endpoint would drain into a hose, which ran along the floor and out an opening in the embalming room's window. A barrel sat outside, collecting the run-off. Where it went from there, Leo didn't care to think of. It wouldn't surprise her to learn the barrels were emptied into the sewer system or the Thames. The last part of the procedure was to fill the cavities of the body with formalin to slow decay and allow the family more time to plan a funeral and viewing.

"Mr. Tate offered his office again," Leo said, eliciting a smile from her uncle.

"The man can barely peek into this room," he laughed. "I'm sure he feels rather emasculated that you handle it better."

Originally, Otto Tate's younger brother had performed the embalming, but when the younger Tate moved to New York City the previous spring, the elder Tate had been desperate to find another embalmer so that he would not be forced to do it himself.

"There," Claude said after putting away his brass plunger, a contraption that looked much like a large needle and syringe. "I'll start on the body cavities after we eat. What have you brought for us today?"

He reached for the basket, but Leo turned away. "Not until you wash your hands—and well, mind you," she chided. "I'll meet you in the back."

There, a cold room, outfitted with a double-hung door that opened wide for corpse deliveries, held a table and a few chairs. It was where they would eat, and today, the hand pies Leo had purchased from a costermonger in Trafalgar Square were still lukewarm. There were, she acknowledged, corpses often stored in this room, but they were at least inside lidded wicker baskets used for collection and transport by Tate's deliverymen.

Entering the chilly room, she found two such deliverymen, Rob and Paul, seated at the table. They were bundled up and having tea but stood from their chairs in a gentlemanly manner when they saw her.

"Good afternoon, Miss Spencer," Rob said. He was a

brawny, middle-aged man, while his counterpart, Paul, was younger and wiry. Both men had their hats off, exposing sweaty temples and foreheads, and their cheeks were ruddy too.

Leo set the handbasket on the table as they retook their seats. "Good afternoon. Did you two have a heavy load today?" She peered at the wicker basket on the floor. It was coffin-shaped, but flexible, with rope handles at the head and foot as well as at the sides.

"We should've brought John with us," Rob answered, dabbing at his forehead with a kerchief. "Could've used the extra muscle."

The body within the wicker basket wasn't visible under the lid; however, Rob and Paul's fatigued states pointed to the occupant as being rather sizable.

"Just part of the job," Paul said with a lift of his shoulder. "At least we don't have to work on 'em, like your uncle does."

"Good man, that Claude," Rob added. Leo took a chair, cheered to hear the praise for her uncle. Rob was right; Claude Feldman was a good man. He did the work not many people would be able to do, and never once had Leo heard him complain.

He'd been trained as a surgeon, as most coroners were, and he'd practiced his trade in a hospital on the isle of Crete for many years. Then, he and his wife, Flora, had been summoned back to cold, foggy London to claim responsibility for the young niece they had never met—and had never planned for.

Childless, Claude and Flora were already quite aged when they took in Leo following the deaths of her parents and siblings. Instead of returning to Crete with their new ward in tow, Claude had accepted a position of assistant coroner at a morgue near Scotland Yard. Inspector Gregory Reid, with whom Leo had been staying for the previous two months, had arranged for the morgue position, and Leo had come to understand that it was the Inspector's way of keeping her close to him. If Leo had not had blood relations to claim her, Gregory Reid would have happily welcomed her to stay with him and his housekeeper, Mrs. Zhao, permanently.

For many years, part of Leo had wished she could have done just that. But now, she felt only guilt at having once thought that way. While Flora had never warmed toward her, Claude instantly had, and she adored him more and more with every passing year.

With a crimp of emotion in her chest as she brought out the hand pies, she thought of how soon everything was going to change.

Claude entered the delivery room then and, after greeting Rob and Paul, took a chair next to Leo. They tucked into their meal of steak and potato Cornish pasties and ate in companionable silence while the two deliverymen chatted between themselves. A minute or two passed, and a question she'd been putting off for a few days continued to poke at her.

Finally, Leo asked, "Have you given any more thought to Chesterton Hall?"

Claude paused as he was taking another bite of his hand pie, his attention pinned onto the greasy, brown paper wrapper where pastry flakes had landed. Leo knew he did not wish to speak about it. However, Chesterton Hall was not a topic they could avoid for much longer.

"I think Aunt Flora would be comfortable there," she said gently. "The house was lovely."

Her uncle took his time chewing. Flora's cognitive decline over the last year and a half had been troubling to watch. Claude cared for her as well as he could, and Jasper's beloved housekeeper, Mrs. Zhao, had also become a fixture in the Feldmans' Duke Street home on the days when Claude worked at Tate's. Only Leo could not manage to care for Flora, though not because she didn't wish to. Her aunt shrank away from her most of the time, and there were moments when she would shout at Leo, calling her a murderer, fearing her niece would kill her.

The accusations had been perplexing until she learned the reason behind them: With her ivory skin, dark sable hair, and serious, hazel eyes, Leo closely resembled her late father, Leonard Spencer, whom Flora blamed for the murders of her sister, Andromeda, and her young nephew and niece, Jacob and Agnes. Letters Leo had found from her aunt Flora to Andromeda had made it clear that Leonard was involved in something dangerous, putting both himself and his family at risk.

Now, of course, Leo knew that he'd been working for the Carters, the criminal family heading the East Rips gang, and that he had betrayed them in some way. His punishment had extended to his whole family. Whenever Flora looked at Leo, she was reminded of Leonard and ultimately, of her sister's senseless death.

Pairing this with the deterioration of her mind, Flora had become increasingly difficult to care for. In late November, Leo and Claude had left Flora with Mrs. Zhao for the day and taken the train west to Isleworth, a town not far outside London. They'd heard from one of

Claude's old friends about a rest home there called Chesterton Hall, which specialized in caring for those who suffered as Flora did. They'd been worried the place would be little better than an asylum for the mentally insane, but Leo and Claude had been pleasantly surprised.

"The home is everything I could want for her," Claude said after a moment, but then sighed wearily. "I suppose I find it difficult to admit the time has come."

Leo understood her uncle's reluctance and his emotional struggle over the decision. For so long, sending Flora to a rest home to be cared for had not been an option; Claude and Leo would never have been able to meet the expense. But now that Leo and Jasper were leasing the fine home they had quite unexpectedly inherited in October, Leo had a tidy sum in the bank.

It felt strange to have split the money with Jasper, especially when she hoped that they might share a home and future together someday soon. But as they'd only recently started courting and neither of them had broached the subject of marriage, Leo had accepted her portion of the settlement from Jasper's solicitor and insisted to Claude that she intended to spend part of it on Flora's care.

It was the least she could do to give them all some peace of mind.

"Perhaps we could bring Aunt Flora to Chesterton Hall after the holidays," Leo suggested. "She could see the house and grounds for herself."

Her uncle had started to murmur his agreement when suddenly, Paul pushed back his chair and jumped to his feet. The chair overturned, clattering to the floor.

Leo swiveled to peer at him in alarm. His coloring,

only a few minutes ago flushed pink from strenuous work, had gone bone white.

"Did…did you see that?" he asked, unblinking. His eyes, round as saucers, stared at the wicker basket that he and Rob had carried in shortly before.

Leo set down her hand pie and looked at the basket. It looked the same as it had before.

"See what?" Rob asked.

As Leo watched, she saw it too: The basket *moved*.

Rob jumped up, his cup of tea spilling onto the table.

"That!" Paul pointed to the basket as it shifted again, and a rustling noise came from within.

Leo stood, her intrigue sharpened, though she wasn't alarmed as the deliverymen seemed to be.

"Cor, it's a live one!" Rob exclaimed.

Sure enough, a soft moaning emanated from the basket.

Claude popped the last bite of his hand pie into his mouth and brushed his hands together as he rose from his chair. "It seems you were too early in removing the body," he said with professional calm.

Leo went quickly to the basket, which encouraged Paul and Rob to also come toward it. She crouched beside it and worked at the toggles holding the lid in place. Freeing them, she finally pushed back the lid of the basket.

Inside, lying on her back, was a woman—who was very much *not* dead. She stared up at Leo, her pale, sweaty brow creased in confusion. She blinked and, slurring her words, asked, "Who are you? And where the devil am I?"

Chapter Two

Amusement wasn't an emotion Jasper ought to have been experiencing as he approached the entrance to the undertaker's premises. In fact, it felt sinful to have to bite back the grin that had been plaguing him on the short walk there from Scotland Yard.

Constable Price had flagged Jasper in the Criminal Investigation Department just as the detective inspector was returning from an arrest in another case, a note held in his raised hand.

"It's from Miss Spencer, sir," Price had said. "Says she'd like a detective sent to Tate's Funeral Service."

The young constable's forehead had crinkled in what looked like skepticism as Jasper plucked the note from his hand. When he read Leo's brief message, he understood why.

A detective is needed at Tate's Funeral Service on James Street.
A woman's corpse arrived. I suspect poison.
P.S. She is not dead.

. . .

Jasper's foul mood—which had set in when the man whom he'd just arrested for housebreaking clocked him in the jaw while attempting to flee—dispersed after reading Leo's peculiar missive.

"A constable from E Division delivered it," Price added as Jasper folded the note. "Said Miss Spencer insisted Scotland Yard be notified."

The note was not addressed specifically to Jasper, but as he'd been the one to receive it, he decided to see what the situation was about. And he much preferred the chance to see Leo to processing the arrest of the housebreaker. So, he'd left that task to PC Price and started out for James Street.

Now, as he entered Tate's, he forced the absurd image of a dead body suddenly sitting upright and alive from his mind. It was nothing to laugh at, to be sure. Especially if Leo suspected poison was involved.

A man wearing a somber black suit came forward at the sound of the brass bell above the door. Jasper withdrew his warrant card from his pocket.

"Detective Inspector Reid from Scotland Yard," he said. "Miss Spencer summoned me."

The man dabbed his glistening forehead with a kerchief. "Yes, yes, she is in my office. It's been quite a shock, Inspector. This sort of thing hasn't happened here before, not once."

"You are...?" Jasper asked as the frazzled man led him toward a door at the back of the parlor.

"Otto Tate, at your service."

Jasper knew Leo's uncle had been working at Tate's,

and that Leo would often bring him his tea, but he'd never had a reason to come here himself. Following Mr. Tate into a back hall, past another room full of portraits of death photography set on easels, he decided he preferred the morgue to a funeral parlor. The elegance of the stuffy rooms, with their displays of glossy caskets and ostentatious funeral wreaths, mourning trinkets, photographs of the deceased made to look alive, and endless urns of flowers, was somehow more miserable to Jasper than the cold postmortem room at the Spring Street Morgue. Perhaps it was because the funeral industry shamelessly capitalized on people's grief, while the work of a coroner at a morgue was simply to seek answers for anguished loved ones.

In the back hall, Mr. Tate opened a door and stepped aside, allowing Jasper to enter. When he did, his attention immediately hooked on Leonora Spencer. She sat perched on the arm of a sofa, looking down over a woman of considerable size, who lay prostrate, a plaid blanket covering her. Claude Feldman sat in a chair next to the woman and was holding her wrist, as if measuring her pulse.

Leo's eyes, the color of honeyed amber, widened when she saw him enter the small office.

"Jasper," she said, her voice husky with surprise. She stood and came toward him in a rush. "I didn't know if my message would be delivered to you. I'd hoped, but I thought you might be out on some other business."

He stifled the potent urge to drag her to him and kiss her; had they been alone, he would have done it. Nearly two weeks had passed since the last time they'd shared a kiss. In the privacy of an enclosed carriage after leaving a restaurant, they'd burned through the five-minute ride to

Duke Street with a feverish kiss. Instead of sating him, it had only left him craving more.

Jasper cleared his throat and tried to focus on the trouble at hand. "I'd just returned to the Yard when Price received your note," he explained. "What has happened?"

Leo turned to view the woman reclining on the sofa. "This is Mrs. Augusta Lawlor. She arrived at Tate's two hours ago."

Taking a cursory assessment of Augusta Lawlor, Jasper placed her in her middle to late thirties. She wore a dark purple gown of fine quality, tailored well to fit her round figure, and she had the soft hands and skin of a woman of some wealth.

Claude released Mrs. Lawlor's wrist; it fell limply onto her stomach. She tried to sit up, but Leo's uncle persuaded her to be still.

"You will feel well soon, Mrs. Lawlor," he assured her. "But you must rest now."

"My husband..." Her voice was weak and winded. "Has someone... sent for...?"

Jasper frowned at her unfinished thought and her slow, slurred words. A clammy sheen of sweat dotted her brow, and her white skin lacked any hint of color. Her lips were just as pale. He'd seen the aftereffects of opium before, and Mrs. Lawlor appeared to be heavily dosed with it.

"Yes, Mrs. Lawlor, your husband has been sent for," Mr. Tate said. "I am sure he will be here momentarily."

Leo touched Jasper's arm and, eyeing the hallway, indicated they should exit the office. Once they stood just outside the door, she parted her lips to speak. But then, her attention landed on his jaw. She lifted her fingers and gently ran them over the bruise that had formed where the housebreaker's fist had caught him.

"You've been injured," she said, concern brightening her eyes.

He covered her hand with his. "It's nothing." Though it must have been purpling quickly if it was already showing through his scruffy, burnished blond beard. "I'm fine, really. Tell me what is happening here."

She lowered her hand and kept her voice low. "The casket bearers who collected Mrs. Lawlor earlier this morning returned to her home to summon her husband. However, they brought back news that he has quit the house. His staff do not know where he has gone."

"A tavern somewhere, I suspect," Jasper said, thinking of where a newly widowed man might go to drown his sorrows. But Leo shook her head.

"You don't understand," she said, even quieter now. "He has left entirely. Taken some of his belongings and disappeared."

Jasper cocked his head, alarm lifting the hair on the back of his neck. "The very day his wife is mistaken for dead?"

"And when she has so obviously been dosed with opium," Leo added. "Uncle Claude has been attending to her, and he agrees that she shows all the signs of an overdose. It would explain why she appeared dead; her heart rate would have been slow, her breathing shallow and slow too."

He supposed someone not trained in the medical profession could have easily made such a mistake in thinking the woman was deceased.

"It is possible she took too much laudanum," Jasper

suggested. The tincture of opium was a popular drug among people of all classes. Women were often prescribed it by their doctors when they suffered from nerves or any number of maladies. Or when they simply wanted to escape from a painful reality. It would not be so out of the ordinary for someone to have purposefully sipped too much of the stuff in an attempt to leave the earthly world entirely.

"But why did her husband flee so swiftly?" Leo asked.

Jasper grimaced. He knew what she was alluding to. "I agree that he needs to be found and questioned. If he gave her too much, the overdose might have been accidental. He could be panicking."

Leo nodded, though she pressed her lips into a tense line that hinted she did not believe that theory. Jasper wasn't entirely convinced, either.

"Does she need to be taken to hospital?" he asked.

Leo peered into Mr. Tate's office, where Claude was still at the woman's side. "No, my uncle says her heartbeat is strengthening already. We gave her some strong coffee, and she vomited, which Uncle Claude believes will help with her recovery."

"Then, once she is ready, I will take her home," Jasper said. He would speak to the woman's staff and see what he could determine about how Mrs. Lawlor came to be mistaken for dead.

"I'll come with you," Leo said and, before he could argue as he was about to do, added, "It would put Mrs. Lawlor at ease to have a woman with her."

He could not dispute that, especially as the woman was clearly of some refinement. Besides, Leo might be able to draw Mrs. Lawlor into conversation whereas he, as a detective inspector, might be viewed with hostility or reservation.

"Very well," he said. "I'll summon a carriage."

The Lawlors' home in the heart of Mayfair was every bit as posh as Jasper had anticipated. When the hired carriage drew up to the elegant home on Hill Street, just off Berkeley Square, the first thing he noted was the wide, black swath of fabric drawn across the front door. It marked the terraced, brick and limestone, four-level residence as a house in mourning. The deliverymen from Tate's Funeral Service had informed the staff that the lady of the house was not dead after all, but clearly, they had not taken the word of two laborers as fact.

Jasper descended from the carriage and helped Mrs. Lawlor to the pavement, her movements still sluggish and weak. Leo descended without his aid and immediately shored up the woman's opposite side. As they approached the front entrance, the door whipped open. An older man in what looked to be a butler's uniform stood upon the threshold, gawping with astonishment.

"We dared not believe the claims made by the two men who came earlier, madam," he apologized, stepping aside to allow Mrs. Lawlor, Jasper, and Leo entry. "But it is true. By the grace of God, you are alive. Come, come."

Hurriedly, he showed them into the front sitting room. Mrs. Lawlor became heavier as her strength started to leave her.

On the short drive to Hill Street, she'd made it evident that, even though she was still dazed and suffering, she would remain as proper as possible. She'd sat upright, her bearing rigid with quiet resolve, though beads of perspiration glistened on her temples. However, now it seemed she was finished with her show of strength.

By the time she had reclined fully on the salmon-pink velvet sofa, the house had erupted with commotion. A housekeeper swept inside the room, her shock just as pronounced as the butler's had been. A maid, her eyes teary and red, jumped in alarm as the housekeeper snapped orders for tea, for the doctor to be fetched at once, and to have Mrs. Lawlor's bedroom prepared immediately.

Jasper and Leo stood back while the servants tended to their mistress, all of their expressions shifting between overwhelming joy and guilt. They had sent Mrs. Lawlor off to a funeral parlor while she was still very much alive and were likely fearful of dismissal for making such a grievous error.

While waiting for things to calm down, Jasper searched the room for any framed portraits or photographs that might show Mr. Lawlor. The mantel above the hearth displayed a few pictures, but they were all of Augusta, at various ages, and a man and woman who appeared to be her parents. While the house itself wasn't much larger than Jasper's home on Charles Street off St. James's Square, it was more modernly decorated and fashionable.

His adoptive father, the late Gregory Reid, had not updated anything inside the house for over twenty years, and its dated furnishings, carpets, and wallpaper had all dulled with the neglect. Gregory hadn't had the money to do anything about it; he'd barely been able to keep the house at all on his humble wages from the Metropolitan Police Force. Recently, Jasper had learned how it had been possible: Every year, his father's former sister-in-law, Francine Stroud, had paid the property tax bill in full, anonymously. The amount was more than what he or Jasper earned in a year.

Much to Jasper's astonishment, he'd also learned Francine had been Gregory's lover after the tragic death of his wife, Emmaline. The pair had found companionship and solace in one another, though Gregory had taken the secret of their love affair to his grave. Only by chance had Jasper and Leo learned of it when Francine had included them in her will.

Now, the fine home on Craven Hill in London that he and Leo had been bequeathed was being leased, and the windfall from that was more than enough to pay the tax the Crown levied on property owners. He supposed he could afford to update some furnishings too, but a part of him wondered if it would be worth the bother. He wasn't yet sure he would stay on at Charles Street. It was his home, but it was also, inexplicably, sad. Haunted, in a way, first by Emmaline Reid and her two children, and now by Gregory, who had at long last gone to join them.

Jasper wasn't certain it was the right place for him to stay forever. He wasn't even sure if London was where he should remain, especially now that Andrew Carter, the youngest of his criminal East Rips cousins, had discovered that Jasper was a Carter himself. His cousin had promised he would keep the secret—so long as Jasper did his bidding. *Illegal* bidding, to be sure.

It had been two months since his return from Liverpool, and so far, Andrew had not approached him. But it was only a matter of time. Staying in London would mean having to navigate Andrew and his threats. It wasn't what Jasper wanted for his future. Or for his future with Leo.

He peered at her now, at her serious expression as she observed everyone in a dither around Mrs. Lawlor. Leo would be securing everything in her memory, he knew, and it could prove useful later, should this situation end up being more than a near-tragic accident. To be safe, before leaving Tate's, Jasper had sent word to the CID that a constable was needed at the Lawlors' residence.

When at last things quieted in the sitting room, Mrs. Lawlor asked, "Where is my husband? I demand an answer, Hastings."

Though the lady's voice was weary, there was no mistaking her authority. The butler stiffened and peered at the housekeeper. She, too, seemed uncertain what to say.

"The inspector and Miss Spencer," Mrs. Lawlor went on, pausing to take a shallow breath, "said he was not at home."

During the short ride to Hill Street, Leo had asked Mrs. Lawlor a few questions about her husband, but she had not been alert enough to answer. An effect of the opium, no doubt.

"I'm afraid, madam, that we are still searching for Mr. Lawlor," Hastings finally said. He was obviously nervous and skirting around the truth as finely as possible. Disoriented as she was, Mrs. Lawlor did not seem to notice.

"I must see him as soon as he returns," she said. "He must be in such a state, thinking I am dead. Oh, however did this happen?"

The butler met Jasper's eye, then coughed furtively

and stepped aside, to allow the housekeeper, Mrs. Vincent, to take over the care of their mistress. Jasper followed Hastings into the foyer, as did Leo. Once the door to the front sitting room closed, the butler exhaled a shaking breath.

Jasper, for the sake of officiality, showed Hastings his warrant card and introduced himself and Leo.

"Can you tell us what happened this morning? How did Mrs. Lawlor come to…pass?" Jasper asked, understanding the absurdity of the question.

"It was awful," the butler said, clasping his hands behind him and shaking his head. "Kitty—Mrs. Lawlor's maid—found her in bed this morning, not breathing. By the time I reached the bedroom, Mr. Lawlor and Mrs. Vincent were there too. It appeared as if she had passed away in her sleep."

"Mr. and Mrs. Lawlor have adjoining bedrooms?" Leo asked. Hastings nodded. It was the typical arrangement for the upper classes.

"Women her age do not usually pass away in their sleep," Jasper said. "Was a doctor summoned?"

"Yes," the butler said. "Mr. Gray. Henry Gray. He had been treating Mrs. Lawlor since she took ill."

"What sort of illness did she have?" Leo asked, beating Jasper to the question. Once, he would have minded. But now, he understood that she was simply never going to be the sort of woman who stood back and allowed others to ask the questions. Besides, Leo had a knack for asking the right ones.

"I couldn't say, not with authority. My mistress is very private and didn't wish her illness to be the subject of gossip," Hastings said but hesitated before adding, "However, from what I did hear, it was an internal malady. Stomach complaints. Quite serious and debilitating, I am told."

A maid with a tea tray shuttled toward them, and the butler paused to open the sitting room door for her.

"When did this illness begin?" Jasper asked once the door had closed again.

"About three months ago. Perhaps four. Shortly after the wedding."

Leo glanced up at Jasper, and he met her look of surprise. "They are newly married?" she asked. At the butler's nod, Leo continued, "The photographs on the sitting room's mantel show a younger Mrs. Lawlor. Is this her home? Did Mr. Lawlor join you here after the wedding?"

"That is correct." He quizzed Leo with a look, as if surprised by her observation. "This is the Hart family residence. Has been for three generations. My mistress grew up here and inherited the holdings after her mother passed. The staff here are devoted to Miss Hart. Or rather, *Mrs. Lawlor.*"

It was an unusual thing for a man to marry and move into his new wife's home. It made Jasper wonder what he had brought to the marriage, if anything.

"Her inheritance was substantial, I presume," Leo said.

"Quite." The raised brow that accompanied Hastings's answer seemed to impart that *substantial* might be putting it mildly.

"The deliverymen from Tate's indicated to us that Mr. Lawlor has quit the house entirely," Jasper said, getting back to what had happened that morning. "Is that true?"

The butler's countenance grew even more grim as he

took a long step farther away from the door. "I believe so, Inspector." He kept his voice low. "It seems the last any of the staff recall seeing him was after Mr. Gray pronounced Mrs. Lawlor deceased. Mr. Lawlor gave instructions for the body to be taken to Tate's, and then he shut himself into his bedchamber. We thought it best not to disturb him."

"What time was that?" Jasper asked.

"Around eight thirty this morning."

"And when did you notice he was gone?" Leo asked.

"Noon," Hastings answered. "He did not emerge from his room when the men from Tate's arrived. I presumed he could not bear to see her taken away. But then, as noon approached, I grew concerned. So, I knocked and called through the door. There was no answer. I looked inside and found the room in a state of disarray. Bureau drawers pulled open, articles of clothing strewn on the bed. Several of his belongings were missing from his wardrobe. His valet confirmed a small valise he used for traveling was also gone." The butler's gray brows tensed. "I can only think that he has lost his mind from grief."

Jasper wasn't convinced grief was the reason for Mr. Lawlor's disappearance, and by the dubious expression on Leo's face, she wasn't, either.

"Is there a safe on the premises?" Jasper asked.

Hastings blinked and flinched, as if struck off guard by the question. "I… Why, yes, of course, in the study."

Leo asked, "And has it been checked since Mr. Lawlor left?" After a moment of staring at her as though she'd spoken in a foreign language, the butler sidestepped them and started up the stairs with a punch in his pace.

Jasper and Leo followed, and when the three of them

entered the study, the suspicion that had been brewing in Jasper's gut was verified. The thick door of the floor safe standing behind the study desk was not shut properly. Hastings crouched to open it, and all that met them were some scattered papers on the shelves.

If money had been kept within the safe, it was now gone. The man had left in such a rush that he had not even bothered to close the safe door fully.

The butler stood back, his initial shock hardening over into understanding. He turned to Jasper and, with all the poise of a well-trained butler asked, "How may I be of service to you, Inspector?"

"You can tell me everything you know about Mr. Lawlor," he answered. "Let's start at the beginning."

Chapter Three

Augusta Lawlor's dining room was overpoweringly pink. It had never been a color Leo gravitated toward, and as she stood at the head of the table, waiting for the next maid to be shown in, the shades of salmon, mauve, and blushing rose began to creep in and prickle under her skin.

So far during her interviews with the staff, Leo had learned that at thirty-eight years of age, Miss Augusta Hart had long since given up any hope that she might one day marry, least of all for love. Augusta's grandfather had accrued a fortune in shipping earlier in the century, and her father had continued to grow the family business and legacy. When her father died several years ago, Augusta solely inherited. She sold the business—as an only child and a spinster, she did not expect to continue the family line—increasing her wealth to an even greater degree.

In her youth, and into her spinsterhood, Augusta received offers of marriage from unscrupulous gentlemen, but she had turned them all away. Her mother, Mrs.

Florence Hart, who had passed two years ago, had even gone to such lengths with one suspicious suitor as to have him investigated by a private inquiry agent. In the end, Augusta had refused the fortune hunter and resigned herself to remaining unmarried.

And so, she had redecorated the home where she'd grown up in her own feminine tastes. Varying shades of pink and rose everywhere.

When, six months ago, Augusta met Sebastian Lawlor at an art exhibit at the Royal Academy, the two struck up an easy friendship. It quickly developed into a romance, and to the staff's astonishment, their mistress accepted Sebastian's proposal of marriage just one month later. They married swiftly and spent the next month in Paris on a honeymoon trip. Kitty, the maid who traveled with the new Mrs. Lawlor, said her mistress started experiencing severe stomach complaints while in Paris. Augusta blamed the rich French cuisine and started to reduce her meals to clear broths and vegetables, but it didn't help. Cutting their honeymoon short, the newlyweds returned to London, but Augusta's health continued to worsen.

Leo, who had offered to interview the maids and housekeeper while Jasper spoke to the butler and footmen, had spoken at length with Kitty.

"Couldn't keep a morsel down," the maid had said during that first interview. "I've been taking in her gowns every week. Must've gone from near eighteen stone to fourteen in a flash."

It was a large amount of weight to lose in so short a time span.

"Has she had any other symptoms of illness?" Leo asked.

"She's grown so weak, she can't hardly hold a pen. Says her hands keep going numb and tingly," Kitty replied. "Her feet too."

That was certainly curious, and it bolstered a hunch Leo was starting to develop.

"And the doctor who has been treating her, this Mr. Gray, what was his diagnosis?"

With a frown, Kitty answered, "Cancer of the stomach."

Leo had come across many corpses at the morgue that had been afflicted by such a cancer. The disease ate away at a person, usually whittling them down to skin and bones by the end. As Augusta Lawlor had lost a good deal of weight, perhaps it truly was cancer of the stomach, as the doctor had concluded. However, Leo was still skeptical.

"What medicine was she prescribed?" Leo asked Kitty next. "Laudanum?"

"Yes. She took eleven drops every morning with her tea in bed," she confirmed. Kitty went on to explain that she would bring a tray at half eight, and Mr. Lawlor would often come through the shared door between their bedchambers to join his wife.

"Who would administer the laudanum to her?" Leo asked. "And where was the bottle kept?"

"It stayed on her bedside table," the maid answered. "I would administer it. Though if Mr. Lawlor joined my mistress, he would do it."

That morning, Kitty had discovered Augusta's seemingly lifeless form upon entering the bedchamber. So, the overdose had to have occurred sometime during the night or early morning.

When the maid's nose twitched and she appeared hesitant, Leo asked if there was anything more Kitty would like to say.

"It might be nothing," the maid said, her hands balled tightly, crushing a handkerchief. "The new bottle Mr. Gray gave her is gone. I noticed it missing from Mrs. Lawlor's night table when I helped her up to bed just now."

That was certainly suspicious. Had Mr. Lawlor taken the bottle after upending the contents into his wife's morning tea?

"Was it there this morning, when you found Mrs. Lawlor?" Leo asked.

But Kitty answered that she couldn't be sure. In all the ensuing commotion, she hadn't thought to check the bottle, which had held just two ounces of the tincture the night before.

As Mrs. Vincent, the housekeeper, showed the fourth and final maid, Marianna, into the dining room to be interviewed, Leo felt restless to know what Jasper had learned in the last hour from those staff members he'd questioned. So far, the maids' information had been mostly insubstantial and repetitive. However, when Mrs. Vincent stated that it was Marianna who went into Mrs. Lawlor's room each morning at dawn to stoke the fire in the hearth, Leo sat up taller with interest.

"How long have you been working for the Lawlors?" Leo asked her.

"Seven months," she answered.

"So, you would very likely notice something out of place or amiss while carrying out your duties?" At Marianna's answering nod, Leo added, "And did you notice anything out of place in Mrs. Lawlor's bedroom this morning?"

"It were too dark to see much of anythin'," Marianna replied, her hands clasped so tightly in her lap, her chapped knuckles whitened. Leo decided against leading her with a question about the missing laudanum bottle and turned to another question.

"Was anyone else awake at the time?' she asked Marianna. "Mr. Lawlor, in the next room, for instance?"

She shook her head. "Don't know."

Marianna's eyes shifted toward Mrs. Vincent, who stood near the door. The housekeeper had insisted on being present for the interviews, and Leo saw no reason to object. Though now, she had the distinct impression that Marianna was nervous to have the housekeeper listening in.

"After Mrs. Lawlor's supposed death, did you see Mr. Lawlor at all?" Leo asked.

Here, every other maid had answered *no*. There had been too much tumult in the house, and they could not specifically recall Sebastian Lawlor shutting himself in his bedchamber as Hastings had said he'd done. However, Marianna did not immediately reply to Leo's question.

Instead, she bit her lower lip in another display of nervousness. She was a slight young woman, probably no older than Leo at twenty-five, with pale blonde hair pinned up under a mobcap. The lace trim on the cap shook as if she was trembling. She continued to clutch her hands together, nervously rubbing the chapped knuckles on her left hand.

"Marianna?" Leo urged. "Did you see Mr. Lawlor?"

Again, she checked over her shoulder. The housekeeper raised her brow in impatience. "Answer the question, girl," Mrs. Vincent ordered.

Marianna faced Leo again. "I seen him."

"Where? When?"

"Mr. Gray had sent word for the body to be taken away, and everyone were weepin' and such, so I…I went out, to get some air." She winced guiltily. "I were standin' just outside the servant's entrance. Mr. Lawlor were on the pavement, out front of the house."

The servant's entrance was set underneath the front entrance, Leo recalled.

"What was he doing?"

"He were hailin' a cab," she answered. At this, Mrs. Vincent breathed in sharply.

"Gracious, girl, why didn't you say this before now?" she chided.

"I weren't supposed to be outside takin' me break, especially with everythin' happenin'," Marianna explained. "I thought I'd be sacked."

Mrs. Vincent sighed irritably. But Leo was more interested in what additional information the maid could provide than in chastising her.

"Marianna, did you hear anything Mr. Lawlor said to the cab driver? Directions, perhaps?" She might have been asking for too much; it would be incredibly lucky if the maid had overheard their exchange. But to her surprise, Marianna nodded.

"Aye, I heard him tell the cabbie he was for Paddington Station."

The breath hitched in Leo's throat and then gusted out in defeat. "Paddington Station. You are certain?"

The maid nodded, and Leo thanked her for her

honesty. But she also felt sorely tempted to chide Marianna for staying quiet for so long. Mr. Lawlor had fled the house even before Rob and Paul from Tate's had come to collect Mrs. Lawlor. Hours had passed, and his train from the busy railway station had surely left by now. Still, she would alert Jasper. He might be able to learn which train Mr. Lawlor had boarded, or if the man had any family he might have traveled to.

As Marianna hurried out of the dining room, Mrs. Vincent stepped forward. "I've searched the house, as the inspector requested, but I cannot find the wedding photographs anywhere."

Jasper had asked for a description of Sebastian Lawlor, or better yet, a photograph. The housekeeper assured him they had a portrait of him, taken with Mrs. Lawlor the day of their wedding.

"It was framed, on the mantel of the drawing room," Mrs. Vincent said. "And another was in Mrs. Lawlor's bedchamber. Both are gone. I cannot understand why Mr. Lawlor would abscond with them."

Leo thought she could. Without the photographs, the police would not know what Sebastian Lawlor looked like when and if they were summoned for an investigation. The man had been deliberate in his actions; he'd anticipated being sought.

"The police have an artist who often sketches portraits based on descriptions witnesses give," Leo said as she exited the dining room. "Inspector Reid may ask for your help with that."

The housekeeper agreed readily, then led Leo to the front sitting room. Jasper was already there, along with Constable Price. The constable peered at Leo with a wariness that many officers at the Yard showed her. A young woman working at a morgue disturbed them, she knew, and many did not like that she had been involved in a handful of Scotland Yard investigations. This was especially true as she'd proved to be as good as they were at their jobs—if not better.

"Mrs. Lawlor is resting," Jasper said as he joined Leo. He was ready to leave, she sensed. So was she. "I'll return tomorrow to question her."

"A maid witnessed Sebastian Lawlor hiring a cab earlier this morning. He gave directions for Paddington Station," Leo revealed.

Jasper grimaced with the same patent disappointment that she had felt.

After bidding Mrs. Vincent a good day, they stepped out into cold, gray, late-afternoon weather.

Jasper addressed Constable Price. "Go to Paddington Station and speak to the ticket office. See if the clerk recalls Mr. Lawlor purchasing a ticket this morning around eleven. Also, talk to porters, station agents, anyone who might have seen him."

Price nodded and left on his task, though Leo couldn't help but think it would be a futile endeavor until they had either a photograph or a sketch of Sebastian Lawlor.

"I've already sent PC Mills to the Central Bank," Jasper said, referring to one of his newer constables. "He's checking to see if Mr. Lawlor was there this afternoon to access their account or safe deposit box."

To clear them out, Leo inferred.

A hired carriage came along the pavement when Jasper flagged the driver, and after settling inside, Leo rested against the cushion, the tension draining from her shoulders. Jasper sat across from her, his feet bracketing hers. Though they weren't touching, the positioning still felt intimate.

"Sebastian Lawlor wasn't liked or trusted by Hastings or the other footmen in the house," Jasper said after a moment. "He owned a moderately successful import-export shop near Wapping Basin on Redmead Lane. But there was the general belief among the staff that he had married Augusta Hart for her money."

"Mrs. Vincent said Augusta was perfectly content as an unmarried woman, and that Sebastian's romantic interest in her came as a shock to them all," Leo provided. "A happy one, for Augusta."

She felt sorry for the woman and for the painful humiliation that would no doubt grip her when she was alert enough to understand what her husband had done.

"A bottle of laudanum is missing from her bedroom," Jasper said.

"I know. It was prescribed as treatment for her abdominal illness, which sounds very much like long-term arsenic poisoning."

He removed his bowler and set it in his lap, allowing a lock of his honey-blond hair to sweep over his brow. "Arsenic?"

Leo nodded. "Her hands should be soft for a lady of her status, and the tops of them are. But I noted that her palms are rough, the skin hard. And there are white lines on her nails. Those and digestive issues are signs of long-term exposure."

Leo had seen it often in bodies that came into the morgue. Most of the time, the poisonous exposure was accidental and tragic, especially when the victims were children who were simply drinking out of a contaminated public well, or young women who worked in factories that used arsenic to dye their products. Last winter, Leo and Jasper had investigated an arsenic poisoning that had been tied to a wallpaper factory that used the chemical in their green dye. Even just papering a home's walls could prove deadly.

"And her illness just happened to start on their honeymoon," Jasper said with marked doubt.

"So, you agree that he was poisoning her?"

"It does look that way, though I would like the chance to find him and ask."

The likelihood of that happening seemed small, however, especially since Leo had started to question if Sebastian Lawlor was even the man's real name. When she suggested that he may have been using a pseudonym, Jasper's grimace deepened.

"I will see what I can find on him, but I fear you're right. That is likely why he took the few photographs there were of him. Someone might have recognized him and shared his real name with the police, should they be circulated to the public."

Leo looked out the window, in thought. "Say he *was* slowly poisoning her with arsenic. Today, she seems to have been given a much higher dose than usual of her prescribed laudanum with the intent to kill her. Why change his method now and not allow the arsenic to take its course?"

"It might have been taking too long," Jasper mused with a shrug. "He wanted to be rid of her faster."

"Just so that he might take the contents of the safe?" Leo shook her head. It seemed too paltry a payout for such an extensive and complex plan. "He would not have even needed to become a widower to access Augusta's wealth. It was already his. He could have taken everything and disappeared. He didn't need to kill her when he could simply spurn her."

Jasper arched a dark blond brow. "Yes, but then she might have contacted the police or a private detective to find him. Filed for divorce, even. Killing her would mean no loose ends."

Especially if the death of his wife was made to look like a long-term illness that had finally taken its toll.

"But then, why did he run?" Leo asked. "He had no reason to. He didn't yet know Augusta was still alive."

Jasper sat back against the cushion, looking worn. "I don't know. Hopefully, Coughlan will agree to opening an official case, and I'll be able to investigate further."

At the mention of Detective Chief Inspector Dermot Coughlan, a prickle of tension threaded back into Leo's shoulders and back. Though she and Jasper had been courting for over a month, she wasn't certain who at the CID knew, other than Roy Lewis. She and Jasper had hardly had much time together to discuss it, or how his fellow officers had reacted to the news. She did not think Chief Inspector Coughlan would be very pleased to receive the news.

Although, the thought of the chief inspector gave her an idea.

"What if I were to lend my help? Officially, I mean. Chief Inspector Coughlan did say that he'd permit me to help in a limited capacity from time to time."

That had been last summer, after Leo and Jasper had solved a few murders and the mysterious disappearance of a child, linked to the Metropolitan and City Police Orphanage.

"And Inspector Lewis did credit me with the arrests made at Gleason's Department Store in October," she added when Jasper narrowed his eyes.

The opium ring she'd uncovered, along with the murder of a female investigative reporter, had been pinned on a Spitalfields Angel.

"Coughlan wasn't pleased with Roy for that," Jasper reminded her.

"And yet, Roy is now Detective Inspector," she pointed out. "You could hire me as a consultant of sorts."

He crossed his arms over his chest. "What is your fee?"

Leo bit her lip against a victorious grin. "I'm very affordable. Practically free."

"I suppose I could use your assistance," he said, attempting to smother a grin as well. "I'll see what Coughlan has to say about it."

Though the chief inspector was not Leo's strongest supporter, there were others, like Constable Horace Wiley and Detective Inspector Tomlin of the Special Irish Branch, who flat out disliked her.

Jasper had insisted that he did not care what they or anyone else at the CID thought about his affection for her, and Leo could only hope that he was not faced with hostility over the matter. Or that she would be rejected as a consultant because of it.

"I wonder if Mrs. Lawlor will even want us to investigate," Leo said. "She will be mortified, I'm sure, and she might not wish to invite a public scandal."

There would be whispers, however, and gossip would spread like wildfire no matter what.

"If he tried to murder her," Jasper said, anger lowering his tone to a near grumble, "he deserves to be arrested."

He was correct, of course. Though unfortunately, too many murders went unsolved. With millions of people in one city and dozens of murders brought to the attention of the police every month, the Metropolitan Police Force could not investigate them all.

"I'll visit the import-export shop after I leave you at the morgue," Jasper said. "With any hope, an employee is there who can tell me more about Mr. Lawlor."

Leo wished she could accompany him, but she had already been gone from the morgue for too long.

"Why does it sometimes feel as though there are too many wretched people out there and not enough good ones?" she asked as their carriage entered the traffic circle around Trafalgar Square.

"Careful," Jasper warned. "You're starting to sound as cynical as I am."

"I don't know why that would be," Leo said, happy to put aside the quandary involving Augusta Lawlor for the time being. "I hardly ever see you."

"I am seeing you now," he replied, moving his foot just enough to align it against hers. "And don't forget about tonight. I think you'll like Roy's wife."

Leo had not forgotten their plans for dinner at the Lewis home.

"I'm glad I'll be able to meet Mrs. Lewis and their sons," she replied, nudging Jasper's foot in return. "But mostly, I'm looking forward to seeing more of you."

It wasn't easy for Leo to express herself so openly, especially when it came to her feelings for Jasper. Like him, she was naturally reserved and serious. But she found that when she took the chance and spoke her feelings plainly, he would reward her with something in return. This time was no different.

As the carriage drew to a stop in front of the morgue on Spring Street, Jasper sat forward. "I'll confess what I am most looking forward to," he said. Though he didn't smile, his eyes gleamed with frank longing. "The carriage ride home. Though I may ask the driver to find a longer route to Duke Street this time."

Leo gaped at his wicked suggestion. He was speaking of their last carriage ride and the several minutes they'd spent grasping at one another. Even thinking of it now brought heat to her cheeks. Especially since she, too, had been hoping for another chance at privacy with him tonight.

Jasper handed her down onto the pavement and, lifting her hand to his lips, told her he'd pick her up at seven o'clock. He then returned to the carriage and carried on toward Scotland Yard.

Hoping the blush would quickly drain from her face, she entered the morgue through the front lobby doors.

Leo had sent word to Connor before leaving for Augusta Lawlor's home, explaining that she would be away longer than anticipated. The assistant coroner would not be too upset, she reasoned, and she was inordinately lucky for his good-naturedness. But when she entered the postmortem room and saw an additional two corpses had arrived, Leo groaned.

"I'm sorry, Connor," she said, removing her coat and hat, and casting them onto an empty autopsy table. She hurried to don her canvas apron. The coroner, wrist-deep in the chest cavity of a male corpse, scowled. Thankfully, it was not a genuine scowl.

"Where the devil have you been? All your note said was that *a dead body wasn't*. What did that mean, exactly?"

Leo pulled down a clipboard, paper, and pencil from where they hung on a peg.

"It's a long story for later. Tell me what we have here."

Connor turned back to his work. "Coronary thrombosis due to arterial embolism. The man's mistress told the police his wife had poisoned him. So, here we are."

Leo noted the cause of death, her mind turning to the arsenic that must have laced Augusta Lawlor's food and drink for several months, weakening her and causing her illness. It would take some time for her body to repair itself.

"The only poison was this man's poor diet," Connor added while resetting the corpse's cracked rib cage in preparation for closing sutures. He looked up at her when she made no response. "That was meant to be humorous."

"Was it? Sorry," Leo murmured, only half-listening. A notion had come to her regarding Mrs. Lawlor's doctor: "Would every doctor recognize the symptoms of arsenic poisoning?"

Connor wiped his bloodied hands on a length of toweling. "Any competent doctor would. Why?"

Mrs. Lawlor's doctor had misdiagnosed her as having cancer of the stomach. Had it been incompetence that had caused the doctor to overlook the signs of arsenic poisoning that Leo had seen?

"Do you know a doctor in London by the name of Henry Gray?" she asked.

Connor had turned to his table of tools, ready for

closing with catgut sutures, but now threw Leo an amused glance. His light chuckle filled the postmortem room. "Henry Gray?"

"Yes, do you know him?"

He returned to the corpse, the catgut threaded into the eye of the hooked needle. "You're not serious?"

"Why shouldn't I be?" she asked, irritated by his amusement.

"Because that is the name of the famous physician who wrote *Gray's Anatomy*," he replied. "The anatomical bible for every surgeon? You must know it."

Astonishment pooled through her. An image of her uncle's worn copy of the textbook dropped into the forefront of her mind, and Leo felt exceedingly stupid.

"I do know of it," she said, furious with herself for not having made the connection sooner.

"Does this have anything to do with where you were for the afternoon?" Connor asked as he set the first closing stitch.

Briefly, she explained who Mr. Henry Gray was and what had occurred with Mrs. Lawlor. Afterward, Connor whistled.

"I can ask around to be sure there is no doctor by that name in London, but from what you've said, it sounds like he might have been using a false name."

Just as Sebastian Lawlor might have been, Leo thought. If that was the case, had the two men been working together? Had the doctor, too, fled?

While Connor finished with the corpse, Leo went into the office and quickly typed the postmortem report for the dead man. As there had been no crime, there would be no inquest, and the report could simply be filed away.

Connor had set the man's personal possessions in a box for his wife, and Leo marked them down in the morgue's registry.

Before Leo left for the evening, she fed Tibia, the morgue's resident cat, a dinner of some tinned sardines, then found Connor in the postmortem room to bid him a goodnight. He told her—only half-jokingly—that she was not to miss work the next day under any circumstances. There were corpses to see to, and he had, after all, hired her on as a paid employee.

"I will be here," she promised, and she had every intention of keeping that promise.

However, as she started home, a yellow brume swimming in the cones of light streaming from the lampposts, she acknowledged that consulting on Mrs. Lawlor's situation and questioning her staff had been far more stimulating than assisting in a postmortem. With every stride, she tried to push the mystery surrounding Mr. Lawlor from her mind and instead think about the evening that lay ahead. She did hope Roy Lewis's wife didn't think her too odd for working at a morgue.

Leo had started along the busy pavements of the Strand when she felt an inkling of premonition skitter across the nape of her neck. Intuition slowed her, then stopped her altogether. When a throat cleared directly behind her, she turned—and found herself looking up at the familiar face of one of Andrew Carter's hired men.

Chapter Four

Leo slid her heels backward to put some distance between herself and the man. "What do you want?"

He was at least two heads taller than her, built like a prizefighter, and had the placid expression of a man who was accustomed to following orders. Which, Leo knew all too well, he received from Andrew Carter.

"Got a message for the inspector," the hired muscle answered, his deep voice as intimidating as his height and brawn. He extended a sealed letter and waited for Leo to take it.

She eyed it warily. "Why are you giving it to me?"

The hired man didn't answer. He simply stood there, letter in hand, waiting. Leo plucked it from his fingers, and the moment she did, he pivoted on his heel and strode away. She exhaled, her knees surprisingly soft, and looked at the sealed envelope in her hand.

Andrew could have just as easily had this letter delivered to Jasper's home. He'd had it brought to Leo for one reason: to show Jasper how easily he could get to her.

She continued on to Duke Street, checking over her shoulder several times before determining that she wasn't being followed. Even still, she didn't allow herself to relax until she'd hurried through the front door and locked it behind her. Releasing a long breath, she transferred the letter from her coat pocket to her skirt pocket. She didn't want to give it to Jasper. Didn't want his shallowly buried worries about his cousin to come forward, into the light.

Mrs. Zhao's voice traveled from the back of the house. She was in the kitchen making supper, Leo presumed, and Flora would be seated in a chair at the table, knitting. Mrs. Zhao had introduced the pastime, thinking it might help to calm Flora. She'd been correct, and Leo's aunt had since created a blanket and a pair of mufflers.

"Shouldn't you be getting dressed to go out this evening?" Mrs. Zhao asked when Leo joined them in the kitchen.

The older woman, stirring a soup pot on the stove, smiled and arched a thin black eyebrow. She'd adopted the teasing expression as soon as Jasper announced he and Leo were courting. Like Claude, Mrs. Zhao had been pleased by the development. Leo wanted to believe the Inspector would have been too.

"Just stopping in to say hello," Leo answered.

Flora ignored her presence, her attention on the blanket she was knitting with violet yarn, now so large it covered her lap.

Leo gathered up a little courage and addressed her aunt directly. "Aunt Flora, that is a lovely color."

Her aunt didn't respond, and after a moment, Leo turned to go upstairs, at least grateful she hadn't been shouted at or accused of murder.

"It is her favorite color." Her aunt's frail voice stopped Leo from taking another step. Both she and Mrs. Zhao whipped around to look at Flora, whose needles were still clicking steadily.

"Whose favorite color, Aunt Flora?" Leo chanced asking.

"Andromeda." Her voice was light. *Happy*, even. It was surprising, considering any mention of Leo's mother usually pushed her into a tantrum.

Leo and Mrs. Zhao exchanged a guarded look; each of them knew how fragile a moment it was. To be safe, Leo backed out of the kitchen to go upstairs while Mrs. Zhao commented that violet was a favorite color of hers as well.

As she climbed the stairs, Leo removed the letter from her pocket. Like Flora, Leo could not think of her mother without also thinking of her violent death. For a reason Leo had never been able to understand, she had trouble remembering anything about her life from before the night of the murders. As perfect as her memory was, her life *before* was trapped behind a dense, impenetrable wall. She wanted memories of her mother; happy, normal ones...but they were impossible to recover.

All Leo had were the facts known to the police about her mother's death.

When the Inspector had given Leo the file he'd kept on the Spencer family murders, he'd advised her to open it only when she was ready. She thought she had been, but after flipping through photographs of her slain family members, some of the images overexposed or blurred, an inexplicable and unrelenting panic had gripped her. She'd closed the file and stored it under her bed. And yet night-mares had persisted, invading her sleep. These night-mares, she knew, were simply memories, startling in their newness and debilitating in their horror.

Although Leo still did not know how her father had betrayed the East Rips, pieces of information had come to her over the last year. The latest had been compliments of a criminal named Eddie Bloom. The owner of a dance hall and casino, it had been Mr. Bloom's opium that was stolen for use in the illegal operation Leo had uncovered at Gleason's Department Store. To thank Leo for her efforts in exposing the thieves, Mr. Bloom had sent Leo a note along with a hefty ten pounds. The note included a strange comment: *You'll make an excellent spy. Must be in the blood.*

Indicating that someone in her family—her father? her mother?—had been a spy had prompted Leo to draw the file out from under her bed for the first time in months. This time, she'd gathered the appalling photographs, flipped them over, and shuffled them to the back. With a clenched stomach, Leo had perused case notes, interviews, constable reports, and newspaper clippings. Unsurprisingly, there had been no mention of Leonard Spencer's involvement with the Carters or anything to do with clandestine spying. Disappointed, she'd stuffed the file under her bed once more. But the papers she'd read were all still in her memory, every typed word, available for perusal whenever she wished.

The temptation arose now and then, but as she entered her small bedroom and lit a paraffin lamp, the only thing tempting her currently was the letter from Andrew Carter. She set it on her bed. Her eyes drifted toward it several times as she changed into a somewhat more stylish ensemble for dinner at the Lewises'. As she sat at her vanity, re-pinning her hair in front of her mirror, the reflection of the white envelope on the bed drew her attention again.

Leo gritted her teeth. "*Blast it.*"

She stood and snatched up the letter. The envelope flap wasn't sealed with wax. Although it was a breach of trust to open, let alone read, someone else's correspondence, Jasper was just going to tell her what Andrew wanted anyway. Surely, he would.

With that in mind, Leo felt marginally less guilty as she withdrew a square of paper. The only writing on it was a place and time: *Charing Cross Station, tomorrow morning, eight o'clock.*

Andrew wanted to meet. Her stomach turned to lead as she sat on the edge of her bed. She replaced the note in the envelope and then dropped it into her small handbag. She didn't want Jasper to go near his cousin. But she had no choice. If she didn't give him the letter, he would not arrive at the meeting place, and Andrew might react badly. Dangerously.

Downstairs, a few knocks on the front door drove her to her feet. It had to be Jasper, coming to take her to dinner. Picking up her handbag, Leo went down to open the door, but Mrs. Zhao had already done so, allowing the detective inspector to come inside. He wore a dark green, woolen Chesterfield coat, unbuttoned to reveal a fine black suit and tie, and a burgundy satin waistcoat. Leo had always acknowledged that Jasper was a handsome man, but only over the last year had she come to recognize just how attractive he was. How a flutter of her pulse and a yearning in the very center of her body came alive whenever she saw him enter a room or step through a doorway.

Like now.

He kept his serious gaze hinged on her, as if he knew where her private thoughts had wandered. Jasper took Leo's coat from the hook on the front hall stand and held it up for her to slip into. After thanking Mrs. Zhao for staying with Flora, they departed for the hired carriage waiting outside. As Leo took a seat on the bench, a bubble of anxiety simmered in her stomach at the thought of giving Jasper Andrew's note. It would plunge him into a wretched mood and distract him during dinner too.

But she had to tell him.

"Jasper," she started to say as he shut the carriage door and took the seat next to her.

Leo didn't get out another word before he'd reached one arm behind her back, the other under her legs, and lifted her from the bench entirely. She yelped in surprise as he hauled her onto his lap—and covered her mouth with his.

She went to pulp in his arms, her shock dissipating as she leaned against him, and into the kiss. Notes of oaked whisky on his tongue and the warm musk of his sandalwood cologne wrapped around her as possessively as his arms did.

With every kiss they had shared so far, there was a slowly dissolving sense of propriety between them, one that they'd yet to discuss but which Leo knew they both felt. There was also growing familiarity and trust. For instance, Leo knew that she could place her palms against his waistcoat and delight in the feel of his muscled chest without startling him. Likewise, Jasper knew she would not draw back from him when his hand explored the length of her leg, from ankle to hip. The barrier of his gloves and of her skirt and petticoats prevented him from touching her skin, but Leo took pleasure in imagining what his warm, calloused palm might feel like on it.

The carriage slowed and hit a crater in the cobbled road, causing their locked mouths to part.

"I thought you said you were looking forward to the carriage ride *home*," Leo teased, gripping his shoulders as the carriage took a corner. With his arms bracing her, she stayed firmly on his lap.

"I'm an impatient man," he replied and then claimed her mouth again.

If they continued kissing like this, the bristle on his chin would abrade her skin—something Roy and his wife would surely notice during dinner. Leo pulled back and told him as much. He groaned in annoyance but did not try to kiss her again. He did, however, keep her ensconced on his lap.

"There is something you should know," Leo said.

The letter in her handbag would ruin the moment. Jasper would shift her from his lap and likely keep space between them. He hated his blood ties to the Carters. When Andrew had told him he was aware of his true identity, Jasper had tried to walk away from Leo, claiming that he would only be a danger to her. She hadn't accepted his stance, though, and Jasper had relented. But if Andrew pressed hard enough, Leo wasn't certain what Jasper might do in the name of protecting her.

With him now waiting for her to continue speaking, his dark green eyes searching hers, she took a breath. "The doctor Sebastian Lawlor hired to treat his wife was likely a fraud and an accomplice," she said, cringing with a smidge of guilt. But the letter, she reasoned, could wait until after dinner.

"Henry Gray is the physician who wrote the famous medical text, *Gray's Anatomy*. Connor believes a real doctor would have noticed the signs of long-term arsenic poisoning. Instead, this Mr. Gray diagnosed stomach cancer."

Jasper made a musing sound in the back of his throat as he frowned. "I wondered about the doctor. Especially after what I discovered on my visit to Lawlor Antiquities earlier."

His palm continued to gently massage her hip, and Leo was tempted to kiss him again. But she was too intrigued to know what he'd found out.

"It appears the shop is owned by a Roger Lawlor, and he has no earthly idea who Sebastian is," he said, his eyebrow arching. "And he's never heard of Augusta Lawlor."

"I knew it," Leo said, happy she'd been correct in her theory...and yet also sorry for Augusta. "He is a fraud. Do you think he selected the last name Lawlor just so he could pretend the shop belonged to him?"

"I'll find out when I track him down."

"What did PC Mills find at the Central Bank?" she asked. "Were the accounts cleared out?"

"The bank manager refused to provide any information without a police warrant. I'll have to go back with one," Jasper said. "That is, if Chief Coughlan agrees to open a formal investigation. He was out by the time I returned to the Yard. I'll speak to him first thing in the morning."

"You'll inform him that I'm consulting?"

"I will, although I can't promise he won't challenge it. I am courting you, after all," Jasper said. "He could see it as a conflict of interest."

Leo shifted on his lap. "You've told him about us?"

"I have."

She waited for him to say more, perhaps what sort of reaction the chief inspector had given. But just then, the driver whistled, and the carriage slowed. They had arrived at the Lewises' home on Oswin Street, a modest, working-class street in Lambeth, lined on each side with brick terraced houses. Roy Lewis promptly opened the door upon Jasper's knock, and they were ushered into a small but cozy home.

It was strange to see the new detective inspector outside of his work at Scotland Yard. Here, his roles were those of husband and father, and as two young boys came running into the front room in a burst of giggles, Roy aptly rounded them up. He snagged them both by the shoulders and brought the boys in front of him.

The elder boy was about eight or nine years of age, and the younger perhaps two years younger than that. Both were gangly limbed, with curly brown hair, and light brown eyes and skin. Previously, Jasper had explained to Leo how Mrs. Lewis was of West African descent, her parents having come to England from the Sierra Leone Colony. Roy had been purposely protective of his private life at the Yard, due to adversarial attitudes toward marriages between people of different races. His own sister had cut him out of her life for marrying a woman with dark skin, and he had lost several close friends too.

"Now, boys, this is Miss Spencer," Roy said to his sons. "You are to show her your best manners."

The younger boy wriggled impatiently under his father's grip, while the older one stood stock still and gaped.

"You're the lady who likes dead bodies, aren't you?" the older one asked.

Leo bit back a grin, and Jasper stifled a snort of laughter as Roy gently reprimanded his son. "Miss Spencer works at a morgue, Fletcher. That does not mean she likes dead bodies."

"Indeed, I do not particularly like them," Leo clarified, still tempted to smile. "I simply assist the coroner in determining how they died."

That impressed Fletcher, if his wide grin was any indication.

"All right, off with you," Roy said, giving his son a nudge. "Take Benji and wash up before supper."

The boys scattered, nearly colliding with their mother as she came into the front room. She only laughed as she narrowly avoided them.

"Forgive our boys, Miss Spencer," she said as she came forward. "They are as fascinated as they are frightened by the idea of corpses."

"Then, they are no different from most people I have met," Leo replied.

"And yet you are unbothered," Mrs. Lewis said, her smile lingering as she seemed to inspect Leo. "I admit, I am impressed. My sons have been told not to ask you questions, but Roy hasn't forbidden *me*." She sent her husband a playful look, then batted his arm lightly. "Take their coats, dear, and get them drinks already."

Dinner was served shortly after Leo and Jasper had settled in, and young Fletcher raced around the table to pull out Leo's chair for her, winning him a pat on the head from his father. As Roy commanded, neither boy asked her questions about the morgue, and when Roy and Jasper began discussing cases, Mrs. Lewis chastised them for talking about murder at the dinner table.

"I cannot stand hearing about all the awful people in this city," she said fervently. "It makes me fearful for our children."

Leo exchanged a look with Jasper, seated next to her at the table, and she sensed he was thinking the same thing she was—that, unlike Roy's wife, Leo did enjoy hearing all about Jasper's cases. They each arched a brow before turning their attention back to the Lewises, just in time to see little Benji flick a pea at his brother's cheek.

It was a boisterous and entertaining hour as they ate and chatted, and Leo couldn't remember the last time she'd had such a wonderful meal.

Once the boys were dismissed from the table and Roy invited Jasper for a whisky in the front room, Leo helped Mrs. Lewis clear the table.

"You have a lovely family, Mrs. Lewis," she said, placing their plates on a counter in the kitchen near a large sink.

"Thank you. And please, call me Thea."

"Gladly, if you will call me Leo."

Thea set about making them tea in the small, but comfortable kitchen. She gestured for Leo to take a chair at the small table set in one of the corners of the room.

"My Fletcher is quite enamored with you, Leo," she

said as they waited for their tea to cool. A conspiratorial grin formed on Thea's lips. "As is Inspector Reid."

Leo shifted in her seat, a bit abashed by what Roy's wife had observed. But also pleased.

Thea picked up her teacup and blew over the surface. "In all seriousness, it is rather impressive work you do. Important work."

"Thank you. I think so too." She reached for her own teacup.

"Will you be sorry to give it up?" Thea asked, causing Leo's fingers to falter and bump against the cup handle.

She frowned. "Give it up?"

"Judging by the way Inspector Reid looks at you, I doubt your courtship will be very long."

"Oh," Leo said, taken aback. She gripped her teacup handle more tightly to keep it from slipping in her suddenly damp palms. "Well, we haven't discussed anything like that yet. But Jasper understands I want to work. Even after…*if* we…marry."

Saying the words aloud brought a tingling flare to the center of her stomach.

"Really?" Thea's eyes widened with evident doubt. "What about when you have little rascals like mine running about?"

Startled, Leo choked as she swallowed a sip of hot tea and then coughed fitfully. Thea seemed to know what had set off her coughing and laughed as Leo recovered, her eyes watering.

"All right, no more questions," Thea said good-naturedly as she patted Leo's arm. "I don't want to be accused of murder, should you choke to death on your tea."

Chapter Five

The carriage ride from Lambeth after dinner wasn't what Jasper had hoped it would be. He'd perceived a change in Leo's bearing when she and Thea rejoined him and Roy in the front sitting room after dinner, though it wasn't anything he could pinpoint. Leo had smiled and made pleasant conversation before they bid their hosts a good evening, but she'd been distracted and slightly flustered.

"What is wrong?" he asked, once they were settled on the bench inside the hired hansom.

Leo blinked up at him, as though her thoughts had been elsewhere. "Wrong?"

"Don't bother denying it. I know you too well." He brushed his thumb against the corner of her mouth. "You've been biting your cheek in contemplation when you think no one is looking at you."

And he rarely did not look at her.

She covered his hand with her own, holding it against

her cheek an extra moment. Then, with a heavy sigh, she reached into her handbag and withdrew an envelope.

"I don't want to give this to you, but I know I must."

The merriment of the evening drained away as Jasper took the letter and read it.

Charing Cross. Tomorrow at eight in the morning. The letter was unsigned, yet he knew who it was from.

He folded the paper, barely resisting the urge to crumple it in his fist. "Where did you get this?"

"On my way home from the morgue this evening," she answered. "One of Mr. Carter's men stopped me and told me to give it to you."

Hot, seething fury quaked through him. As did something else that he didn't often feel—fear. Andrew had sent one of his thugs to approach Leo and relay the message just to prove how easily he could find her. How easily he could harm her, if he wished.

"I didn't want to ruin the evening, so I waited to give it to you," she explained.

Jasper pocketed the letter. "You've read it, I presume." There had been no seal, and Leo's incessant inquisitiveness would never have allowed her to not read it.

"I have," she admitted. "I'll come with you to Charing Cross."

"No." He nearly growled the single word. "I don't want you involved."

"I already am, Jasper."

Hell. She was right. She was involved, merely by being part of his life. He'd always hated that he was a Carter by birth but never more so than right then.

There was no choice. He would have to meet with Andrew. If he didn't, he risked Scotland Yard learning the truth about who he really was. It would mean complete ruin for him. A colossal lie had formed the bedrock of Jasper's life, and Andrew could demolish it if he wanted. Not only that, but if he were to inform the rest of the Carters and East Rips about what their long-lost cousin James had done, Jasper would have a target on his back. So would Leo and anyone else he loved.

As their carriage crossed the Westminster Bridge, he scrubbed his palm against the bristle of his beard. "I will go alone to see what he wants."

But Jasper would not—*ever*—compromise his duty to the Yard. Or his oath to the law. Though he hadn't yet spoken of it to Leo, he'd given it some thought over the last six months. Jasper would rather step down from the Metropolitan Police Force and implore Leo, her uncle and aunt, and Mrs. Zhao to leave London with him, if need be, than submit to Andrew Carter's blackmail. Of course, he hoped it would never come to that. But Jasper was prepared.

"Please don't shut me out, Jasper," Leo said. "I want to know what Mr. Carter asks of you."

He abhorred the idea of coming to heel like a dog for his cousin. Possessing Carter blood plagued him in a way Leo could never understand. If he allowed it to, it would taint his entire life.

"I will tell you," he promised. "And I am also sorry."

"Whatever for?"

"For ruining our carriage ride home." He tried to make light of the moment, wanting only to see her smile. It worked.

"Don't be daft." She took his hand and leaned closer to him. Jasper reveled in the weight of her body against his and was tempted to bring her onto his lap as he had earlier on their way to Lambeth. But with the letter, Andrew's presence had infiltrated their carriage, blotting out any chance of focusing solely on one another.

"I'm going to visit Mrs. Lawlor tomorrow," Leo said, thankfully changing the subject.

"I'll be calling on her as well after I speak to Chief Coughlan about the case," Jasper replied. "So, we should go together."

Genuine pleasure lit Leo's face. "I like that idea."

"I'll meet you at the morgue at ten o'clock. If Connor can spare you," he added.

She pursed her lips with consternation. "I'm sure he will complain. But leave it to me."

Charing Cross was a busy hub at all hours, but the crowds were especially dense at quarter to eight in the morning. Jasper had arrived early for his meeting with Andrew and had taken up position in the forecourt of the hotel and station, at the base of the Queen Eleanor Memorial Cross. Carriages, hansoms, and pedestrians flowed around the ornate spire memorial while Jasper kept an eye peeled for one of Andrew's hired men.

A lead weight had sat heavy in his stomach all night. Andrew must have had someone watching Leo, following her, and that Jasper had been oblivious to his machinations was infuriating. It only proved that there was no way he could protect Leo at all hours of the day. Even if they married and she lived with him, he would not be able to keep her by his side at all times. If anything, being his wife would only make Leo more of a target. Or a pawn.

It was in despondent moments like this one when Jasper wished he had left the Inspector's home long ago. Before he could fall in love with Leo. It was too late now, of course. There was no going back, so Jasper would just have to find a way forward. How it would be done eluded him.

It didn't matter that he was a man of thirty years, he still would have liked for his father to be alive, so that he could ask for his advice.

Jasper kept his hands in his coat pockets as he stood immobile at the memorial's pedestal. These thoughts were like thorns, pricking him from the underside of his skin. The only balm for them was to replace them with thoughts of Leo.

Last night, while having dinner with Roy's family, Jasper had felt something rare: envy. He hadn't experienced that feeling since last summer when he'd been under the impression that Leo and Connor Quinn might have formed some attachment while working together at the morgue. That suspicion had been unfounded, to his great relief, but this envy was different in form. Watching Roy interact with his wife and children, seeing them at home, at ease and happy, had put Jasper in mind of what it would be like to have those same things for himself. Going home to Leo every night and waking up to her each morning had become part of a vision he could not deny wanting to make a reality.

A carriage pulled up in front of the memorial, severing the satisfying image of Leo, morning sunlight burnishing her dark hair as she lay in bed beside him. It scattered like road dust as the bulky man riding next to the driver climbed down. It was one of the two brawny hired men Andrew kept.

"Weapon," the man ordered.

Jasper held aside his coat panels so that the man would see he had no weapon, unlike the last time Andrew had forced him into a carriage ride. He'd anticipated there being constables patrolling the busy train station this morning and didn't want to be seen handing over his police-issued gun.

The hired man grunted and opened the carriage door. Jasper stepped in and took the bench across from his cousin. Andrew wore a fur-collared coat, a top hat, and leather gloves, looking more like a financier than a criminal. He was five years younger than Jasper but over the last several months, he'd grown a mustache that made him look a little older.

"I see our Miss Spencer gave you my message," Andrew said with a note of cheerfulness that did not match his intense, ice-blue stare.

Jasper held himself back from saying that she wasn't 'our' anything. Andrew wanted to prod him into a reaction, and he had no plans to give it to him.

"Games are for children, Andrew. If you want to talk to me, come to *me*."

His cousin bristled infinitesimally. He maintained his façade of pleasantry with a tight, coy smile.

The carriage began to move. The last time Andrew had picked him up, Jasper had believed he was going to be killed and dumped into the Thames. He supposed there was still a chance of that, but he didn't see why his cousin would dispose of him before even trying his hand at extortion.

"What do you want?" Jasper asked.

"Lower your hackles, Jamey. I'm helping you."

"In what way?"

Andrew's coy grin vanished. "By not telling my brothers what I know about you. You should be grateful I didn't, especially after you disappeared to Liverpool."

"I was seconded by the police, and it is hardly disappearing if you knew where I was."

Andrew lifted his chin and flared his nostrils. "Well, now you're back. Lucky me. Especially since now, I have a use for you."

Jasper braced himself.

"Sean's only son hasn't been seen in six days," Andrew said. "Cillian's a troublemaking wanker, and I'd be just as happy if the little shite never turned up. But you know how Sean is, or have you been out of the family fold for so long you don't remember your oldest cousin?"

Try as Jasper might, it would be impossible to forget his cousins. The sons of Patrick Carter, the late head of the East Rips, had grown up as privileged bullies who'd always known that they would inherit their father's criminal empire. Sean was the eldest and at least twenty years Jasper's senior. He was followed closely by Brian, then William—the black sheep of the family who'd tried to divest himself of the Carters but wound up shot and killed last January. Rory was next in the succession of brothers and was the closest in age to Jasper. Then, there was Andrew.

"Get to your point. What is it you want me to do?" Jasper asked.

His youngest cousin tapped his foot impatiently. Then stilled it. He didn't seem to like that Jasper wasn't cowering before him. Andrew has always been the quietest of the five brothers. The most observant and patient, and Jasper suspected he was also the most intelligent. Instinctively, he knew there was only so far that Andrew would allow himself to be pushed.

"I want you to find Cillian," he answered.

Jasper exhaled, the knot in his stomach loosening if only a little. The request didn't make sense. "You could approach any detective at the Metropolitan Police Force. You could hire a private inquiry agent."

"But I'm not asking any detective, am I?" Andrew replied. "I'm asking you."

Jasper regarded him another moment, his mind churning with questions. "How does it benefit you if I find him?"

The carriage slowed and turned. It had done that a few times, and Jasper determined they were circling Whitehall.

Andrew clasped his hands together in his lap. "It'll make Sean happy. And a happy Sean is a stable Sean. He's been ill lately. It's put him in a foul temper. More foul than usual, at least." He shrugged. "Besides, I'd like to put our new relationship to a test."

"We have no relationship."

Andrew wagged his pointer finger. "Wrong there, Jamey. We share blood. And as Cillian is also your blood, you owe it to him to look for him."

"Who else is looking for him?" Jasper asked.

"Sean's not sitting on his thumbs, and Brian has some of his trusted men scouring Cillian's known haunts,"

Andrew answered. "He had a piece of muslin whose husband might have caught wind of their affair."

"Who is the husband?"

"An Angel," Andrew answered casually, with an arched brow.

"A Spitalfields Angel?"

"No, the kind sent down from heaven. Yes, a bleeding Spitalfields Angel," he said with a scoff. "And before you ask why we haven't approached him, no Carter is at liberty. There's an accord in place between Sean and Barry Reubens. Sean's adamant about it—at least until we have proof one of Barry's men has done for Cillian."

That Cillian and his mistress had run afoul of the woman's husband seemed the most likely possibility. The request Andrew was making wasn't illegal. It wasn't immoral, either. And yet, Jasper's instinct was still to say no. But that was something he couldn't do, unless he was prepared to face the consequences.

As the carriage came to a stop again, and the hollow moan of a train whistle cut the air, he determined he was back at Charing Cross.

"If I am going to find him, I'll need the husband's name," Jasper said, chewing words as though they were gristle.

Andrew's puckish grin returned. "That's what I'd hoped to hear, detective."

Chapter Six

It was colder indoors than it was outside when Leo arrived at the morgue early the next morning. Shivers twinged along her arms as she lit the lamps in her office and went straight to the cottage range in the corner to put a kettle on the hob for tea. Tibia, still curled up in her nest of flannel blankets by the stove, glared at Leo with accusing pale green eyes.

"I'm sorry for waking you earlier than usual, Tibby," she said, her hands held above the stove to coax feeling back into them. The gray cat mewed, unimpressed, and closed her eyes again.

Leo had been too restless to sleep past dawn. Jasper's meeting with Andrew worried her. As much as she wanted to show up at Charing Cross Station at the appointed hour, she knew she could not. It would infuriate Jasper...and it might even be what Andrew was hoping she would do. Surely, he'd factored in that she might read the note before giving it to Jasper. She wondered if the East Rip suspected that she wasn't totally in the dark about Jasper's identity. If Andrew was angling to find out, she wouldn't give it to him.

She'd left the house on Duke Street shortly before six o'clock, thinking it better to get an early start at the morgue, especially since she would be leaving with Jasper at ten to call on Mrs. Lawlor. If Leo could prepare the postmortem room for Connor and finish typing outstanding reports and notes, he might not grumble as much when she told him she'd been hired as an investigative consultant to Scotland Yard and needed to leave for an hour.

When Connor arrived at the morgue at his usual time of eight o'clock, the cottage range had warmed the office just enough so that Leo's breath did not cloud the air. Her hands had also warmed as she'd typed, and thankfully, Tibia had curled up on her lap, which benefited them both.

Connor peered at the stack of completed reports on her desk on his way to the range for tea.

"You either could not sleep, or you came in early to make up for the time you were out yesterday," he said, taking the kettle from the hob.

Leo squirmed at what she had to confess. She lifted Tibia from her lap and stood, joining him near the stove.

"It's a little of both." Clasping her hands behind her back, she added, "It is also for the hour I will spend out of the morgue this morning."

With his back turned to her, Connor slowly lowered the kettle back onto the hob. Too slowly, she observed. The pause that followed hinted that he was carefully considering his reply.

"I've been hired by Inspector Reid as a consultant for the case involving Mrs. Lawlor," she explained.

"The woman who was poisoned by her husband and the false Henry Gray?" Connor turned to face her. He didn't appear angry, and yet, he also didn't appear pleased. "Miss Spencer, while I understand, and even applaud, your interest in crime solving, there are two corpses awaiting examination."

"Three," she corrected while wincing. Earlier, she'd discovered Mr. Sampson, the night attendant, had taken in another body during his shift.

Connor scrubbed his chin and groaned. "Three corpses, then. I can perform postmortems on my own, but I move much faster when I am assisted, and if our backlog grows, Mr. Pritchard is going to take notice."

It was already something Leo had considered. Mr. Pritchard was the deputy coroner, and if he marked Spring Street Morgue as falling behind in its assigned duties, he would undoubtedly blame the fact that a woman was employed there. He hadn't wanted Leo hired on to begin with. The worst part was that he'd be correct: Leo *would* be at fault—though not because she was a woman. But Mr. Pritchard, and ultimately Chief Coroner Giles, would not take into consideration the reasons for her absence.

While she had come into a nice income with the leasing of the house on Craven Hill, and she no longer needed to worry about how to provide for herself and her aged aunt and uncle, Leo did not want to be out of a position that she'd fought so hard to keep.

"You're right." She smoothed the front of her skirt with damp hands. "I'll let the inspector know I won't be joining him." Her stomach dropped at the decision, and she turned so that Connor wouldn't see the disappointment on her face.

"Wait," he said with an aggrieved sigh. "Since you came in early today, you may take an hour with the inspector."

With that, Leo's stomach buoyed. "If you are certain? Because it might stretch into two hours, depending on what Mrs. Lawlor has to say."

He bobbed his head and grumbled that yes, *this time*, it would be acceptable. Then, with a look at his watch, he announced they should begin. The next two hours passed quickly, and they were finishing the examination of the first corpse when Jasper arrived.

"I'll take it from here," Connor said, trying—Leo sensed—not to grumble.

"Thank you," she said as she placed her notes on a table near him, considering his hands were busy returning the spleen to its proper place.

He merely grunted in response.

Jasper's narrowed eyes met hers as they exited into the lobby. "Did the two of you argue?"

"It was more of a discussion than a disagreement. But it doesn't matter. What happened with Andrew?" For that was what she was truly interested in.

Jasper didn't respond as he handed her into the hired carriage, and when he'd taken the seat across from her, he continued to be silent, his expression flinty.

"Did he ask something of you?" she pressed.

As the carriage moved toward Trafalgar Square, Jasper held himself like he'd become a block of stone. "I'd rather not say."

"Jasper—" she began, but he held up his hand.

"It is better if you aren't involved."

Leo clenched her jaw. She ought to have known he'd resist telling her, and yet, she had trusted that he'd at least give her some scrap of information.

"That isn't acceptable," she replied. "You promised that you would tell me."

"I regret making that promise."

"That is too bad. What if Eddie Bloom summoned me to meet," she went on, "and when you asked me what he wanted, I chose to leave you in the dark?"

Leo had met Mr. Bloom on several occasions, and while he was a dangerous man whom Jasper disliked greatly, Leo wasn't entirely convinced Mr. Bloom was a danger to *her*.

Jasper crossed his arms, fixing her with an inflexible glare. "That would be an entirely different situation. Bloom has at least proven that he's not going to kill you at the drop of a hat."

Andrew Carter could not be trusted in the same way, she knew. But that wasn't her point.

"I'm not upset that you wish to keep me from potential harm. I'm upset because you don't trust me with the truth."

"I do trust you, Leo," he said, some of his stony edge smoothing out. "I am asking that you trust me to handle the position I am in. Trust me to do what I can to keep us both safe from Andrew and the rest of the Carters. You have my word that I would never compromise my oath to the police force."

"Of course, you wouldn't. I never believed you would."

Frustration overwhelmed her, and Leo sat back. Silence filled the interior of the carriage, their conversation stymied. She didn't know what to say that would not lead to more of an argument between them, so she said nothing as the driver took them into Mayfair. Jasper followed her example, and after several more minutes of fraught quiet, they arrived at the Lawlors' home.

Jasper briefly met Leo's eyes as he helped her to the pavement, but she was still perturbed. He wanted to handle Andrew Carter on his own, without her, and it felt like a door closing in her face. However, right then, they needed to focus on Augusta Lawlor and what so far appeared to be her attempted murder.

They were shown inside by Hastings, who took their coats and hats before leading them to the front parlor. Mrs. Lawlor was expecting them, though she didn't stand when Leo and Jasper entered the room. She was seated in a cushioned chair before a blazing fireplace and was wrapped in a voluminous blanket. Though she was still wan, the tip of her nose was red, as were her eyes. Evidence that she had been weeping.

"Forgive me, but yesterday is quite a blur," she said as her small, plump hand peeped out of the blanket, and she gestured weakly for them to be seated. It would take time for Mrs. Lawlor's body to rid itself of the arsenic that had built up in her system and for her to regain her strength.

"I recall seeing you both, but it is all very fragmented. I am told by my staff that you are Miss Spencer and Inspector Reid from Scotland Yard." A hesitant smile quivered over her lips. "A woman working for the police?"

"Miss Spencer is not employed by the Metropolitan Police Force," Jasper explained—a bit *too* rapidly. "However, she does consult from time to time on certain investigations."

Leo appreciated the added clarification, but as she sat on the sofa and Jasper took the cushioned chair opposite Mrs. Lawlor, the friction from their quarrel in the carriage remained firmly in place.

"I'm glad to see you are recovering well today, Mrs. Lawlor," Leo said. "You gave us all quite a fright at Tate's."

The other woman closed her eyes and emitted a sad chuff of laughter. "I may be alive, Miss Spencer, but I am not confident I shall recover."

Leo shifted on the sofa cushion, surprised by the vulnerable statement.

"I am aware that my husband has fled. He took the contents of the safe, nearly one thousand pounds that I am aware of," she said as she turned to stare, transfixed, at the flames leaping in the hearth. "Mrs. Vincent said he… he might have accidentally given me too much laudanum. Perhaps, he panicked."

The theory was a generous excuse for Sebastian Lawlor's actions, and Augusta's servants had likely presented it out of care for their employer's fragile state. But with what Jasper had discovered the previous day at Lawlor Antiquities, her husband's deceit could no longer be concealed from her.

"It isn't our intent to upset you any further, Mrs. Lawlor," Jasper began. "However, Scotland Yard has opened an investigation into your husband's actions. Miss Spencer and I have spoken to your staff, and we have some questions for you, if you are feeling well enough to answer them."

Augusta lifted a linen handkerchief from the folds of her blanket and touched it to her nose. "Of course, but I am certain Sebastian merely made a terrible mistake. I want him found, if only so that he knows I am not dead."

Jasper coughed lightly. "If you could start at the beginning and explain how you met your husband?"

Lowering the square of linen, Augusta drew a long breath, then commenced telling what might have been a romantic tale, if Leo did not already have concerns over Sebastian Lawlor's duplicity.

"We met at the Royal Academy," Augusta said. "I've been a patron for ages, but Sebastian had only recently discovered an interest in the arts. He comes from trade, you see, but I am not so conceited that I would discredit him for it." She paused, as if now wishing she *had* been arrogant, as most other women of her class would have been.

"Your butler said he is in imports and exports, with a storefront on Redmead Lane," Jasper said.

"That is correct," she answered.

"Have you been to the shop?" Leo asked, curious as to how the woman had never realized the truth.

"I nearly went once." Augusta frowned at the memory. "We were set upon by ruffians as soon as we stepped out of the carriage. Sebastian ushered me back in, and we got away unharmed, but he forbade me from ever visiting again. He worried for my safety, you see."

Leo thought it more likely that Sebastian Lawlor had arranged for the ruffians to attack, though not before his wife saw the shingle bearing his last name—all the evidence Augusta would require to believe he owned the shop. The event would certainly frighten her enough for her to stay away in future.

"Mrs. Lawlor," Jasper began slowly. "I visited the shop

yesterday after leaving here. I met a man named Roger Lawlor. He owns the shop, and I'm sorry to say, he does not know anyone by the name of Sebastian Lawlor."

For several seconds, Augusta merely stared at Jasper with incredulity. She scoffed, then laughed tersely. "That is impossible, Inspector. You must have visited the wrong shop."

"I was at the correct address on Redmead Lane, near Wapping Basin," he insisted.

She blinked rapidly, her incredulity transforming into consternation. "I don't know what to think."

"It appears," Leo said, as gently as she could, "that your husband told you a falsehood about his business."

Augusta kept shaking her head and again lifted her handkerchief to her nose.

"Did any of your husband's family or friends attend the wedding?" Jasper asked, changing the topic. It seemed to relieve her. At least for the moment.

"No. His parents are deceased, and he has no brothers or sisters. As he hails from Leeds, there was no one nearby to stand up with him. We had a small ceremony here, in this very room." She looked about it, fighting back tears.

Leo imagined his lack of family had reminded Augusta of her own deficit, and it had united them in a way.

"I know what you are thinking," Augusta said. "I know it because I thought it myself when we were first courting. That a man as handsome as he could not possibly want a woman of my age and appearance for anything more than her money."

Leo sat forward, suddenly furious on Augusta's behalf. "Please do not disparage yourself, Mrs. Lawlor."

She shook her head. "I am no beauty; I have always known that. But I believe we cannot help who we love. That it sometimes makes no sense."

Leo couldn't dispute that. If people could choose whom they loved, life would be simpler. She peered at Jasper and thought of Constance Hayes, the pretty and wealthy cousin of his good friend, Viscount Oliver Hayes. Jasper had courted Constance for several months. Had he loved her, he would have asked for her hand in marriage. But because of his irrepressible feelings for Leo, as he'd once admitted, he'd been unable to. Certainly, it would have been far more beneficial for him at the Yard to have a woman of Constance's ilk and refinement on his arm. But as Augusta seemed to believe, the heart wanted what it wanted.

"I know my acquaintances and my staff were suspicious of his intentions. I do not blame them, of course. There have been duplicitous suitors in the past," Augusta remarked.

"Your housekeeper mentioned that your mother once hired a private agency to look into one such suitor," Leo said. "When was this?"

"About four years ago. My mother had a bad feeling about a man who'd taken an interest," Augusta explained, looking slightly humiliated. "She hired Mr. Castelan to investigate him—quietly. He found that the man was steeped in debt and that he'd attempted to court other heiresses, albeit unsuccessfully."

Leo sat up taller. "Castelan, you say?" It was the same agency her good friend, Nivedita Brooks, now worked for.

"Yes, and I suppose if my mother was still alive, she

would have hired Mr. Castelan again to look into Sebastian." She fiddled with her handkerchief. "I admit, his actions yesterday do appear to be reprehensible. I cannot explain why he would lie about his shop. Perhaps he was ashamed that he had no business at all. But I am certain there is a reason—a good, logical reason—for his behavior."

It didn't surprise Leo that Augusta did not believe or even want to suspect that her husband had lied to her. To face that truth would mean facing another: that her husband might be guilty of something far more nefarious.

Jasper got to his feet and withdrew a folded piece of paper from his coat pocket.

"Last evening, your housekeeper sat with an artist who works for the police. Mrs. Vincent described your husband in detail. This is what the artist produced." He handed her the paper, and Leo craned her neck to try and view the rendered portrait.

Augusta's chin crumpled. Then, as if the picture pained her, she held the paper away from her. Leo took it before Jasper could.

Sebastian Lawlor was, as his wife claimed, a handsome man. He had a strong, square-shaped chin, a generous bottom lip, the top obscured by a well-trimmed mustache. His eyes, though drawn and shaded with graphite pencil, exuded vibrancy. The only flaw in his facial features was the crooked line of his nose. It bent ever so slightly to the left, as if it had been broken at some point in his life.

"It looks very much like him," Augusta confirmed once she'd recovered from the brink of another sob. She dabbed the corner of her eye with her knuckle. "Disappearing like this. Taking money and our wedding photographs… I just don't understand why."

Leo returned the sketch to Jasper, her chest tight with pity. Sebastian Lawlor—if that was even his real name—had manipulated Augusta, and he'd done a good job of it.

Jasper tucked the sketch into his pocket and cleared his throat. "Is it true that you began feeling ill while in France, on your wedding trip?"

When speaking of her mysterious illness, Augusta became less despondent and more animated. She spoke of how bewildering it was that she'd suddenly taken so ill. Her constitution, she claimed, had always been robust. With ladylike blushes and avoiding Jasper's eyes, she recounted in the vaguest terms the gastric attacks she had suffered while in Paris.

"I could hardly leave my hotel room," she whispered. "I was too weak to even go for a stroll with my new husband." At the mention of him, the despairing pull of her brow started to return.

"And when you came back to London earlier than expected, and you continued to be unwell, Mr. Lawlor summoned a physician?" Leo asked to keep Augusta from weeping again.

"Yes," she answered, sniffling. "Mr. Gray is my husband's physician. Sebastian was sure he would make me well again, and yet, I only worsened. Mr. Gray told us last month that it was cancer of the stomach. That I was… Well, that I would not live much longer." She fluttered her lashes, and a few tears spilled down her cheek. "And now, I will die all alone."

Leo met a glance with Jasper. He nodded, granting permission, she presumed, to tell Augusta the truth about her illness. And thus, what they suspected Sebastian had done to her.

"Mrs. Lawlor," she began, "you are not ill. At least, not terminally, as Mr. Gray led you to believe."

The blanket covering Augusta shifted as she hinged forward in her chair, her stare suddenly razor-sharp. It sliced into Leo. "What do you mean by that?"

As gently as she could, Leo explained. "It is my belief, as it is Inspector Reid's, that your illness has been caused by long-term exposure to arsenic. The poison is tasteless and odorless, so you wouldn't have known you were consuming it. The gastric symptoms you've been experiencing along with other things, like the white lines on your fingernails, the rough patches of skin on your palms, the numbness in your hands and feet, are all in line with arsenic poisoning."

Telling someone they'd been poisoned was new for Leo; most poison victims she'd encountered had been past the point of help.

As expected, staunch denial spread across Augusta's face.

"No." She lurched to her feet, the blanket falling away. "No. That cannot be."

"I understand that it is a shock—" Leo began, stopping when Augusta made a strange noise in her throat, something between a growl and a wail of pain. She turned away from them.

"My uncle works at Tate's and is a surgeon by trade; however, he has spent nearly twenty years as a coroner. I assisted him for several years." At this confession, Augusta peered over her shoulder at Leo with distaste, as was usual when someone learned of her work. "We've seen many arsenic poisoning victims. We've also seen morphine overdoses, which we suspect is what happened to you yesterday. May I ask, Mrs. Lawlor, who last administered your laudanum?"

Augusta's stare went distant as she considered the question, and as horror dawned in her eyes, Leo knew what answer she would give.

"Sebastian," Augusta whispered. She reached out to grip the back of the chair. "I woke in the night, feeling ill. He must have heard my distress because he came into my room and poured me a glass of water. He added drops from the bottle Mr. Gray had recently brought, but... Sebastian would only ever add eleven drops of the tincture. Just a teaspoon."

"Did you witness him administering just those eleven drops, Mrs. Lawlor?" Jasper asked.

She pressed her fingers to her brow, as if in pain. "I cannot say. It was dark, and I was so nauseous."

How easy it would be, Leo considered, for Sebastian Lawlor to slip in more than the normal amount with his wife distracted or still half asleep.

"The current bottle is missing from your bedside table, according to your maid," Jasper said. "None of your staff seem to know what has become of it."

"You are suggesting Sebastian took it?" Augusta asked, almost angrily.

"Yes," Jasper answered brusquely. "We are considering the possibility that he gave you a high dose of laudanum, with the intent to end your life. If he emptied the bottle into your glass last night, he wouldn't have wanted to leave the evidence for your maid to find. It would only inspire suspicion."

Kitty had informed Leo that the two-ounce bottle had been new. If Sebastian had mixed that amount, or near to it, into his wife's glass of water, the potency could have certainly led to her death. However, Augusta Lawlor may have developed a tolerance to laudanum over the last few months. It was also possible that her generous size had helped to protect her from succumbing to the tincture's effects. A proper dosage of laudanum was administered according to a person's weight. A heavier person would need a larger dose of the drug to feel the same effects as a slighter person would with a smaller one.

Had Sebastian incorrectly calculated how much laudanum was needed to kill his wife? It was an awful thought. And Augusta was not ready to believe it. She lifted her chin and firmed her expression. "That suggestion is abhorrent, Inspector. I cannot entertain it. I will not! I would like you both to leave."

They could not refuse. She had welcomed them in and had every right to toss them out. Though clearly feeling thwarted, Jasper nodded tightly.

"Very well, Mrs. Lawlor. I do have one last question for you, however. Where is Mr. Henry Gray's office located?"

They would need to visit. Or rather, Jasper would. Leo had been gone from the morgue nearly three-quarters of an hour now and would surely not have time to accompany him.

"I'm sure Hastings will get you the address," Augusta answered, her demeanor so chilled she would not even look at them. Still, they thanked her and wished her well.

Hastings was waiting for them in the front hall, and when Jasper asked for the doctor's address, the corners of the butler's mouth pulled even lower in a downward slope. "I am afraid none of the staff know where to find the doctor. Mr. Lawlor was always the one to summon him, you see."

Once they were in the hired carriage again, on their way back to the morgue, Jasper doffed his bowler and groaned as he rested his head against the cushioned wall.

"I doubt Mr. Gray's address will be found within the London Directory, but I'll put PC Drake on the hunt as soon as I've checked in at the Yard and updated Chief Coughlan."

"What did he say about my consulting?" Leo asked, though she was nervous for the answer. Jasper sighed and lifted his head.

"To tread carefully," he replied. "Though I don't know if the order was directed at me or you."

"Probably both," she presumed.

Silence grew between them, and as it did, their earlier argument regarding Andrew Carter came to mind again. Leo didn't want to discuss it, as she didn't wish to quarrel with him. To prevent Jasper from broaching the topic, she stayed focused on Sebastian Lawlor.

"Mr. Lawlor, if that is his real name, has certainly pulled the wool over his wife's eyes," she commented. "It makes me wonder if he has had some practice at this sort of deceit before. And if Mr. Gray does turn out to be an imposter, perhaps the two of them have a history of working together as partners."

Jasper drummed his fingers on the crown of his black bowler. "That would explain Lawlor's thoroughness in taking the photographs from the house. And in deciding upon a surname and business that was already established. The trip to the antiquities shop had to have been well coordinated."

"It was a nefarious scheme," Leo agreed. "But this type of marriage ploy could be easily replicated."

She considered it: A handsome man approaches a wealthy, unmarried woman, someone who never expected to marry. He charms her into falling in love, and after they marry, he begins to slowly poison her, making it look like ill health is claiming her. Once he is a widower, he receives the entirety of the woman's wealth. That would include property that he could sell, if it wasn't entailed. Augusta's property was surely worth far more than the one thousand pounds taken from the floor safe.

Why would Sebastian rush away? Why disappear before the con was seen through to its end?

"We need to find his past victims," Leo said. "If, of course, they exist."

"A family member might have lodged a complaint." Jasper shrugged. "But if he selects his victims carefully, he wouldn't make the mistake of choosing someone who has family."

He would select a woman like Augusta.

"If he targets wealthy women," Leo said, "their deaths would be reported in the gossip rags."

She sometimes read the society pages in the newspapers, if only out of curiosity—although, she avoided the *Times*. It was petty of her, she knew, but Constance Hayes was a typist there, and though she had no byline, Leo was aware she typed those columns.

"Can you recall anything?" Jasper asked. He was thinking of her photographic memory, and even as she answered, "I'll work on it," she was busily shuffling through her mind's endless images of society pages that might have mentioned the death of a newly married heiress.

"I'll put PC Mills on it when he and Warnock return from the Central Bank. They were bringing a warrant there this morning to see if the Lawlor accounts have been cleared out."

As they entered Trafalgar Square, Jasper sat forward. Before he even spoke, she knew what he was going to say. "Leo. About earlier—"

"Unless you are going to tell me what it is Andrew Carter wants, I don't wish to talk about it." It was brusque and a bit harsh, but it was how she felt. She also didn't want to argue again.

Jasper sat back, his mouth a firm line.

The carriage drew up to the morgue on Spring Street, and she reached to open the door. Jasper caught her wrist.

"I don't want us at odds, Leo."

She didn't want that, either. But she was also too perturbed to make amends right then.

"Have dinner with me tonight." His whispered request danced along her spine and curled around her heart. She longed to forget their dispute and simply bask in his affection. If she were to dine with him, perhaps at his home, they could spend time alone afterward in his study. The temptation was nearly physical. Gracious, her attraction to him was becoming unruly.

"I'll accept," she said, "*if* you'll reconsider and tell me what Andrew Carter wants from you."

Jasper grimaced. "No."

She pulled her wrist free. "Then, I believe I will spend the evening with Uncle Claude and Aunt Flora.

I've been remiss in spending time with them lately, anyhow."

Disappointment doused her as Jasper opened the carriage door, descended, and then helped her down. He appeared conflicted for a moment but then shook his head.

"We'll speak later, then."

She didn't trust herself not to take back her decision and agree to dine with him, so she bid him a good day and rushed to enter the morgue.

Chapter Seven

Jasper flexed his hands, enjoying the dull ache of bruised knuckles. He'd lasted a few rounds in the boxing ring, and though he and his opponent were evenly matched, the man had a particularly hard jaw and a torso like metal plating. Not to mention a left hook that felt more like a ship's anchor sailing up out of the water to collide with his chin.

"Barney's taken the measure of you tonight," Oliver Hayes said as Jasper collapsed into a club chair across from him. Tables surrounded the raised ring inside Fortune's, the gentleman's boxing club that Jasper had a standing invitation to frequent thanks to his friend, the viscount.

"What is that supposed to mean?" Jasper asked. A waiter had poured him a whisky while he'd been in the ring with Lord Barnstable, the third son of a duke, and he now took a healthy swig of it.

"You're angry, and it has made you sloppy," Oliver answered with an amused grin. He was reclining in his chair, one ankle resting on his opposite knee, his attention fixed on the two men who'd climbed into the ring after Jasper and Barnstable had finished. Or rather, after Barnstable had finished with Jasper.

He flexed the hand not holding his drink and groaned. Oliver wasn't wrong. He'd been in a foul mood most of the day. His meeting with Andrew had started it off; his argument with Leo had exacerbated it; and his inability to locate any doctor in London by the name of Henry Gray had cemented it.

Now that Jasper was certain Lawlor and Gray were accomplices, he would need to send the sketch artist, Mr. Gibbons, to Mrs. Lawlor's home on Hill Street. With any hope, a member of the staff could provide a description for a rendering of the doctor's face. He'd put it and Sebastian Lawlor's sketch into the *Police Gazette* for circulation, and he'd send the likenesses to Fleet Street too, for inclusion in any newspaper that would run them.

Constable Price had taken a copy of the sketch of Sebastian Lawlor to Paddington Station, but no porters or ticket salesclerks recognized his face. There was no way to know if the man had purchased a ticket and boarded a train; hundreds of people passed through the station every day. Porters couldn't be expected to remember them all.

If Sebastian had left London, at least Jasper knew he had not first gone to the Central Bank. The judge's warrant had loosened the bank manager's lips, and Sergeant Warnock and PC Mills had learned the Lawlors' account—originally in Miss Augusta Hart's name and transferred into her husband's after their wedding—had not been accessed for over a week. But looking through the account ledgers, the manager revealed that a significant withdrawal of four thousand pounds had been made the previous week.

Jasper presumed that Lawlor must have stashed the amount in the study safe, in preparation for the morning he would overdose Augusta and flee.

However, four thousand pounds was a fraction of what had been left in the bank account and of what Mrs. Lawlor's other assets and investments might have raked in. So, the question remained: Why had Sebastian left without trying to take his full due?

Frustrated, Jasper had arrived at Fortune's with a desire to hit something. But so far, none of the punches he'd thrown—or absorbed—had alleviated the pent-up aggravation inside him.

"Is it one of your cases that has you in twists?" Oliver asked as a waiter set a shallow bowl brimming with chipped ice before Jasper. "Or is it the lovely Miss Spencer?"

Jasper plunged one fist into the ice and sent his friend a warning glare. Oliver only chuckled, as if knowing he'd hit the mark.

He'd expected Leo would be upset when he refused to tell her what Andrew wanted. Had he explained, she would have insisted on helping him search for Cillian Carter, and that was something Jasper did not want. Her assistance wasn't the issue; it was the fact that the assignment involved both the East Rips and the Spitalfields Angels, two enormously dangerous gangs. Jasper had thought that keeping her clear of it all would be worth fielding her disappointment, even her anger. Now, however, he wasn't sure he'd made the right choice. She'd accused him of not trusting her. How could he make her understand it was the Carters and the Angels he didn't trust?

"How are things progressing with your ladylove these days?" Oliver asked when it was clear his first question would go unanswered. This one would as well.

Jasper gritted his teeth against the ice numbing his sore knuckles. "I hear you're becoming serious about a certain debutante," he asked his friend instead.

The viscount rolled his eyes at the obvious redirection. "That is what my mother is feeding to the gossip mill."

His mother had recently returned from a long stay in Italy, following the death of her husband and Oliver's father. Since the widowed viscountess's arrival at Hayes Manor, Oliver had been complaining about her insistence that he find a wife and settle down. He'd been forced to curtail his vice-ridden soirees—and his habit of falling in love on a weekly basis.

"I don't read the society pages, but Leo does," Jasper replied. "She mentioned a Miss Vachon."

Oliver scowled and raised his empty glass to signal the waiter for another pour. "She is perfect in every way, as my mother has expounded upon countless times," he said with a distinct lack of enthusiasm. "I'll probably marry her, though I'm not in any rush."

Jasper removed his numbed fist from the ice and buried his other bruised set of knuckles next. "I'm not sure how any woman could resist such a romantic declaration."

Oliver laughed. "I could be an ogre, and she wouldn't bat an eyelash. It's the title and the money Miss Vachon's kind wants. You can see for yourself when you meet her at the Home Secretary's dinner next week."

Jasper peered across the table. "I'm not aware of any dinner at the Home Secretary's."

Oliver grinned as his glass was refilled with more Spanish port. "Your invitation is on its way. I made sure one was extended to you."

"This day needs to end," Jasper groaned. "It is only getting worse."

"Oh, come now, you can bring Miss Spencer."

"She would hate it even more than I would."

"You are attending, and that is that."

Jasper pulled his knuckles from the rapidly melting ice chips. He detested the political elbow rubbing that came with being an inspector in the Metropolitan Police Force. The higher up one rose in rank, the closer one was to the politicians at the helm of the force, such as the Detective Chief Superintendent, Commissioner, and Home Secretary. Jasper didn't have the polished temperament that his father, Gregory Reid, the former Detective Chief Superintendent had possessed, and nor would he need it if he remained a detective inspector...as he preferred to do.

That meant, of course, that he needed to solve most of the cases he was given. On that note, Jasper turned his thoughts to work and the possibility that the man known as Sebastian Lawlor had pulled off this fraudulent ploy more than once. He would have targeted a wealthy woman. Possibly one within the aristocracy.

Briefly, Jasper laid out the Lawlor situation to the viscount, who nearly choked on his port when he heard a woman had risen to consciousness while inside a wicker transport casket.

"Christ, I don't want to think about what might have happened had the poor woman not woken up before Miss Spencer's uncle commenced the embalming process," Oliver said, his complexion taking on a greenish hue.

"We don't believe this was Lawlor's first confidence trick," Jasper said.

"We?" Oliver echoed, raising a brow.

Of course, he would have picked up on that one word. "Miss Spencer and I," Jasper clarified, though his dour tone advised Oliver against pressing the subject. "Can you think of anyone from your set who experienced something similar? Perhaps within the last few years?"

Oliver swirled the dark ruby port in his glass, a look of concentration pulling at the corners of his mouth. It was the expression he wore when playing cards with a losing hand.

"I'm sorry, no," he said after a moment. But then he brightened. "However, I can think of someone who might have a better idea than me."

Jasper knew to whom he referred. His cousin Constance typed the society pages for the *Times*. She'd been employed there for about two years, much to the discontent of her parents. If a newly married heiress had died of a mysterious wasting disease, Constance would likely recall the announcement.

"I can pay her a call and hope she speaks to me," Jasper said. The last time he'd seen her had been over the summer, when her younger brother went missing. Thirteen-year-old George Hayes had been kidnapped by his birth mother, after he had been stolen from her as a baby. Leo had managed to track him down, which led to his safe return to his adoptive family.

"Don't worry. She's over you," Oliver replied. "In fact, she has a new beau."

"Does she? I'm glad." The sentiment was sincere. Jasper felt no envy that Constance had found another man; he'd ended his courtship with her for the undeniable reason that he did not love her. He could not. Because he was already in love with Leo, even if he had not yet admitted it to himself.

"She's calling on my mother tomorrow at Hayes Manor. If it would be helpful, I'll put the question to Constance then," Oliver offered.

It would free up Jasper to attend to other aspects of his investigations—including the unofficial one he'd taken on to appease Andrew Carter. So, he thanked Oliver, threw back the remainder of his whisky, and rose from his chair.

"Getting back in the ring?" his friend asked, smirking.

He shook his head. "Going home while I still have all my teeth."

Jasper collected his coat and hat at the front of the club and started home on foot, the scent of cigar smoke lingering on him. He arrived home too late to find Mrs. Zhao still awake. Attempting to bathe in the room off the kitchen would have stirred her from her sleep, so he washed up quickly and fell into bed, his mind still churning.

He rose at dawn, and when he joined his housekeeper in the kitchen, the bruising on his knuckles drew her attention.

"Police work or that boxing club again?" she asked, her meaning unequivocally clear: Men pummeling each other for sport was barbaric.

"Whichever you would rather it be," he answered. It earned him a string of muttering in her native Cantonese.

He ate the sausage and soft-boiled eggs she'd prepared, then left the house earlier than usual. From Charing Cross Station, he took the railway to Liverpool Street. When he emerged, the morning fog was lifting. Jasper hired a cab and directed the driver to Newton Close.

The previous morning, Andrew had provided the information he possessed on Cillian's mistress, Tabitha Pierce, and her husband, Desmond. The couple lived in a common lodging house, like many others did in the East End. Desmond held a job at a casino in Stepney, and when he wasn't working, he often loitered with other Angels at the Black Parrot, a public house owned by Barry Reubens, a cousin to Desmond.

With the pact for amity between the two gangs in place, no East Rip—not even Sean Carter—could approach Tabitha or Desmond on Angels' territory now to ask questions about Cillian. Jasper doing so would still draw attention, and it could be dangerous, but Andrew didn't much care about that.

The cab traveled through narrow, crowded streets filled with shopfronts for butchers, shoemakers, silk weavers, taverns, and garment makers. Costermongers had set up their carts; children in thin clothing and pitiable footwear were collecting horse droppings and bits of dropped coal from the streets to burn at home or in rubbish bins for heat; and too many bedraggled men and women were lounging in alleyways as though it was where they'd spent the night.

The cabbie stopped at the corner of Newton Close. Doss-houses lined the short and narrow dead-end street, with people's laundry strung crisscross overhead. At the far end, children kicked a ball amongst themselves and against a crumbling brick wall that sealed off the close.

Jasper paid the cabbie and asked him to wait, then started toward the address Andrew had given him. A man emerged from one doss-house, caught sight of Jasper, and stopped to stare. He likely knew Jasper was a copper: He had the unmistakable look of a policeman, his father had once told him. Somehow, Gregory had added, Jasper's promotion from a uniformed constable to a plainclothes detective sergeant had only made him appear more like a policeman. It was in his bearing, and that was something Jasper could not disguise.

He'd tucked his Webley in a holster under his coat, though he would rather not find himself cornered in this dead-end street.

With the man in the doorway continuing to stare, Jasper found the building he wanted and dipped inside its dank entry hall. Taking the stairs to the next floor, he considered how he would approach the Pierces. Prancing around the reason for his visit would only waste time. Besides, Jasper preferred to employ straightforward questions. How people reacted to them was often telling.

He found the door he wanted and, taking a bracing breath, brought down his fist. No sound came from within the rooms. Jasper knocked again. It was early still. If Desmond had returned home late after his shift at the casino, he might still be abed. Tabitha, Jasper hoped, would answer the door, and he could pose his questions about Cillian Carter to her.

But when the door did open an inch, that hope scattered. A man with dark eyes stared out at Jasper. He looked as if he hadn't slept in days, with his shaggy black hair, a patchy beard, and clothes in need of a thorough washing. Three deep gouges scored his neck, peeking out above his stained collar.

"Desmond Pierce?"

The man's glare sharpened. "What do you want?"

"I'm looking for someone. I think you might know where he is."

Desmond sniffed, unimpressed, and started to close the door.

"Cillian Carter." He trusted the name would stop Desmond's retreat, and it did. The door reopened, and Desmond's stare turned hawkish. Though he stood a full head shorter than Jasper, he had the thick, brutal look of a man who knew how to throw a debilitating punch.

"You're a copper," he stated.

"I'm not here on police business," Jasper replied. "I've been hired privately."

"And why would you think I know where this Carter fellow is?" Though he tried to sound it, Desmond wasn't ignorant as to who Cillian Carter was. Every Angel would know the name of the East Rips leader's only son.

"I've been told your wife is an…*acquaintance* of his," Jasper said bluntly, prepared for any sort of reaction the man might give. An incoming fist, for example, or the sudden appearance of a blade. But all Desmond did was squint.

"Bollocks," he said, and with a genuine snort of disbelief.

Jasper peered over Desmond's shoulder into the shabby room. "Is Tabitha in?"

Desmond came forward, shutting the door behind

him, to hamper Jasper's view. His upper lip curled into a sneer. "Where did you hear my wife's name, copper?"

"Part of a rumor, I'm afraid."

The man glowered but said nothing.

"It isn't my intention to malign your wife," Jasper continued. "But my client wants no stone left unturned. Mr. Carter has been missing for several days, and his loved ones are concerned."

Desmond's nostrils flared, but his swelling temper seemed to cool. "How many?"

"How many what?"

"Days," Desmond ground out. "How many days has he been gone?"

The question took Jasper by surprise. "Seven, now. Have you seen him?"

A shade of nervousness seeped through Desmond's scowl. He bumped his heels into the closed door as he took a step back. "No. Now, leave off." The order lacked any teeth.

"When will your wife be in?" Jasper asked as Desmond backed into his room. He slammed the door without answering.

The tension in Jasper's chest eased as he descended the soft, corky wooden stairs and exited the doss-house. Desmond hadn't said much, and Jasper was still no closer to finding out where Cillian might be, but the Angel hadn't seemed to know Cillian was Tabitha's lover.

And by asking how many days the young Carter had been missing, he'd also let something more slip: Jasper was almost certain Tabitha Pierce had been missing for the same length of time.

Chapter Eight

Nivedita Brooks was standing at the cottage range, up close to Connor Quinn, when Leo entered the morgue's office just before eight o'clock. The two of them —sipping tea, conversing in low voices, grinning bashfully —were so entranced with one another that Leo's presence did not register until she closed the back door with a firm tug.

"Oh, good, Dita, you are here," Leo said brightly.

Connor cleared his throat and stepped away from the range. Dita followed the coroner with a lingering gaze.

Before she had met Connor, even the thought of dead bodies had turned Dita's stomach and made her dizzy. Daring to cross the threshold now was testament to Dita's serious interest in the assistant city coroner. Though she still refused to enter the postmortem room. Once the heat and humidity of summer set in, Leo doubted Dita would even be able to stand entering the office or front lobby.

"Hmm?" Dita murmured distractedly, then reluctantly peeled her attention away from Connor.

Leo only shook her head and laughed. "I wanted to ask you about a case Jasper and I are investigating."

"Oh, yes, Connor told me all about it. A dead woman who came back to life at Tate's?" Dita's interest was now completely on Leo rather than her new beau. "And the doctor who named himself after that textbook?"

Leo set her bag down and removed her gloves. It was icebox-cold in the office, but she would warm them on a cup of tea, as Dita was.

"Mrs. Lawlor did not come back to life, as she wasn't dead to begin with," Leo clarified.

"As I explained," Connor said to defend himself.

"All right, all right. What did you want to ask me?" Dita inquired while scowling playfully at Connor.

"Mrs. Lawlor's mother hired Mr. Castelan a few years ago to investigate a suspicious suitor. He turned out to be a fortune hunter," Leo explained. "However, I'm wondering if Mr. Castelan has investigated, or heard of, any attempted murders like this one that was perpetrated against Mrs. Lawlor."

Dita furrowed her brow in thought. "I'm not sure. Not since I've been there, at least."

She had been employed by the private inquiry agency for just two months. At first, Leo had been envious of her friend. However, she changed her mind when Dita was assigned to an undercover job at Gleason's Department Store with the objective of luring the store owner into a compromising situation to prove he was conducting extra-marital affairs.

Women were too often hired by agencies like Mr. Castelan's to act as spies, exploiting their womanly wiles to tempt men into bad behavior—which would then be caught out and turned against them. They didn't seem to truly investigate as Leo enjoyed doing. However, Dita seemed to be enjoying her new job, and Leo had come to terms with the fact that her friend had a different perspective.

"I can ask Mr. Castelan," Dita said as she lifted her wool cloak from a peg near the door. "Or better yet, you can join me for lunch there and ask him yourself. He still wants to meet you, you know."

"And I am still not interested," Leo replied, repeating what she'd already told Dita several times.

Mr. Castelan had been angling for an introduction to her since reading a few articles in the *Illustrated Police News* earlier in the year that mentioned a lady morgue assistant had aided Scotland Yard in some of its recent investigations. The publicity had angered Jasper's superiors, who said a woman's help made the department look weak. Mr. Castelan, however, clearly disagreed.

"He isn't going to give up, so you may as well get the meeting over with. Join me at noon," Dita commanded, then with a beseeching glance at Connor, "if Mr. Quinn can spare you."

He met her flirtatious look with something just shy of real annoyance. "It seems all I do lately is spare Miss Spencer. But what is another hour when there have already been so many?"

Had Leo not been present, Dita would have likely kissed Connor's cheek in thanks. Instead, she restrained herself and left through the back door while wearing a coquettish grin. Leo stifled her amusement and followed Connor into the postmortem room, collecting an apron on the way.

"You are smitten with her," she observed.

Connor didn't bother to deny it. "And you are benefiting from my smittenness."

"I'm not sure that is a word."

He ignored her as he entered the closet filled with tools and supplies for his trade, as well as aprons, gloves, and vulcanized rubber boots for him to wear.

She raised her voice to be heard within the closet. "How do you feel about her work at Mr. Castelan's?"

"I want her to be happy," he replied, "but I worry she will find herself in some trouble during one of her assignments. I especially worry that no one will be there to help her."

He was thinking, no doubt, of Lydia Hailson, his former betrothed. She'd been the investigative reporter working undercover at Gleason's Department Store, gathering information on what had happened to Mr. Bloom's opium. She'd been discovered and killed. Connor and Lydia's relationship had ended several months before her body had arrived at the morgue, much to his shock and dismay. But he had still mourned her.

"You're quite talented at detective work, you know," Connor called, still shuffling items around in the closet. The unexpected compliment flummoxed Leo for a beat too long, and before she could thank him, he added, "However, we do have two postmortems this morning before you go off gallivanting again."

Leo pursed her lips. "I would hardly call it gallivanting."

She wasn't looking forward to meeting Mr. Castelan, though she was interested in what he might know about any private inquiries like what had happened with Augusta Lawlor.

"Did you send in for that new sharpening kit?" Connor asked as he emerged from the closet.

"Last Wednesday," Leo answered. She approached one of the corpses. A man, still clothed in a black suit. She reached for the postmortem request that arrived with the body.

"The bone saw is going to need replacing soon too," he informed her.

She regularly kept a list in her mind of all the supplies Connor went through in his duties and now added the bone saw.

"Who do we have here?" Connor asked as he joined her, outfitted for the procedure.

"A John Doe," she read. "Found in Blackfriars. Appears to be a stabbing."

Like with other John and Jane Does, Leo would send a description of the victim to Constable Elias Murray later in the day to be included in the next issue of the *Police Gazette*.

She set down the postmortem request and joined Connor at the top of the table, near the man's head. She would need only to look fully at the victim once to remember the details of his appearance, then type them later for Constable Murray. She would include his clothing and any other identifying marks too. However, as she took in the victim's face—his square chin, the crooked line of his nose—Leo went utterly still.

"Miss Spencer?" Connor was waiting for her assistance in removing the man's coat. "Is something wrong?"

"Not exactly," she replied, noting the corpse's full bottom lip. Even without the mustache that had trimmed his upper lip before, his features were unmistakable. "I believe I know who this man is. Or at least, the most recent name he'd been using: Sebastian Lawlor."

Connor was in the middle of conducting the postmortem on the body of Augusta Lawlor's husband by the time Jasper arrived at the morgue. The brass bell chimed in the lobby, announcing a visitor, and as Jasper had a standing invitation to enter, the detective inspector joined them without first knocking.

As he crossed the room toward the autopsy table, a feeling charged through Leo, one that had started to occur with more regularity. It was pleasure and longing, tangled up into one urge to stand closer to him, to hear the resonating timbre of his voice. Even now, as they stood over the body of a slain man, his postmortem underway, she felt an irrepressible delight that Jasper had arrived, scowl and all. And scowl he did as he peered at Sebastian Lawlor's face.

"Damn it," he muttered. "Did he have anything on him? Any identification or something that might give us a clue as to who he truly was?"

"I checked his pockets," Leo replied. "They were empty except for these."

She took from her apron pocket a flat brass skeleton key and two gold bands, one larger in circumference than the other.

"Wedding bands," Jasper said as he took the gold rings first.

"They were tucked in the ticket pocket of his trousers," Leo said. The small slit in the waistband might have been easy to overlook if his killer had been rushed.

"Mrs. Lawlor was still wearing her wedding band yesterday," Leo recalled. "The larger band fits on Mr. Lawlor's ring finger." Which, Leo had noted, did not sport a wedding band at all. He'd removed it before he was killed.

Jasper held up the smaller ring. "He had another wife, in the past?"

"Or he still had his other wife when he married Mrs. Lawlor," Leo suggested.

With a disturbed tuck of his mouth, Jasper gave the rings back to her and took up the brass skeleton key. It had been engraved with a number: 146. "This appears to be a key to a safe deposit box."

"That was my thought too," Leo said. "Could Mr. Lawlor have taken it from the study safe and gone to the bank to empty it?"

Jasper shook his head. "Warnock and Mills spoke with the Central Bank's manager. Lawlor wasn't there two mornings ago. He did, however, withdraw four thousand pounds the week before from their account."

It was a staggering amount for most people, though Leo presumed he'd left behind far more than he'd taken.

"The bank manager said the safe deposit box hadn't been touched," Jasper went on. He pocketed the key. "I'll hold on to this and check with Warnock to see if the number matches."

The bank would have the second, matching key required to open the box, Leo knew.

"Whoever he was, the cause of death is clear," Connor said. He pointed a bloody, gloved finger toward the damage within the open chest cavity. "Stabbed twice in the heart, and once in the stomach. The blade was about three inches long and thin, likely a slip joint folding knife. The bruising here, see?" He indicated some discoloration on the sides of the chest punctures. "The handle of the blade struck the victim as the knife was plunged in, each time."

"And those four round marks?" Jasper said, his attention on four identical round bruises at the puncture sites. Each round bruise measured three millimeters in size and were darker in contrast to the rest of the bruising.

"Something on the knife handle made them," Leo answered. "Some ornamentation."

"The killer got close with a small blade, which would have been easily concealed, before attacking," Jasper said. "A man of some strength, I would guess. A mugging?"

"It could appear that way. He was found with no belongings," Leo said. "Most notably, none of the money he'd taken from Mrs. Lawlor's safe."

"But why would his assailant leave behind the wedding bands?" Connor asked. "Muggers would check every pocket, I imagine, and gold is easy to fence."

"If a mugger saw the bounty in Lawlor's bags, he would not bother with his ticket pocket," Jasper suggested.

He lifted the coat from the pile of clothing that Leo had folded and set on a vacant autopsy table. It was a common sack coat, frayed at the cuffs and worn at the elbows.

"These are not the clothes of a wealthy woman's husband," Jasper said.

Leo had noted that too. The manufacturing labels on high-end clothing would have been woven into the lining, while the paper labels on cheaper clothing would disintegrate after a few washings. Sebastian Lawlor had been found in the latter type of clothing, the paper labels already gone.

"I think he must have either purchased secondhand clothes or changed into items he had set aside somewhere," Leo said. "And he shaved his mustache too."

"To be less recognizable as Sebastian Lawlor," Jasper concurred. "The maid said she overheard him telling a cabbie to bring him to Paddington Station. Why go there if he planned to stay in London?"

"To meet someone?" Leo suggested. "Henry Gray, perhaps."

He and the false doctor might have had plans to meet after Augusta's body was removed and brought to Tate's. There was no way to truly know, at least not that Leo could figure.

"He died yesterday," Connor said after a moment of quiet. It was best, Leo knew, to return to the facts they did have. "By the current phase of rigor and the lack of digestion of his last meal, I'd estimate he was killed between four and seven o'clock, the latter of which was when constables were summoned to an alley off Creed Lane. The victim's last meal was within an hour or two of his death. Standard pub fare. Ale, a steak and kidney pie, and carrots."

That meant Sebastian had spent a full day in London

after fleeing the Lawlor home on Hill Street. Why linger if he had the money?

"I'll have my constables show Lawlor's sketch around at pubs near Creed Lane," Jasper said. "It's possible someone will remember him and if he was with anyone. I have a sketch being done of Henry Gray. We can show them both."

It was a good start, although Leo wished there had been more on the body, like a tattoo, or something among his belongings that would have helped them narrow down their search for his identity.

"What of Mrs. Lawlor?" Leo asked as she walked with Jasper toward the lobby door. Augusta was already devastated; if her heart wasn't yet completely broken, learning her husband was dead would finish the job.

"I'll inform her." Jasper took the watch fob from his waistcoat pocket and checked the hour. "I have some time before luncheon."

She looked askance at him. "Since when do you take time out of the day for *luncheon*?"

"Since Superintendent Monroe invited me this morning to join him at one." He didn't sound at all pleased.

"Has he ever invited you to luncheon before?" she asked as they crossed into the lobby.

"No," he answered once he'd pulled back. "And to be honest, I don't look forward to it. I don't have the time to spare. However, since it is the superintendent..." He didn't need to finish his thought. Leo knew well enough he could not have refused his superior.

A hush settled between them. Instinctively, she knew they'd both turned to thoughts about the night before. She hadn't liked the way they'd parted. She'd been angry, and he'd been pigheaded. Even so, all night, Leo regretted refusing to dine with him.

Jasper spun his bowler slowly in his hands. "There is something I want to say."

Apprehension churned her stomach. "That sounds ominous."

"Andrew has asked me to find someone. A nephew."

The information rendered her speechless, especially as he'd been so unyielding before about shutting her out.

"I still don't want you near it, so that is all I am going to share," Jasper said. "For now, at least. Unless I can see some way you might be able to assist without drawing Andrew's attention or putting you directly in danger."

It wasn't exactly enough to fully appease her, but it was more of a concession than she'd expected.

Jasper reached for her waist. "I don't want us to quarrel."

It would have been petty of her to pull away, and she didn't want to do that anyhow. So, she allowed him to bring her closer.

"Neither do I," she admitted.

A flicker of a grin touched his mouth, but instead of leaning forward and kissing her, he only bussed his lips against her cheek. As he did, he whispered, "Tell me I will see you tonight. Come to my home for dinner."

The unruly longing that had afflicted her for a little while now flared again. She would not refuse him this time.

"Seven o'clock?" she asked.

With a grin of satisfaction, Jasper stepped away. "Now that is a meal I *can* look forward to."

Chapter Nine

Jasper approached the arched entrance to Verrey's with curious trepidation. Although he hadn't dined at the posh French restaurant before, its reputation and exorbitant prices weren't the reasons he hesitated on the pavement outside. His qualms were due to the person who was waiting for him inside.

That morning, after returning from Spitalfields—and before he'd been summoned to the Spring Street Morgue to view the body of Sebastian Lawlor—he'd found two letters waiting on his desk at Scotland Yard. One, a large envelope, had contained a heavy card embossed with the details of the Home Secretary's dinner party. He was being invited, just as Oliver had promised. He'd tossed it aside, preferring not to think about the dinner just yet. The second letter had been a brief note from Superintendent Clive Monroe, asking Jasper to meet him at Verrey's for luncheon at one o'clock.

He'd been baffled…and slightly aggravated. As he'd told Leo while on his way out of the morgue, he was already pressed for time with his caseload—both official and unofficial. The idea of taking a leisurely hour or more to dine with the Criminal Investigation Department's superintendent made him itch.

Jasper gave his name to the host, uncertain why Monroe—a man he didn't know well—had invited him to a fine restaurant rather than to the Rising Sun pub next to the Yard, where most officers stopped for a pint or something to eat. Soft strains of a violin floated through the air as he was led through the restaurant toward the center of the dining room. Round, white linen-draped tables held crystal glasses and silver cutlery, along with vases of hothouse flowers. Jasper's dark wool suit wasn't on par with the refined threads the other patrons were wearing. It looked especially shabby in comparison to the starched suit the superintendent wore.

Monroe was already at the table, though he wasn't alone. A young man, no older than twenty, and a young woman, perhaps a few years older than that, were seated with him. They were both dark-haired, like the superintendent, and possessed his same arrow-shaped chin. His children, Jasper presumed. He recalled that the superintendent's wife had passed away a handful of years ago.

"Ah, Inspector Reid, I'm pleased you could join us," Monroe said jovially as the host pulled out the last chair at the small, round table for Jasper.

"Thank you for the invitation," he replied as he sat. "It was unexpected."

There was no reason to pretend it wasn't.

A waiter poured champagne into a fluted glass at Jasper's place setting. The superintendent was seated directly across from him, while Monroe's daughter was to Jasper's right, and his son to his left.

"Allow me to introduce my children, Christopher and Rose."

Jasper gave them each a tight grin and nod. While Christopher didn't bother to meet Jasper's eyes or respond, Rose smiled gamely.

"I've heard much about you, Inspector," she said. "Father has been singing your praises for months now."

The invitation to Verrey's had surprised him, but this statement set him back in his chair. He hadn't known the superintendent gave him any thought at all, let alone enough to speak to his children about him.

"Resolving that counterfeiting case in Liverpool made the Yard look good, Reid, and as you well know, good press is not easy to come by," Monroe said. "I think Gregory would be proud of you, son."

Jasper nodded his thanks, even though he was, again, unsettled. His father had been superintendent at the CID until his illness had become too debilitating. Monroe, a detective chief inspector from Birmingham, had moved into the position and had only met with Gregory a few times. Claiming to know what the late superintendent would feel and addressing Jasper as 'son' raised his hackles.

"Following in your father's footsteps is an admirable thing," Monroe went on when Jasper remained quiet. He glanced toward his son. "As I've been telling our Christopher, there are futures to be made in policing. But for now, he is attending Cambridge."

The young man picked up his glass of champagne. "My

father has not given up in his mission to see me follow in *his* footsteps."

"Now, now," Monroe said with a tense chuckle. "Let's not bore the inspector with family politics, son."

"You were the one to bring them up, Father," Christopher replied in a bored tone.

"Inspector Reid, I hear you solved a case concerning the murder of a viscount's granddaughter recently," Rose said in a smooth, yet obvious attempt to interrupt her father and brother's squabbling.

"My Rose does not shy away from the topic of murder, Reid, as you can see," Monroe said with a doting glance toward her.

"Viscount Cowper's granddaughter, yes. Mrs. Helen Dalton," Jasper said.

"Do tell us more," Rose said.

"I would rather not, Miss Monroe. The details are unseemly."

Murder had been only one part of that case. The incestuous lust the viscount's son felt for Helen, a niece close in age to him, and his choice to kill her, to cover up his previous murder of Helen's younger brother, would surely ruin appetites around the table.

Rose raised a thin, dark brow. "I see. You're quite the gentleman, Inspector."

The simpering grin she formed was artful. It reminded him of Constance Hayes. Like Constance, Rose had likely been trained in refined comportment and social graces from a young age. Monroe, Jasper knew, was a wealthy man, with ties to a successful manufacturing family in Birmingham.

As they ate their lunch, he found that like Constance,

Rose had a cheery, confident exterior and the ability to encourage those around her into lighthearted conversation, even if the topics were ultimately shallow. Still, Rose adeptly kept the conversation flowing, in turn preventing her father and brother from making sniping remarks at one another.

They were nearly finished with their meals, and Jasper still couldn't be sure why he'd been summoned to dine with the Monroe family. He suppressed the urge to glance at his pocket watch, but he could not restrict his eyes from wandering toward the tall case clock across the room.

As he'd told Leo he would, he'd paid a call to Augusta Lawlor's home after leaving the morgue. As expected, she had refused to permit him entry. So, instead, Jasper had told the butler, Hastings, the news of Mr. Lawlor's death. Hastings relayed the information, and only then had Mrs. Lawlor allowed Jasper to enter the home. But she had been inconsolable, and ultimately, unable to answer any questions without devolving into gasping hysterics.

The sketch of Henry Gray that Mr. Gibbons had been creating with the aid of the housekeeper, Mrs. Vincent, hadn't been finished when he'd left Hill Street, but by now, it was surely completed and waiting on his desk back at the Yard.

The superintendent cleared his throat. "So, Reid," he began, taking Jasper's thoughts away from the Lawlors. "I am told you are attending the Home Secretary's dinner this Saturday?"

Jasper set down his fork and knife; he'd made an effort with his joint of beef but was restless to leave.

"I received the invitation this morning. It appears Lord Hayes arranged for it."

"Ah yes, I heard you were connected to the viscount. A beneficial association to have."

"He's a friend, sir," Jasper said, another burr lodging under his skin. The implication that he associated with Oliver for his connections was an insult.

"Yes, good, good," the superintendent said. "We will be in attendance as well."

"There seems to have been no dinner parties all autumn, and I've been starved for some dancing," Rose said. "Do you dance, Inspector?"

Christopher snorted softly, as if he already knew the disappointing answer.

"No." Jasper recalled how Constance had often lamented that fact while he'd been courting her. "We had a lesson or two at Cheltenham, but they didn't take."

For the first time during luncheon, Christopher straightened with interest. "You were at Cheltenham?"

Sending Jasper to the boys' school in Gloucestershire had been an extravagant choice for Gregory, but he'd claimed to have enough money put aside to afford it. He'd planned to send his late son, Gregory Junior, to the private boys' school and had seen no reason not to send Jasper instead.

"That's right," Jasper answered.

"What about university?" Christopher asked.

Jasper knew why he asked; all the boys in his year at Cheltenham had gone on to attend Oxford, Cambridge, or King's College, or into the Queen's army. He would have wagered none had gone on to work in the police force.

"It wasn't for me," Jasper said simply. The only thing he'd wanted to do was join the force and, as Monroe had said, follow in his father's footsteps.

"Admirable," Monroe said, his loud voice close to a bellow. "The man knows his vocation, Christopher."

It was praise for Jasper as much as it was criticism for Christopher's choice to attend university. The young man squirmed with a desire to shout at his father, and likely seeing it, Rose changed the subject.

"I will save you a dance, Inspector." She reached the short distance between them and rested her palm on his hand, which had been lying flat on the table, his fingers drumming impatiently. They now went still, her touch surprising.

"As I said, I'm not much of a dancer," he reiterated as she slowly removed her hand, allowing her fingertips to brush his skin as they lifted away.

"You will just have to relearn your steps," Rose said in a light, teasing tone. Once more, he recognized it as a tactic Constance had employed when flirting.

Expecting a scowl or reprimand from the superintendent, Jasper drew his hand from the table and looked to him. But he only saw a gleam of approval in Monroe's smothered grin.

Christ.

So, that was what this lunch had been about? Introducing him to Rose, setting them up to dance at the Home Secretary's dinner this Saturday. Monroe aimed to align him with his daughter. And Jasper was a complete dolt for only realizing it now.

The servers cleared their plates, and at last, it was time to leave. Jasper stood from his chair, uncertainty weighing him down. He had no intention of being rude or of embarrassing the young woman by insisting they would not be dancing at the dinner party, but he also could not allow any misconceptions that Monroe or Rose might have in mind to flourish.

Rose and her brother fell back in some whispered discussion as the four of them left the restaurant. Jasper was grateful for the moment alone with the superintendent.

"Thank you for inviting me, sir."

"Glad to have gotten some time with you, son," he said, the endearment causing Jasper to grit his teeth again.

"Superintendent Monroe, I feel it is only right that I make something clear before there can be any misunderstanding," Jasper said. "I am courting someone, sir."

They stepped outside Verrey's into a light, cold rain that had started to fall while they'd been dining. Monroe breathed in deeply, and when he exhaled, it was accompanied by a grumble of impatience.

"Yes, I have heard." His good humor, which had been firmly fixed throughout lunch, ebbed.

"You've been doing well, Reid," the superintendent went on, his eyes peeled on a carriage rolling forward along the curb. It wasn't a hired cab, but a polished, dark red landau. Monroe's private carriage. "You could make a name for yourself, in your own right, at the Yard. In the Home Office even, if you wanted."

"I don't aspire to the Home Office, sir." He cared for law and order, but he would rather arrest criminals himself than govern over the police forces charged with doing so.

"Didn't Gregory ever advise you not to limit yourself?"

Monroe countered. He faced Jasper. "Not in your work, nor in your personal affairs. I want you to be sure you take the right steps on your way up."

There was little doubt what he meant by that. Those *right steps* involved associating with the right people. Evidently, to Monroe, Leonora Spencer was not one of them.

For a moment, the differences in rank and status between him and Clive Monroe vanished, and Jasper was left with the overwhelming desire to tell the superintendent to go directly to hell. Only the arrival of Rose and Christopher, and the brougham, saved him from doing so —and throwing his job into the gutter.

"Can we give you a lift, Reid?" Monroe asked, ignoring the hard glare Jasper was leveling him with.

"I prefer to walk." He stepped away before Rose could look to him for help in being handed up into the carriage. Instead, he tipped his hat to her and moved along the pavement.

Bloody hell.

Regret and fury spooled out in his wake as he moved swiftly in the direction of the Yard. Monroe had known about Leo, and yet he'd still arranged for this meeting with his daughter. There were other detective inspectors at the Met, other men with the ambition Jasper didn't share in rising to higher branches of the police force. And yet Monroe seemed to have chosen him to lavish with praise and take under his wing.

He could be overthinking it or jumping to conclusions. But his instinct disagreed.

Walking did not prove curative; when he finally arrived at Met headquarters, his rigid shoulders and a knot of hostility in his gut remained. That the superintendent viewed Leo as an inadvisable attachment inflamed him. Jasper knew, however, that he would need to stifle his incensed mood when he saw her that evening. She would sense his anger and ask him what had happened. She was already worried his superiors would disapprove of her and their courtship. He would not tell her what Monroe had tried to do.

Entering the detective department, Jasper passed Constable Wiley's desk. The irritable and peevish officer who greeted and approved visitors to the department had recently applied to, and been rejected by, the Special Irish Branch at the CID. He'd been a morose lump ever since.

"This came for you," Wiley said, holding up an envelope. He did not move to rise from his desk. "Heard you were at lunch with the superintendent."

Jasper ignored the comment, keeping his attention on the letter. It was too small to be Gibbons's sketch of Henry Gray. "When did that arrive?"

"I don't know. An hour ago, maybe."

"Why is it still on your desk and not on mine?"

Wiley only shrugged. Jasper plucked the envelope from his hand, thankful once more that the man was not one of the constables assigned to his team.

He tore the seal on the way to his office, and giving it a quick perusal, his spirits lifted. It was from Constance Hayes.

Oliver had informed her about their conversation at Fortune's the night before, and yes, in fact, she did recall something that she'd included in a society column the previous year. A newly married heiress had taken ill shortly after her wedding, and within a few months of returning from her honeymoon trip, she had died. Constance remembered the announcement because she'd felt pity for the woman. *At age thirty-five, after being resigned to a life of spinsterhood, she'd unexpectedly found love and a husband, only then to die,* she'd written.

"Warnock," Jasper called to the sergeant, who followed him into his office. "A woman named Victoria Herrington died in December of 1883. Find her death certificate. I want to know what happened to her."

Chapter Ten

The exterior of Castelan Private Inquiries was far more polished and professional than Leo had expected. In her mind, whenever Dita spoke of the agency, Leo pictured a set of dingy, cramped rooms. The surprising reality, however, was a street-front office on High Holborn, with large, bowed windows, a fresh, glossy coat of dark green paint on the wood trim, and a shingle above the door with the agency's name, both engraved and gilded.

A costly lease, Leo imagined, and after inhaling a fortifying breath and opening the door, she saw additional expenses in the several employees scattered around the large front room.

There were three desks, two men to each, and they were either typing or sorting through stacks of papers while smoking cigarettes. It resembled the newsroom at the *Times,* which Leo had visited on a few occasions. Only here, each man looked up with rapacious eyes to see the woman who'd just entered.

One man came forward. “Welcome to Castelan Private Inquiries, madam. My name is Mr. Hutchins. How may I be of assistance?”

“I am here to meet with Miss Brooks,” Leo replied.

Dita was not in view, though there was space enough for there to be another room in the back, perhaps for the women employees.

“Ah, you must be Miss Spencer,” Mr. Hutchins said. “Do come in. Mr. Castelan is expecting you.”

He turned on a heel and started away, expecting her to follow. She did, though with a rolling of nervous tension through her. The owner’s office was located off the main room, and when Leo stepped inside, she didn’t find Dita, but a man seated behind a desk piled high with papers.

“Miss Spencer is here, sir,” Mr. Hutchins announced and then left, shutting the door behind him.

Mr. Castelan stood from his chair, his gray eyes alight with interest. “Welcome, Miss Spencer. Miss Brooks said you would be paying our office a visit today. I was pleased to hear it. Forgive the mess on my desk. I’m out of the office for one day, and this is what I return to,” he said with a laugh.

Leo took a tentative step into the room. It was furnished well, with a button-tufted leather sofa, a thick Oriental rug in hues of red and gold, gold-framed paintings on the walls, a few licensing certificates for his agency on display, and opulent, cut-glass shades over gas lamps. The snug touches of elegance were proof that Mr. Castelan was either doing exceedingly well in the private inquiry business, or that he came from money. By his cultured, almost aristocratic tone, Leo presumed he was an educated man too.

"It's a pleasure to meet you, Mr. Castelan," she said as she removed her gloves. A fire in the grate left no trace of chill in the air. "I must admit, I didn't realize you had so many detectives on staff. But is Miss Brooks not in?"

"She is out on a new assignment," Mr. Castelan replied as he came out from behind his desk. "We are a fast-moving agency, and I am always in need of skilled investigators."

He gestured to one of the chairs positioned in front of his desk. "I hear you'd like to discuss a case you're handling. I hope you don't mind that Miss Brooks imparted some details?"

Leo stayed on her feet until Mr. Castelan lowered himself into one of the chairs. Only then did she settle into the opposite one, not wanting to loom over him.

"I don't mind," she said. "Which details did she share?"

He crossed his legs and laced his fingers over his pin-striped waistcoat. Mr. Castelan was in his early forties, perhaps, with an athletic build and short, dark auburn hair. He wasn't conventionally handsome; his nose was short and sharp, his forehead broad, and he had reddened, chapped skin. A result, she presumed, of the cold and dry December air. However, his eyes, light gray and lively, were striking.

"Mrs. Augusta Lawlor, née Augusta Hart. Independently wealthy and newly married," he began to recount. "She appears to be growing increasingly ill, but in truth, her husband has been poisoning her over the course of several months. He administers an overdose of some kind —laudanum, most likely—which appears to finish her off, then disappears the same day, possibly with a large amount of cash, taking with him any photographic evidence of himself."

It was a concise summary of what Leo had explained to Connor, who must have then informed Dita.

"Did she mention the false physician as an accomplice?" Leo asked.

Mr. Castelan nodded enthusiastically. "Indeed. A truly diabolical scheme, which could be carried out several times, if the two actors were meticulous. But they weren't, were they?"

Leo agreed. "Not in this instance."

"The overdose was not planned," Mr. Castelan identified. She was reluctantly impressed.

"Exactly," Leo said. He laughed delightedly at her obvious surprise.

"Miss Spencer, I may run this agency, but I am a detective to my marrow. I can't help it; solving puzzles is something I've always been drawn to. We are a lot alike, you know."

"How so?" she asked, curious—and skeptical. He clearly wanted to make a good impression in his bid for her to join his agency.

"Your uncle is a surgeon, as was my father and grandfather. You have contacts with the police, as do I. From what I know of you—all of which is, admittedly, derived from others—you like puzzles as much as I do. More importantly, you are skilled at solving them."

With such compliments, Leo rather felt like she was being courted by another potential suitor. Platonically, at least. It was unsettling, and yet also unpredictably...*nice*.

"Thank you, Mr. Castelan. Perhaps we do have some things in common. You are right that I do like puzzles.

Now, getting back to the one at hand…" she said, eager to direct them back to the Lawlor case. "If the intent was to make his wife's death appear natural due to illness, Mr. Lawlor could have waited for the arsenic to do its job. Instead, he sped things along with the opium overdose."

The private detective nodded. "And then disappeared, rather than stay and inherit the property and holdings, as was due to him."

Leo was about to reveal that Mr. Lawlor was now dead, discovered stabbed in Blackfriars. But she held her silence. She didn't need to discuss every detail of the ongoing murder investigation with Mr. Castelan.

"Mrs. Lawlor claimed her late mother hired you four years ago to investigate a suitor," Leo said.

He reached for a thin folio on his desk. "Yes. I anticipated you'd learned as much. This is the file, if you'd like to see it. To summarize, Sir Walter Priestly, an impoverished baron, had already tried his luck at courting two other heiresses before setting his sights on Miss Hart. All three women had lackluster prospects regarding marriage, and Priestly used his extraordinarily good looks and charm to woo them. Covering the fact that he was up to his ears in debt, of course."

Leo opened the folio and took a cursory look at the typed-up report inside.

"His intent was reprehensible, but as you can see, nothing as nefarious as what this Lawlor fellow undertook," Mr. Castelan said. "It is too bad Mrs. Hart did not have me look into him as she did Priestly."

She closed the folio and handed it back. "Mrs. Hart passed a few years ago, or else I'm sure she would have."

"As I always say, it pays to be suspicious," he said. "Miss

Brooks inquired if my agency has handled any cases with similar circumstances. But I'm afraid the answer is no."

The odds had been long, Leo supposed, but she was still disappointed.

"There are many private inquiry agencies in the city, and there is the League of London Private Detectives," she said, eyeing the framed certificate hanging on the wall marking Mr. Castelan as a member. "Have you ever heard your colleagues speaking of a scheme such as this?"

"I'm sorry, no," Mr. Castelan said again. He cocked his head. "Are you working with Scotland Yard on this? Miss Brooks also mentioned you have a partnership of sorts with a detective inspector."

She wondered just how much Dita had shared about her partnership with Jasper, though by the glint of mischief in the private detective's eyes, she thought she might know.

"I am consulting," Leo answered. "I was one of the people who found Mrs. Lawlor alive in a casket that had been delivered to the undertakers."

Mr. Castelan flashed his teeth in a full smile and barked a laugh. She peered at him, bothered.

"A woman was nearly killed by her husband," Leo said. "I don't see how you can find that amusing."

He uncrossed his legs and held his hands up in surrender. "I apologize. I am not amused by what the poor woman endured but only surprised by your calm manner while speaking of it. A discovery like the one you made would undo most young ladies."

His explanation didn't help, as he likely thought it would. She stood, deciding she was in no mood for patronizing men.

"Thank you for meeting with me. However, I should be going," Leo said. He could provide nothing on the Lawlor case, and that was the only reason she'd come, after all.

Mr. Castelan got to his feet quickly. "Wait, please. I do apologize, Miss Spencer. My laughter was tactless."

Grudgingly, she nodded, accepting the apology.

"Before you go, I wished to speak to you about my proposal," he went on. "Miss Brooks has told you, I hope, that I'd be honored if you would join my agency?"

"She has," Leo replied warily. "And I'm sure she has informed you that I'm not interested."

"But you *are* interested in crime solving. You've assisted Scotland Yard on numerous occasions," Mr. Castelan continued as though not hearing her rejection. "As I said, I have contacts within the police force. I'm aware that you and Inspector Reid work well together."

Leo hitched her chin, curious to know who his contacts were. Some detectives hired outside help from time to time when caseloads became too heavy. Perhaps Mr. Castelan contracted with the Yard on occasion.

"I work with Inspector Reid when I have an interest in a case or a connection to it. And I work with him in an unofficial capacity," she said as she pulled on her gloves in preparation for leaving.

"For which you receive no credit and no compensation."

"I am interested in neither, Mr. Castelan," she assured him as she picked up her handbag. "I thank you for the offer, but I'm not going to change my mind. Good day."

She started for the closed door.

"What if I could tempt you with information?"

Leo pursed her lips, hemming in an exasperated sigh. "You have already revealed that you have no information on the Lawlor case."

He crossed his arms, and again, mischief sparked in his direct stare. "I wasn't referring to that case, Miss Spencer."

She indulged him, though she was quickly becoming irritated. He might like puzzles, but he also seemed to enjoy playing games, and there was nothing she disliked more. "Then what *were* you referring to?"

"To the case that brought Inspector Reid to Spitalfields this morning."

The glint in his eyes tamed, his gaze becoming more serious. Leo faced him fully, reluctantly intrigued. *Jasper had been in Spitalfields that morning?* Then, with a quiver of alarm, she realized he might have been there attending to Andrew Carter's request.

"Are you having Inspector Reid followed?"

Mr. Castelan chuckled as he returned to his desk. "I can assure you, I am not. My detective spotted him while he was out on his own assignment."

Bewilderment held Leo back from stalking out of the office in annoyance. "Why would you think Inspector Reid needs information?"

Mr. Castelan retook his seat behind his desk, his smug expression beginning to grate. "I believe my detective and Inspector Reid are working parallel cases. We may be able to help each other."

Now, she was well and truly provoked. If Jasper had indeed been in Spitalfields to search for Andrew's nephew, Mr. Castelan seemed to know about it. Any link made between Jasper and the Carters could be damaging.

With a shrewd smile, Mr. Castelan held up his hands.

"What do you say? Give working for my agency a try? It doesn't have to be official. An evening of your time, at most, to assist on a case."

Leo shook her head, attempting to look as if his knowledge about Jasper's movements in Spitalfields wasn't worrisome.

"I don't think so, Mr. Castelan," she said, then turned for the door.

"I know that this pursuit Inspector Reid has undertaken is quite hazardous, Miss Spencer. And that he wasn't there in his capacity as a Scotland Yard detective, was he?" came the nettling man's reply. "I wonder…who sent him?"

A chill slowed her legs, pulling her to a stop. She looked over her shoulder at Mr. Castelan, who appeared satisfied to have affected her.

"Good afternoon, Mr. Castelan." Leo left his office without another backward glance.

Chapter Eleven

The study inside Number 23 Charles Street was the room Jasper gravitated toward each evening after he returned home. His bedroom, the kitchen, and dining room were the only other rooms within the large townhouse he normally entered, though Mrs. Zhao kept the front parlor dusted in the unlikely event he received a visitor, and a single guest bedroom ready for the same reason.

The study, however, was where he felt most at home. The reason why wasn't complicated: It had been his father's favorite room. No matter the season, as night fell, Mrs. Zhao stoked the coal brazier and lit the lamps, a routine she'd kept with Gregory Reid and one that she continued now with Jasper.

That evening as he tossed his jacket onto the sofa, Jasper glimpsed the leather swivel chair behind the desk. He'd yet to sit in it since his father's death. For some reason he couldn't explain, the idea of sliding into the button-tufted leather chair, the seat soft and worn, felt disrespectful. As if sitting there would cause the memories he held of his father to fade, or even to erase.

Gregory had been gone nearly a year now, and yet, Jasper sometimes still caught himself expecting to see his father in that chair. To hear his voice greeting him as he walked into the study. Jasper touched the chair's arm and gave it a nudge. It turned on its base, revolving outward as if to beckon him to sit.

"Well, this is becoming ridiculous," he muttered to himself, and then before he could change his mind, he settled into the chair. Jasper shifted and leaned back.

It turned out, it was just a chair. Sitting in it hadn't changed anything.

Sighing, he opened the file Sergeant Warnock had delivered to his desk just before the end of the day. The young detective sergeant had succeeded in finding the death certificate for Mrs. Victoria Herrington at the General Register Office at Somerset House. However, in Warnock's enthusiasm, he'd also taken it upon himself to visit the records room at Scotland Yard. It had proved to be an astute move.

Not only had the attending doctor, *Mr. Henry Gray,* signed Mrs. Victoria Herrington's death certificate in a broad and scrawling hand, but Warnock had found a police report on the woman's death filed in the records room. A single-page report described a concern brought forward by Mrs. Herrington's maid, who believed her employer had been poisoned by her new husband.

There had been little additional information written in the report, and it had been filed as *unfounded,* meaning the investigating officer had determined the alleged crime had not occurred. However, as the investigating officer had been Inspector Bruce Tomlin, Jasper had even less confidence that the finding was correct.

Now a lead inspector in the newly formed Special Irish Branch, Tomlin had been a detective inspector at the CID in December of 1883, when Victoria Herrington had died. Tomlin's shoddy police work during the Scotland Yard bombing last May had nearly led to an innocent woman being tried in court for treason and attempted murder. Thankfully, Jasper and Leo had discovered and arrested the true perpetrator behind the bombing. It had caused Tomlin some embarrassment and cemented his hatred for Jasper, but it had also proven that Tomlin's lazy police work could not be trusted.

A knock at the study door fired up Jasper's spine, and he sat forward in the swivel chair. He knew his housekeeper's knock—a single rap of the knuckles. This was three quick taps—Leo's knock.

She entered the study, her coat and hat already discarded, her cheeks flushed from having been outside in the December evening air. Jasper stood, and Leo tucked her chin, a trace of surprise in her tentative smile.

"You were in the Inspector's chair," she observed.

Jasper stepped out from behind the desk. "It was time."

She had noticed, it seemed, that he'd been avoiding it. She crossed the room, toward the table of decanters in the corner.

"Mrs. Zhao says dinner will be served in ten minutes," Leo announced as she upended two glasses and poured them each a drink.

She had begun to join him in sipping whisky rather than the sweet cherry brandy she and Gregory had shared a preference for. As she brought him his glass, and their fingers met briefly, Jasper thought how satisfying it would be if this was what he could look forward to every evening. Arriving home from work, having Leo join him for a drink before dinner. And then, instead of having to put her in a cab and sending her back to Duke Street...she would stay. All night, by his side.

Watching Leo sip her whisky and claim the desk chair for herself, he was grateful that she could not read his immodest thoughts. He hoped Gregory, wherever he was in the afterlife, could not read them, either.

How the Inspector would feel about Jasper and Leo becoming romantically involved still concerned him. He wanted to think Gregory would approve, but the truth was, Jasper's blood ties to the Carters put Leo at risk. The Inspector would expect Jasper to do whatever was necessary to keep her safe. Marrying her would only further mire her in danger.

But it was something he didn't want to think about right then.

"How was your luncheon with Superintendent Monroe?" she asked as she slowly swiveled side to side in the chair.

Jasper's stomach only grew more leaden at the question. "Uncomfortable," he answered honestly.

"What did he want?"

Jasper downed half his whisky in one toss. His throat afire, he answered, "To praise my successes."

There was no need to mention Miss Rose Monroe had been present.

Leo tapped the side of her glass with her fingertips, lost in thought. "Perhaps Chief Inspector Coughlan is due to retire soon, and he is considering a promotion for you?"

"I haven't heard anything. And I'm too busy with my own job to think about Coughlan's." Before more about the lunch could be said, he tapped the file he'd left on the desk. "This will interest you."

Leo ceased swiveling. She set her glass down and picked up the file. As she read swiftly through the death certificate and police report, Jasper felt slightly guilty for distracting her, but he would have felt worse had he told her the truth about the strange luncheon with Monroe and his children.

Leo stood up as she read and shifted to sit on the edge of the desk. "Henry Gray was Victoria Herrington's doctor. This is another one of Sebastian Lawlor's victims. Or as he called himself that time, Rupert Herrington." She lowered the file and looked up at him. "How did you find her?"

Damn. He hadn't thought of this potential muddle. Finishing his whisky, he answered, "Miss Hayes."

Leo blinked, then dropped her eyes to the file again. "Oh?"

It was one word, and yet he knew she was surprised, unpleasantly so.

"I boxed at Fortune's last evening and spoke to Oliver about the case. He suggested Constance might know of another such situation, given her standing in society and her job at the *Times*."

Leo nodded, still looking at the police report and not at him. "That was a good idea."

He joined her at the desk. "She sent a note to the Yard with what she could recall about Victoria Herrington."

Leo seemed to gather herself before looking up at him again. "That's excellent. Really. And as cavalier as Inspector Tomlin seems to have been in investigating the claim, at least he took down the maid's name and place of residence so you can pay her a call."

Tomlin had noted that the maid, a Miss Isabelle Chandler, had been *hysterical* and *overwrought*, and when Rupert Herrington could not be tracked down to question, there was no choice but to close the case as groundless.

"When will you go?" Leo asked.

"Tomorrow." Jasper came to stand in front of her at the desk. "You've memorized that report by now."

She closed the manila file and set it aside, on the blotter. "Yes, I have."

His legs brushed against her knees, and Jasper could not stop his attention from wandering toward her lap, and the belted waist of her skirt.

"You know, I remember a time when I would have to peel police files from your hands." He reached for her waist. "Now, here I am giving them to you."

Leo covered his hands with hers, then skated her palms up his forearms. "I much prefer this way."

"As do I."

Although, he no longer wanted to talk about the case. He only wanted to kiss her. Touch her. His palms grazed her hips and along the sides of her legs, eliciting a soft gasp from her. Unable to tolerate another moment without her mouth against his, Jasper kissed her. Leo welcomed him, her hands reaching to his shoulders. Gently, she tugged him closer. One of his thighs slipped between her knees, and when her calf curled around the back of his leg, he thought he might go blind with desire.

A pert knock on the study door burst through the bubble that had seemed to form around them. Mrs. Zhao entered, only to stop in her tracks when she saw Jasper and Leo, and their intimate position at the desk.

"Mrs. Zhao," Jasper muttered as embarrassment flooded in. He released Leo and stepped far away from the desk, while she hastily stood and smoothed her skirt.

The housekeeper unsuccessfully smothered her amusement. "Dinner is served," she said, twittering laughter as she departed.

Jasper, his body still coiled with longing, gestured for Leo to go ahead of him. Color tinted her usually pale skin as she fell into step behind the housekeeper. Thankfully, Mrs. Zhao had set Leo's place at the dinner table to his immediate left, rather than at the far, opposite end.

"Won't you join us?" Leo asked her.

"Thank you, Miss Leo, but I have already eaten my supper." Crossing behind Leo's chair, the housekeeper winked at Jasper. He nearly groaned with embarrassment.

She left them to serve themselves, and after an awkward beat, Leo reached for the ladle in the soup tureen.

"I need to tell you something," she said once Jasper had filled his bowl with Mrs. Zhao's mulligatawny soup. He returned the ladle to the tureen and narrowed his eyes on her.

"Why do you sound as if you're about to confess something I'm likely to be angry about?"

"It's nothing I've done," she replied. "It is what you may have been seen doing."

Jasper set down his spoon. "And what might that be?"

Leo bit her bottom lip, then said, "I went to Castelan

Private Inquiries today to discuss Mrs. Lawlor. Mr. Castelan informed me that he knew you were in Spitalfields this morning."

Jasper went rigid in his chair. He'd gone to visit Desmond Pierce early to try to avoid being seen. What were the bloody chances?

"Why should that concern me?" he asked.

"He says you and his detective are working parallel cases. And he seems to know you weren't there for anything sanctioned by Scotland Yard."

Hell.

"You were searching for Andrew's nephew, I presume," Leo went on, stirring her soup while her eyes speared him.

"Yes," he answered, his appetite gone. He tossed his napkin onto the table. "I doubt Castelan has been hired to look for Cillian Carter, though."

"Cillian?" Leo's spoon went still.

He groaned. At this juncture, there was no longer any reason to hold back. "Sean Carter's only son. He's twenty-one and was having an affair with Tabitha Pierce, the wife of a Spitalfields Angel named Desmond Pierce. That was who I visited this morning."

Leo's expression honed with interest. "Andrew thinks he may have harmed Cillian after finding out about the affair?"

"He does, and Pierce does have recent scratch marks on his neck that point to a fight of some kind," Jasper said, recalling the gouges inflicted by fingernails. "But I'm not convinced Pierce even knew his wife was stepping out on him with Cillian. And when I told him Cillian was missing, he understood that the East Rips were looking at him with suspicion. He became scared."

"Perhaps because he did kill him?" Leo suggested.

"He'd have to be a half-wit to kill the heir to the East Rips and then stick around, waiting to be found out." Jasper thought of Pierce's interest in how many days Cillian had been missing. "No, I think I understand what Mr. Castelan meant by parallel cases. And how he knew I wasn't visiting Pierce on Scotland Yard's orders."

He could only think of one way, in fact. If Tabitha Pierce was also missing, as Jasper suspected, Pierce must have hired Castelan to find her. He didn't know where the Angel would gather the blunt to afford an agency like Castelan's. But if determined, he could have fenced some of his belongings—or something he'd stolen—to afford it.

"Well? Are you going to tell me?" Leo asked when Jasper stayed quiet.

He sat back in his chair, his resolve to keep Leo out of this hunt for Cillian Carter diminishing rapidly. He gave in and explained his theory, including how Desmond Pierce had likely told Castelan's detective all about Jasper's visit and line of questioning.

"So then, if both Tabitha and Cillian are nowhere to be found," Leo said afterward, "they have probably run off together."

"That is what I'd like to think too," Jasper said. "But Andrew told me Cillian left behind all his belongings. For him to totally disappear, there is another possibility I can't overlook."

Leo caught on. "That he is dead."

"Tabitha could have killed him and fled after it happened," Jasper said.

"Or she knows who did kill him, and she's gone into hiding somewhere," Leo added. "She very well could be dead too."

The inquisitive gleam in her eye, the way she nibbled her lower lip in thought, concerned him. "I would like you to concentrate on Mrs. Lawlor's case, Leo. Not this one."

She blinked, as if coming back to herself, and picked up her spoon again. "Mr. Castelan and his detective are going to put together that you're working for Andrew Carter, if they haven't already."

"Let me worry about that." It wasn't so unbelievable that an inspector at the Yard might take on a private inquiry, just as he'd said to Desmond Pierce. Though he didn't want it getting out that he'd accepted a job from an East Rip. It wouldn't reflect well on him at work and could tarnish his reputation. Rightly so, too.

"What happens to you also happens to me," Leo said with a pointed stare. "Let me in, Jasper."

It was a command as much as it was a plea. *Heaven help him.* Once Leo got her teeth into something, she would not let go.

"What do you suggest?" he asked.

"The fastest way to get Andrew off your back is to find Cillian, dead or alive," she said. "Tabitha Pierce seems to be the one person who might know where he is or what has happened to him. If you believe her husband has hired Mr. Castelan to find her, then I might be able to find out what the agency knows. He has offered me information if I try working for his agency."

"*No.*" It was practically a bark, but Leo only looked at him with exasperation.

"I'd just be joining him on a case for one day. One

evening at the most, he said. If it will help you find Cillian, it will be worth it."

Restless to move, Jasper pushed his chair away from the table and stood. "You are going to do this no matter what I say or think, aren't you?"

"If you would please stop trying to control everything around you for a moment, including me, I believe you would agree this is a good idea," she argued.

Dismay sealed his boots to the floor. "I do not try to control you."

Did he?

Leo gaped at him, and then she let out a tinkling of laughter. She covered her mouth with her hand. "I'm sorry, you just looked so offended. I know that you don't mean to be controlling, but it is what you do. Especially when you think something is dangerous."

"I want to protect you. Is that so wrong?"

Leo pushed back her chair and stood, as he had. "I want a partner, not a protector."

He swallowed whatever argument he'd been about to make. Her statement walloped him as good as a smack on the back of the head. She'd spoken one sentence, just a few words, and yet they'd laid out the flat truth: He'd been an idiot.

In the corner of the room, the steady rhythm of the old tall case clock's pendulum marked the passing seconds. Jasper gestured for her to retake her seat, and then he did as well.

"I want you as my partner too," he said once they were seated adjacent to each other again. He slid his hand across the corner of the table and was bolstered when Leo slipped her fingers into his palm. "I will always tell you if I think something is dangerous," he said. "But I will work on trusting you to make your own decisions."

She squeezed his hand as an effusive grin formed. "Thank you." Leo retracted her hand and picked up her spoon once again. "Now, I really am starved for Mrs. Zhao's cooking. I propose no more talk about investigating, at least until we finish dessert."

Jasper accepted the proposal, especially looking forward to after dinner drinks in the study. "On that, I wouldn't dream of arguing."

Chapter Twelve

The address listed in the police report for Miss Isabelle Chandler was not, as it turned out, where Jasper found her the next day. He spent the morning crossing the Thames into Kennington Cross, only to learn that Miss Chandler had given her sister's address as that had been where she'd lived for a short while after Victoria Herrington died. Thankfully, after her sister heard Jasper's reason for seeking out Isabelle, she told him where he could find her. And so, he'd gone back across the river up to Clerkenwell, where the modestly well-to-do Mr. and Mrs. Jones employed Isabelle as a housemaid at their home on Percival Street.

He'd wasted more time than he cared for when he finally arrived at the servant's entrance, and it put him in an unusually surly mood. The weight of disappointment seemed to keep stacking up on his shoulders. He had wanted to find Sebastian Lawlor alive, not dead and unable to give up the identity of his accomplice, the false doctor. There were already so few leads to begin with. Then, there was the search for Cillian Carter that had stalled out, and Leo's decision to accept Castelan's cleverly dangled bait. Jasper would have much rather worked with Leo to find the missing Tabitha Pierce, which he agreed would likely lead him to Cillian. However, if his involvement in the case had reached Castelan's agency, how long until it reached someone within the Yard? He didn't need anyone connecting him to the Carters, least of all a shrewd private detective like Castelan.

The one thing that lifted the pall of frustration was last night's dinner with Leo. Or rather, their time in the study before and after dinner. It had been alluringly comfortable sitting with her on the sofa, nursing a whisky and reading through the *Illustrated Police News* together. Leo had leaned against his side, resting her head on his shoulder. He'd remained gentlemanly, of course, though he'd wanted to kiss her, touch her... Hell, he'd wanted to scoop her into his arms and bring her to his bedroom with a fierceness that could have easily silenced his good judgment. Perhaps that was why he'd held back and, after finishing their drinks, walked with her to the cabstand and paid a cabbie to take her back to Duke Street.

Determined as he was to not let his personal frustration interfere with his interview with Miss Chandler, Jasper quieted all thoughts of Leo Spencer. He brought down his fist on the servant's entrance door. A maid greeted him, and when he showed her his warrant card and asked if he could speak with Miss Chandler, the young maid fetched a matronly woman who looked him over with a skeptical sniff.

"I'm Mrs. Seymour, housekeeper here. What is it you want with our Miss Chandler?"

"I have some questions for her." When it appeared the housekeeper would not permit him to step inside the house, he added, "I will only need a few minutes of her time."

"Has she done something the mister and missus should know about?"

"Not at all," he said, understanding that a Scotland Yard detective turning up did not shine favorably upon the maid. "This has to do with her former employer, Mrs. Herrington."

Mrs. Seymour cocked an ear toward him. "Oh, that business, is it?"

"You recall the lady's death?"

She pondered a moment, then stepped aside, allowing him over the threshold. Jasper entered the warmth of a kitchen redolent with the scent of baking bread.

"It was strange, is all. Miss Blake, as she was called before she married, had been the picture of health. Had her home near here, on King Square. A big place, all to herself, spinster as she was."

The suddenly chatty housekeeper snapped her fingers at the maid who'd answered the door and told her to fetch Isabelle.

"What can you tell me about her husband, Mr. Herrington?" Jasper asked the housekeeper.

"Heard he was a solicitor," she said. "Rumors were that he'd married Miss Blake for her fortune."

"Was it a substantial fortune?"

Mrs. Seymour shrugged. "Her grandfather was Edward Blake, of Blake Sugar."

Jasper hadn't heard of the company, but purveyors of sugarcane out of the West Indies often accrued impressive fortunes.

"Miss Blake had no previous suitors before him?" Jasper asked.

The housekeeper shook her head. "She was a bit eccentric. Private, with very few friends. Certainly surprised me when I heard she'd married."

Just then, a woman, perhaps in her late twenties, entered the kitchen. Her distrustful eyes met Jasper's, and he presumed the other maid had informed her that he was a police detective. Still, he introduced himself and showed his warrant card.

"You may use my room, Miss Chandler," the housekeeper offered. "No more than ten minutes, mind you, Inspector."

Miss Chandler's eyes widened with uncertainty, cutting away from him as she led him to the small room the housekeeper kept as an office off the kitchen. He only closed the door halfway, not wanting to frighten the maid any more than she already appeared to be. He gestured for her to take one of the chairs set before a coal brazier.

"Have I done something wrong?" she asked right away.

"Not that I am aware, Miss Chandler. I've come to speak to you about the complaint you brought to Scotland Yard after the death of your previous employer, Mrs. Victoria Herrington."

At this, her chin drew back into her neck, affecting a look of surprise. "But that was nearly two years ago. And the detective I spoke to then said he was closing the case."

"He did close the case," Jasper said. "However, a recent occurrence has led me to take another look at that report."

"What occurrence?"

"An attempted murder," he provided, at which Miss Chandler sat forward with interest. He continued before she could ask more questions. "The police report for your petition to open an investigation into your employer's death was lacking in detail. I'd like to ask you some questions about it now."

The woman scoffed. "The detective I spoke to all but dismissed me the moment we met."

Tomlin was, Jasper admitted, a lazy arse. But he would not take time to disparage his fellow inspector to Miss Chandler.

"You thought the death of Mrs. Herrington was suspicious and that her new husband might be involved. Can you tell me why?"

"Miss Blake—" the maid stopped, then corrected herself. "Mrs. Herrington fell ill while on their honeymoon trip to Italy. I was with them, as I was her maid."

"What sort of illness was it?"

"Stomach complaints," she replied. "She was bedridden most days."

So far, it matched Augusta Lawlor's experience.

"And the illness continued after their return to London?"

Miss Chandler nodded. "It worsened. She would..." Here, she turned bashful but, averting her eyes, continued, "She would produce a lot of blood in the chamber pot, and her skin erupted in sores. The doctor who came said it was a cancer, and there was nothing he could do but ease her pain."

"With laudanum?" he asked.

The maid nodded.

"How long did she languish?"

Tears turned Miss Chandler's eyes glassy, and she sniffed. "About three months. Near the end, her whole body would be taken with spasms. There was one final convulsion, worse than the rest. She didn't wake afterward. The next morning, she passed."

That sounded slightly different from Mrs. Lawlor, Jasper thought, who had been found seemingly dead in her bed one morning. There had been no mention of convulsions from her or her staff, either.

"And then what happened?" Jasper asked.

The maid composed herself with a deep breath and another sniffle. "Mr. Herrington seemed bereaved at first. But within the month, he'd sold the house, sacked all the staff, and disappeared."

So, he had taken everything he stood to inherit as a widower. Unlike his abrupt disappearance the day of Mrs. Lawlor's supposed death.

"Tell me about their courtship," Jasper said. He was curious to know if it resembled that of Sebastian and Augusta's.

"It happened quickly," Miss Chandler said. "They met at Regent's Park. Miss Blake would take her pair of Havanese dogs for a stroll around the boating lake every other day, no matter the weather. She was very regimented, you see. Very particular. On one such walk, Mr. Herrington approached her with compliments on her dogs. They became caught up in conversation. This happened twice more before it became clear he was not meeting her by chance." She sighed. "We were happy for her, of course. She was older and never thought she would marry."

"Why not?"

The maid winced. "I don't want to say unkind things about the dead. But Miss Blake was a difficult person. She didn't get on with many people. And she wasn't what one might view as handsome, you see."

"Was she a difficult employer?" Jasper asked.

"She was never unkind, only fastidious and blunt. She treated her servants respectfully for the most part. Even apologized profusely to one of the other maids when she mistakenly accused her of stealing some jewelry. Miss Blake felt awful about it once she learned it was one of her few acquaintances who'd done it."

"One of her friends stole from her?"

Miss Chandler nodded. "She had a hard time keeping friends. Spoke her mind, even when she wasn't trying to be cruel. This friend claimed she took the brooch out of revenge for an offense Miss Blake had given her."

"But she had no trouble with Mr. Herrington? No… awkwardness?"

"He was charming. Doted on her and deferred to her completely."

Jasper took both sketches Mr. Gibbons had created from his coat pocket. He showed the one depicting Sebastian Lawlor first. "Do you recognize him?"

She peered at it only a few moments before confirming that she did. It was Mr. Herrington, only she remembered him as having a trimmed beard and a thicker mustache.

"Have you seen Mr. Herrington?" Miss Chandler asked. Then with a look of dawning comprehension, "Is he involved in this recent occurrence you mentioned?"

Jasper didn't mind answering her question. "He is." He

showed her the sketch of the false doctor next. "What about this man?"

Immediately, Miss Chandler bobbed her head. "Oh, yes. That is the doctor who treated Miss Blake. Mr. Gray, his name was."

"No changes to his appearance? Same facial hair?"

"He appears the same," she confirmed. "Goodness. Are they both involved in this occurrence?"

As he pocketed the sketches again, Jasper wondered why Sebastian Lawlor had altered his appearance slightly, while the doctor hadn't. Maintaining the same name, Henry Gray, also seemed peculiar, though perhaps he'd felt no one would look twice at a doctor.

"Both men are suspects, yes," Jasper said. "Have you seen Mr. Gray since your employer's death?"

She frowned and shook her head. "No. I didn't think it very odd, though. He was Mr. Herrington's doctor. Miss Blake never had one, as she was never ill before her marriage."

It was what the Joneses' housekeeper, Mrs. Seymour, had said too. It reminded him that his ten minutes were just about up.

"How many servants did the Herringtons keep?" He wanted to question as many of them as he might be able to find.

"Six," Miss Chandler answered readily.

She provided the names, which Jasper wrote down. Luckily, she knew where the Herringtons' former house-keeper, Mrs. Michaels, had found new employment.

"Oh, wait. I forgot Marion," the maid said as Jasper stood from his chair. He took out his notebook again and added her name. "I can't recall Marion's surname, though. She was new."

"How new?"

"She'd been on staff for about six months. Maybe seven. Mrs. Michaels might know where Marion is now."

The housekeeper appeared within the frame of the partially closed door, her arms crossed. "If you're finished, Inspector, Miss Chandler needs to get on with her duties."

The maid shot to her feet and stepped toward the housekeeper, then hesitated.

"Will you find Mr. Herrington, Inspector?" she asked.

There didn't seem to be any reason not to tell her the truth. "I have already found him. He is dead."

Miss Chandler's expression slackened with shock.

"I'm now seeking Mr. Gray. If you see him, or hear anything about him, contact me at once."

Jasper was shown out, and as he started along Percival Street toward a cabstand, he considered the differences between the Lawlor and Herrington cases. Unlike Sebastian Lawlor, Rupert Herrington had maintained his false identity long enough to fully claim his dead wife's fortune. A significant amount, Jasper imagined, though he would learn just how significant once Sergeant Warnock returned later from another trip to the probate registry offices at Somerset House.

Something—or someone—had caused Sebastian Lawlor to rush the death of Augusta with a large dose of an opiate, and before he knew she had *not* died, he'd fled with the contents of the household safe, and four thousand pounds withdrawn from the bank the previous week. Had he been preparing to bring about her death faster than originally planned? Had he been preparing to run? It was a strong possibility.

And now, Sebastian was dead.

Jasper needed to find Henry Gray, as he was now the prime suspect.

Chapter Thirteen

Throughout the morning and afternoon, Leo found herself continually needing to tame her mind, as her thoughts kept drifting back to the previous evening at Jasper's home.

The cozy contentedness of lounging with him on the Chesterfield sofa in his study while a coal fire hissed and popped in the grate kept claiming Leo's attention, diverting her focus from her tasks at the morgue. To spend every evening in such a manner, reading the newspapers, sipping whisky, and making easy conversation would be gratifying, she admitted. So much so that Leo imagined she would be waiting all day for the hour to depart the morgue so she could make her way home to Jasper.

Of course, they were merely courting for now, and Leo didn't wish to jump too far into the future, as Thea Lewis had done the other evening after dinner. Roy's wife's mention of marriage and *little ones* had kicked up

Leo's pulse. They were two things she wasn't entirely sure she was ready for just yet.

As she and Connor made their way through a busy day at the morgue, he caught her woolgathering a few times.

"Are you well, Miss Spencer?" he inquired in between postmortems and the careful handling of two grieving families that had arrived at the same time. "You aren't yourself today."

"Oh? A lot on my mind, I suppose," she replied.

"Having to do with the case you're consulting on?"

She nodded, though in fact, she had not been thinking of Mrs. Lawlor's case at all. With any hope, Jasper would gain some information from Victoria Herrington's maid that could further the investigation. Leo's mind had been stuck, selfishly, on Jasper.

And on her upcoming visit to Castelan's Private Inquiries that evening.

As the burnished late-afternoon sun slid through the stained glass windows of the postmortem room, Leo grew restless for the five o'clock hour to strike. A part of her had wondered if she might see Jasper before the end of the day. If he might implore her to change her mind. She would not, of course. She'd already sent a note to the private inquiry agency earlier that morning, alerting Mr. Castelan that she would be calling on him. While Jasper had come around to the plan last night at dinner, she knew he despised the idea of her working with Mr. Castelan's private detectives to find Tabitha Pierce. Leo wasn't overly eager to accept Mr. Castelan's offer, either, as he'd struck her as manipulative and a little unscrupulous at the close of their last conversation. However, if she could help bring the search for Cillian Carter to a conclusion, it would be worth the time spent with him.

She bid Connor goodnight and left the morgue. There was no sign of Jasper as she made her way toward a cabstand at Trafalgar Square. She took a seat on an omnibus heading for High Holborn and stepped off at the nearest stop to Castelan's agency.

The bowed front windows of the offices glowed with electric light. This time when she stepped inside, there were only three men present—and Dita was there too.

Leo's friend sprang from where she'd been perched on the edge of a desk while speaking to a man.

"I heard you were planning to come," Dita said excitedly, coming forward to greet Leo She wore a maid's uniform, complete with white pinafore and frilly mobcap. "Sorry I missed you yesterday. I was out on assignment."

"I heard," Leo replied as she eyed the uniform. "You're assigned as a maid somewhere?"

Dita huffed and rolled her eyes toward the ceiling. "Another fine lady wants proof her husband is conducting an affair. She had me hired on as a charlady to discover who his mistress is. She suspects it is a servant within the household."

So far, this was the only type of inquiry Dita had been assigned to. It couldn't have been very rewarding, Leo thought. But then, it was what Mr. Castelan's agency was known for.

"Any idea who it is yet?" Leo asked.

Dita raised a brow. "I think so, and with any hope, I'll have proof soon. Being a charlady is awful. I've never had a single blister in my life, and now I have two!" She pouted as she rubbed her palms.

It was a challenge to imagine Dita cleaning hearth grates, scrubbing floors and windows, or any of the other lowly tasks a housekeeper would assign to her. Charwomen weren't members of a regular full-time staff but were hired out on a part-time basis, and they were often given the jobs other maids didn't wish to do.

Some middle-class families could afford the expense of a charlady. Listening to Dita explain about her undercover role, Leo recalled an interview included in the Inspector's file on the Spencer family murders. When she'd finally sat down and forced herself to go through the entire file, a brief report from a constable had caught her interest. The constable had questioned a charwoman, Opal Rosen, aged fifty-two, who had cleaned for the Spencers three times a week.

The memories Leo had from before the killings were often sparse and fragmented, but one had always stuck with some clarity: an older woman, in the kitchen of their Red Lion Street home, speaking a language other than English. Leo had asked her aunt if they'd had a cook or a servant, but Flora had scoffed, saying Leonard and Andromeda could never have afforded it. But it seemed they had been able to, after all.

The constable's report on Opal Rosen had been meager: Mrs. Rosen had not worked that day. She had not seen or heard anything suspicious the last few times she had come in. Mr. Spencer paid her wage every quarter, on time. She couldn't think of anyone who would want to harm the family.

Surely, Opal Rosen was the older woman from Leo's disjointed memory, though little good that information did her.

"At least you're lucky," Dita said, drawing Leo from thoughts of the past and bringing her back to the present. "It sounds as though you'll be doing something exciting tonight."

"How do you mean?"

"Mr. Castelan has plans for you." Dita sent her a mischievous wink as she went to the coat stand. Leo wasn't sure what to make of it. "Well, I ought to get home. I've finally told my father about my position here, and you can imagine how he reacted."

Sergeant Byron Brooks would have reacted just as Leo had, and Jasper too: with distrust of the private inquiry agency in question.

"He hasn't demanded you quit?" Leo asked.

"No, but he's insisted I only accept assignments that don't demand that I stay overnight anywhere."

That seemed reasonable enough.

"Ah, Miss Spencer. You've arrived." Mr. Castelan stepped from his office. "Why don't you join us?"

Dita gave Leo's arm a squeeze of encouragement before leaving. She seemed to know about the lump of unease that had settled in Leo's stomach. It only grew larger as she crossed the room to meet Mr. Castelan. Stepping into the office, she spied another man standing by the desk. He was perhaps thirty years old, a few inches taller than Leo, and handsome with a strong, square jaw and defined cheekbones.

"Allow me to introduce Detective Silas Palmer," Mr. Castelan said.

Detective Palmer followed Leo with a pair of serious, dark blue eyes.

"How do you do?" she said. He did not smile or respond to her greeting in any way.

"Palmer is one of my lead detectives," Mr. Castelan explained. "I hope, Miss Spencer, your visit tonight is what I think it is? An agreement to work with us? For this evening, at least?"

The flat glare Detective Palmer was leveling her with did not express that same hope. She shrugged it off.

"We have an agreement. I will try working for you this one evening. And in return, you'll provide information on Tabitha Pierce."

Mr. Castelan grinned. "Excellent. Then you'll be pleased to know that Palmer is handling the Pierce case."

"I'm curious to know why a Scotland Yard detective inspector is working for the Carter family," Detective Palmer said, his tone loaded with stony skepticism.

"I'm not at liberty to divulge any information," Leo said.

"Is that right? But we can give you all sorts?" Detective Palmer shook his head, making it evident where he stood on this agreement between Leo and Mr. Castelan.

"Now, now," Mr. Castelan said indulgently, "let's all get along, shall we? Miss Spencer is giving us her time and her mind, which I have heard is rather skilled in the art of deduction. I suggest you give the lady the benefit of the doubt."

Detective Palmer harrumphed but did not argue further.

"Now, as it is Tabitha Pierce you both wish to find, I suggest the two of you make your way to the Golden Harp," Mr. Castelan said. "Palmer has learned Mrs. Pierce has been seen there on several occasions with a man.

Cillian Carter, perhaps? Inspector Reid did, after all, inform Mr. Pierce that was the name of Tabitha's lover."

"I am assisting Detective Palmer?" Leo asked, surprised. For some unsupported reason, she'd imagined she would be helping Mr. Castelan himself. Then again, Dita had hinted he had something exciting in store for Leo that evening,

"This is the case you're interested in, isn't it?" Mr. Castelan said.

"Well, yes, it is," she admitted.

"Good. I try to keep all my detectives happy, you know," he added in another obvious bid. Detective Palmer snorted, as if to dispute his employer's claim. Mr. Castelan ignored him.

"Go to the pub, have a drink, and see what you can find," he said.

A disgruntled Detective Palmer started toward the office door. He did not want her company, and she certainly didn't wish to spend any more time with him than was necessary. However, she'd made her agreement with Mr. Castelan, and she would adhere to it.

"Very well," she sighed.

Detective Palmer stopped at his desk in the main office, where he took up his coat and hat, and tugged them on with short, sharp movements. As Mr. Castelan watched them leave through the front door, he did not hide his amusement in throwing the two of them together for what would certainly be an awkward, if not hostile, evening out.

Jasper really wasn't going to like this.

Detective Palmer flagged a cab, and though he held out his hand to help Leo up, it was with an ungracious scowl fixed on his mouth. The driver took them along Holborn to Newgate Street and Cheapside, all while she and Detective Palmer remained silent.

Leo could not entirely blame him for being churlish; she had barged in on his investigation, after all. But he didn't need to be so impolite about it.

"Cillian Carter has been missing for a week," Leo finally said, breaking the silence. "I highly doubt he will be at a pub."

"We'll speak to a barmaid or the barkeep," Detective Palmer said. "And as it is Tabitha Pierce I've been hired to find, not Cillian Carter, we can ask if anyone has seen *her* recently."

"How long has she been missing?" Leo asked, overlooking his bite of sarcasm.

"About seven days."

It was the same amount of time as Cillian, as Jasper had predicted.

"Does she have no other family she might have gone to? No other friends?"

Detective Palmer squinted as if marking her as a dullard. "I wish you'd been here to suggest that earlier," he said, his sarcasm plain. "I cannot believe I didn't think of asking her husband those questions."

"You needn't be surly," she said with a roll of her eyes. "Or are you the type of man who feels an injury to his pride when he is made to work with a female?"

"I do not care to work with anyone, Miss Spencer, male or female," he replied.

"You don't value help?"

"I don't require it." His astounding arrogance only made her shake her head and smile. "That amuses you?"

"It sounds lonely," she replied. "And in my experience, two minds are always stronger than one."

Detective Palmer pressed his lips firmly, as if to stifle a rebuttal. Several more minutes passed, the scent of brine announcing that they had neared the docklands.

Just when Leo thought he would not speak to her for the remainder of the evening, he said, "Desmond didn't know or even suspect his wife was stepping out on him until a neighbor asked where Mrs. Pierce was working now that she was going out nearly every evening after Desmond would leave for work."

"Did Mr. Pierce confront her?" Leo asked, tentatively pleased for the shared information.

"He did. They rowed, but she wouldn't give up the name of her lover."

"That row is how Mr. Pierce received scratches on his neck?" Leo presumed, recalling that Jasper had mentioned them. Detective Palmer nodded, frowning.

"He had no idea it was a Carter until your inspector showed up, asking about him."

The cab drew up along a curb and let them out. It was a grubby, riverside street, bustling with lower working class, sailors, street urchins, and prostitutes. It was not the sort of place Leo would have ever ventured on her own.

The Golden Harp public house was busy, but there were a few tables left to choose from when she and Detective Palmer went inside. He was still grouchy, but at least he held the door open so it would not shut in her face.

They slid into wooden chairs at a round table near the center of the pub, and as Leo removed her gloves and cloak, she peered around the room. Though the Golden Harp catered to working-class men and women, there were some suited men interspersed with laborers. Loud voices, guffaws of laughter, and a man sitting in the corner by a coal stove, playing a lively tune on a fife, were proof that this pub was a popular spot.

"What does Tabitha look like?" Leo asked, trying to raise her voice above the noise of the crowd, but also keep it quiet enough to not be overheard by their neighbors.

Detective Palmer sat with a rigid back and shoulders. "Twenty-eight, curly auburn hair, light brown eyes, and freckled skin."

Leo peered at the several women seated around the pub or standing around the long bar with men. None matched the description.

"At twenty-eight, she is a bit older than Cill—" Leo stopped herself from forming his name. "Than her lover." It wouldn't do to be overheard mentioning a Carter.

A barmaid came for their orders. Detective Palmer took it upon himself to order Leo a beer and a steak and kidney pie, same as his fare. She bit back the urge to change her order but didn't want to draw unnecessary attention. It would be better to appear as two people content to be out having a meal together. Remaining pleasant might also buy them a few moments of the barmaid's time when she delivered their meals.

"She's still closer in age to her lover than she is to her husband. Mr. Pierce is at least twenty years her senior," Detective Palmer commented once the barmaid left. "Whatever his age, the young man was reckless for dallying with an Angel's wife."

"Perhaps it was that danger that drew them to one another," she said. "I wonder how they met."

Especially since the territories belonging to the East Rips and the Angels did not intersect.

"I would wager it isn't some romantic story, Miss Spencer. Save those hopes for the novels you read."

She bristled. "I am not seeking romantic stories. If we knew how they met, we might have another lead to follow."

"Desmond hasn't any idea how they met. He said his wife's routine was consistent. She went to work at Mary Hobson's bakery Monday through Saturday from seven until three. Sundays, she went to church. Religious sort."

"No children?"

He shook his head, his eyes continuing to rove over the tables in the pub. Leo did not believe Tabitha Pierce was going to suddenly appear.

The barmaid returned to deliver their mugs of dark amber beer. Leo raised a hand to stop her from leaving. "We are looking for a friend of ours and wondered if you'd seen her."

Detective Palmer met Leo's eyes over the rim of his beer mug. She couldn't tell if he was annoyed or impressed by her audacity to question the barmaid.

"Aye?" The woman, who appeared wise to the world and fed up with her job, waited with a furrowed forehead. "What's her name, then?"

"Tabitha," Detective Palmer answered. "She comes here now and then. Thought we'd meet up with her."

He tried on a smile, and to Leo's astonishment, it was somewhat charming. The barmaid, however, was immune. She pursed her lips, peering at them with suspicion.

"How d'you know her?"

"Church," Leo answered swiftly. "We usually share a pew, but we didn't see her last Sunday."

"Haven't seen her, sorry," the barmaid said. She took a chary glimpse toward the bar, then said, "Take my advice? Stop askin' 'round. This ain't the sort of place wants you stickin' your beak in." She left their table swiftly.

"She clearly knows something," Leo said, gripping the handle of her mug. She didn't care for beer, but nerves had made her thirsty. She sipped the bitter, room temperature brew and tried not to grimace.

Detective Palmer suddenly garbled a crude oath under his breath and lowered his chin. He turned his face to the side as if trying to avoid being seen.

"What is it?" Leo asked, twisting to see what had affected him.

"Don't look—"

His warning came too late. The sounds of the busy pub muffled beneath a rush of blood in Leo's ears as Andrew Carter entered the Golden Harp.

She faced forward again, wishing for the ability to melt into the wood of her chair and sink from sight entirely. Briefly, she imagined that in a crowd as large as this, he would not see her. Awareness bored into her, however, and she knew she'd been noticed.

Slowly, Andrew passed their table. Leo lifted her eyes and met his icy blue ones, which were already pinned on her. His flat, cold gaze rested on her, a flex of his brow the only sign that he was surprised to see her. He wasn't alone; the same men he kept with him at all times were at his side. Andrew's lips curved into a slight grin, and he tipped his hat before continuing past their table. Andrew stepped behind the bar, as if he owned the place, and then through another door into a back room.

Once he was out of sight, the sounds of the pub came rushing back. Including Detective Palmer's harsh voice: "How in the bloody hell do you know Andrew Carter?"

She snapped her attention back to the private detective. "I saw his wife die," she explained. "Inspector Reid and I worked together to solve her murder."

Detective Palmer took a long gulp of his beer, then pushed back his chair. "That's just fantastic. You've drawn the kind of attention we don't need. I knew Castelan was making a mistake with you. Time to go."

As he reached into his pocket to pay for their meals, Leo stood. Coming here *had* been a mistake. And something told her it would be Jasper who paid the price.

Chapter Fourteen

Leo and Detective Palmer split up after leaving the pub, taking separate cabs to bear them each home. She anticipated trouble, though she didn't quite know what form it would take. Having been seen at the Golden Harp by Andrew Carter had been a serious misfortune. Whether it was for her or for Jasper, she did not know yet.

She unlocked the front door to her house, and as she entered the narrow front hall, her stomach dropped for a second time that evening. Jasper's black wool overcoat and bowler were hanging on the coat stand. Voices emanated from the kitchen. Leo hung up her cape and hat and made her way toward the back of the house, uncertain what to prepare for. Jasper had not said anything about coming over tonight, but perhaps he'd wanted to be here for when she returned from Castelan's agency.

He and Uncle Claude were seated at the kitchen table when she entered, her damp palms smoothing the sides of her skirt. Both men stood to greet her, but only her uncle appeared pleased. Jasper shot her a dark look brimming with grievance.

"Oh, good, you are home. The inspector was hoping to see you, but I wasn't sure when you might be in," Claude said.

"I hope I haven't kept you too long," Leo said.

"I've been telling Inspector Reid about Chesterton Hall," Claude went on. Leo suffered a pang of guilt. In all the commotion of the last few days, the rest home that she and Claude had been considering for Flora had slipped to the back of her mind.

"I will look into it, to be sure no complaints have been filed against them," Jasper told him. It was a kind offer. Placing his wife in another home for care was something Claude dreaded, and knowing the governors of Chesterton Hall were to be trusted would put him at least a little more at ease.

Her uncle thanked Jasper and then, as if sensing she and Jasper wished to speak alone, excused himself. It dashed Leo's cowardly hope that he would retake his seat and stay.

Once she and Jasper were alone in the kitchen, she braced herself. He said nothing at first, only crossed his arms and glared at her.

"You're upset," she observed.

"I went to the morgue earlier. Miss Brooks was there with Connor."

Leo grimaced, now understanding. Dita had known what Mr. Castelan had in store for Leo that evening. "She told you I was sent out on an assignment."

"You went to a public house owned by the Carters."

Stunned, she pulled back a step. "The Carters own

the Golden Harp?" That must have been why Andrew had felt so at home going behind the bar to the back room.

Jasper broke from his stoic posture and shoved his chair hard into place at the table. "It is one of Andrew's businesses. He explained Cillian and Mrs. Pierce would meet there often. It's how he knew what his nephew was up to and with whom."

She could not believe her ears. "Why didn't you say anything about this before?"

"If you will remember, I was trying to keep you uninvolved."

"If you had shared this with me, I would not have gone there."

"Don't try to turn the blame on me. You were supposed to be getting information from Castelan, not going out on assignment to an East Rips pub. And to dinner with another man, I might add."

There, at the ferocious glimmer in his sooty green eyes, Leo saw it: jealousy. Sometimes, his shows of envy did not bother her. But tonight, this one did.

"You had to have known that working with Mr. Castelan could lead to an undercover assignment," she pointed out. "And I was not having dinner with Detective Palmer in that sense."

She hadn't even seen her plate of steak and kidney pie before rushing to leave.

"Palmer." Jasper's glower narrowed. "*Silas* Palmer?"

"You know him?" The detective had certainly made no mention of knowing Jasper.

The muscles already clenching his jaw jumped. "We worked at E Division together." He provided no more explanation than that, and yet, his formidable frown said plenty.

"For what it is worth," Leo began, "I found him to be quite unpleasant."

Jasper groaned and raked his fingers through his honey-blond hair. "Did you at least learn anything about Cillian or Mrs. Pierce?"

Leo deflated. "No. A barmaid seemed to know something, but she warned us to stop asking around."

"There was no point in going there at all," Jasper said. "Tabitha would be a fool to show up at the pub now that Cillian is missing."

Leo went to the hob to put on the kettle. He was correct, of course. It led her to wonder why Mr. Castelan would have suggested they go. Though perhaps he hadn't known who owned the Golden Harp?

Andrew Carter. Leo closed her eyes and nibbled the inside of her cheek. Jasper was already perturbed. But she could not keep what had occurred a secret. Jasper would learn of it eventually, and she would rather it come from her than from Andrew.

She faced him. "I saw Andrew there. And he saw me."

Jasper went to stone. Unblinking. Not breathing. And then, he turned away from her. He set his hands on his hips, his head bowed.

"I knew this would be a mistake." The disappointment in his voice was worse than a shout would have been.

"It might not be that serious a problem," Leo said. "I was there with a man. Andrew might only think I was out to dine."

Jasper faced her again, no longer appearing angry, only exhausted. "Andrew will contact you, Leo. He'll want to know what you were doing there with an undercover detective. Men like him know a copper when they see one. That's what Palmer is, or at least it's what he used to be."

Leo shivered at the idea of Andrew finding her, the way his hired man had the other evening when he'd stopped her in the street. It disturbed her that he should have the power to make her feel so unsettled and unsafe.

Jasper shook his head and abruptly left the kitchen.

She followed on his heels. "Where are you going?"

He arrived at the coat stand near the front door before answering, "To the Golden Harp."

Leo reached for his arm before he could take down his coat. "Are you mad? What if other Carters are there?"

Jasper peeled his arm free and grabbed his coat. "I will be fine. I need to speak to Andrew."

"And tell him what, exactly?"

"The truth. Cillian's mistress is missing and that you've been working with a private detective to find her." Jasper tugged on his coat.

"You don't have to go there. I can tell him that myself when he contacts me."

Jasper tore his bowler from the stand hook and practically shouted, "I do not want him anywhere near you, Leo."

She straightened her spine and balled her hands into fists, startled by his flaying tone. As if he'd belatedly heard it himself, he closed his eyes. "If I talk to him first, he won't need to speak to you. That is how I prefer it. Goodnight."

He put on his hat as he opened the front door and then was gone.

When the Golden Harp came into view, Jasper was still steaming hot. He'd walked along the Embankment to Blackfriars Bridge before hailing a cab to take him the rest of the way. He'd needed to move, to burn off his frustration, but it had not worked as he'd hoped.

Dread pooled in his stomach as he eyed the pub from the pavement. He couldn't go in there, blazing hot. Entering any precarious situation without being sound of mind could spell disaster. So, he took several breaths and rolled his shoulders, attempting to loosen the tension stored there. He was angry, yes, but in finally setting eyes on Andrew Carter's pub, he realized his anger didn't rest solely with Leo and her outing to the Golden Harp with the ex-copper, Silas Palmer.

While he loathed the vision of her dining out with Palmer—who'd only ever ridiculed Jasper for his connection to a higher-up at Scotland Yard, in turn setting him apart from the other men in their division—it wasn't that, or even that Leo had been seen by Andrew, that made him feel like he'd swallowed glowing hot coals. Jasper was furious with *Andrew* and the fact that there was nothing he could do to disentangle himself from the sodding East Rips.

Once his heartbeat slowed, Jasper went inside the busy pub. It wasn't yet ten o'clock, so the night was young for many here. He scanned the crowd, searching for any face that tugged at his memory. None did.

The barkeep eyed him as he approached, and hitched his chin, indicating he'd take his order.

"I'm looking for Andrew," Jasper said.

The barkeep's expression didn't flinch. "Might be a few men here by that name. I can get you a drink while you ask around."

"The owner. I know he was here earlier," Jasper said, fully aware that the man was stalling. "Tell him James is here. He'll want to see me."

The patrons on either side of him weren't being subtle in their interest. Stating his name or connecting himself in any way to Scotland Yard would have been a blunder. James was a common enough name, though.

The barkeep only scowled another few seconds before signaling to a barmaid to go into the back. In the minute that followed, Jasper considered how many ways this visit could go wrong. That it might have been a hasty move to come here. But the alternative of waiting for Andrew to approach Leo was untenable.

The barmaid reappeared through the swinging door, and with her was the orange-hatted man Andrew had sent to follow Jasper for some time last summer. Muncie was his name.

The man's nostrils flared in recognition, and then, though he looked highly displeased, he jerked his chin. An invitation to join him. Jasper went around the bar. Muncie led him into a kitchen and storage area, and from what Jasper saw before being greeted with Muncie's snub-nosed revolver, it was busy, clean, and orderly.

Jasper opened the panels of his coat, and Muncie took the holstered Webley. He next crouched to pat down Jasper's ankles, then felt around his back, to be sure the one weapon was all he'd had. Satisfied, Muncie swung his pistol toward another open doorway. "Down there."

The doorway topped a narrow set of stairs. The cool,

dank air of a cellar enveloped Jasper as he descended, with Muncie following. The cellar glowed with lamplight, illuminating crates, shelves of food, barrels of ale, a slab of beef slung on a hook, and two men—only one of whom was alive.

Andrew Carter stood over the body of a man, lying on a wooden table. Jasper took cautious steps forward and met with the unmistakable rotten stench of the Thames.

"You didn't do too good a job finding my nephew," Andrew said, glaring daggers at him. The cellar air turned even more foul now.

"I take it this is Cillian," Jasper replied.

"Pulled from the river this afternoon," Andrew confirmed. "He was brought to the deadhouse near the Tower. A man there recognized him and sent word to me."

Jasper's skin crawled at the sight of Cillian's bloated corpse. By the state of him, he'd gone into the water days ago. But he hadn't drowned. His throat gaped wide where it had been slit. Though the freezing water temperature of the Thames had preserved him somewhat, the gash was black and raw.

Andrew bared his teeth in fury. "Pierce did this."

"No," Jasper countered. "Based on the state of the body, Cillian was murdered days, possibly a week, ago. Pierce had no idea who his wife was seeing until yesterday morning."

"What happened yesterday morning?"

"I spoke to him. It was the first he'd heard that Cillian was his wife's lover. I'm certain of it."

Andrew walked along the opposite side of the table, his eyes pinned on his nephew while his jaw shifted side to side. "Even if I were to believe you, Sean is going to go after Desmond's head. Cillian was his only son. Unless you can tell me who killed his boy, Sean is sure to break the peace we've got with the Angels and start a goddamned war. That's something the East Rips don't need."

Jasper shrugged. "I don't know anything more than you do."

Andrew sneered at him. "You know that Miss Spencer was here with a copper tonight. It's why you're here, isn't it?"

As Jasper had predicted, Silas Palmer still must have had the look of a police officer about him.

"She's working with a private detective agency. Desmond Pierce hired them to find his wife, Tabitha."

A predatory shine lit his cousin's eyes. "She's missing too, is she?"

"For about a week," Jasper said. "And while I initially wondered if she had harmed Cillian before running, I no longer think that is the case. Women hardly ever have the strength necessary to carve a blade that deeply into a man's throat."

With a rock sinking through him, Jasper was beginning to fear Tabitha had been killed as well. That her body would be the next to be pulled from the river.

"I'll determine that when I find her." Andrew chuffed a laugh. "I'd ask you to do it, but I'm beginning to think you're not a very good detective. Or maybe you just didn't have the right incentive to get the job done."

Jasper knew what Andrew was trying to do. Threats were all he had as leverage. If only Jasper had something to threaten *him* with.

"You'd best leave, Jamey. My brothers are on their way here, and they won't be in gracious moods."

Meeting up with his older cousins and seeing whether they recognized him, as Andrew had, wasn't something Jasper wanted to test out. Andrew gestured toward the other end of the cellar, where a set of steps led up to a closed hatch.

Jasper looked at Cillian's body one last time, and then Muncie, still standing guard, returned his Webley. As Jasper climbed into the alley behind the Golden Harp, he wondered why Andrew hadn't just killed him in the cellar, adding another body to the tally. Jasper had failed at this first favor, after all. Cillian was dead, and he hadn't even been the one to find the body. Why protect him now from the other Carter brothers?

There was something to it. And it might be the leverage Jasper was seeking.

Chapter Fifteen

Frost glittered on roofs and windows as sunlight broke through milky clouds. Leo buried her hands in the pockets of her cloak as she walked swiftly along the Strand toward Spring Street. As it was Sunday, the morgue would be closed to the public, but Leo still had work to do. Being out during the workday a few times that week meant that there were reports to catch up on. Besides, she popped into the morgue every Sunday to feed and water Tibia.

She'd remained agitated all night after Jasper left. Not knowing what had happened at the Golden Harp—if he'd spoken to Andrew or if he'd been seen by other Carter family members—gnawed at her. She'd done nothing wrong; how was she to have known the pub was owned by Andrew Carter? Nonetheless, she felt an infuriating pinch of guilt. It stole her hunger that morning when she and Claude met in the kitchen, and though she toasted some bread for him, she couldn't stomach more than a few bites herself.

"I heard raised voices last evening when the inspector was here," her uncle remarked with some caution. He didn't want to pry, Leo could tell, but his concern was evident. "Is all well now?"

The answering prick of tears had surprised her. Aggravated her too. Though she had once been accustomed to verbal sparring with Jasper, last evening's dispute had bothered her more than it ever would have in the past.

"Not entirely," she'd answered her uncle. He'd only patted her hand and assured her that things would be repaired. To give it time.

But time could not fix everything. It wouldn't help Jasper escape Andrew, or his own past.

At Trafalgar Square and Charing Cross Road, Leo hesitated—then turned toward Scotland Yard. Jasper might not be in his office on a Sunday morning. But something told her that he'd slept just as poorly as she had, and whenever he could not sleep, he found solace in his work. If he wasn't there, she'd try Charles Street after finishing up at the morgue. She needed to know what had happened at the pub.

She came through Craig's Court and into the yard, for which the police headquarters was named. She moved aside to avoid uniformed constables and the ragtag men they were leading toward the building in cuffs, as well as a few police wagons coming and going. It was busy already, though it was not yet eight o'clock. Instantly, Leo felt the thrum of excitement she always experienced when at Scotland Yard. The commotion and purpose gave her a thrill, and as she entered the lobby, she realized how much she'd missed it.

Ever since she and Jasper had started to court officially, she'd sent reports to the CID via messenger, and now she considered that she might have been unintentionally avoiding the place out of concern for how Jasper's fellow officers and superiors would react to the change in her status.

An unfamiliar constable manned the lobby desk, rather than Constable Woodhouse, who was likely enjoying his day off at home with his family.

"Can I help you, miss?" the constable said.

"I'm looking for Inspector Reid. Is he in this morning?"

The constable looked her over. "Name?"

"Miss Leonora Spencer. I am an acquaintance of the inspector's."

The constable's eyebrows shot up. "Of course, Miss Spencer, do go in."

She entered the narrow corridor, strangely rattled by the man's instant graciousness. He'd recognized her name. Was Jasper's courtship with her really so well-known at the Yard?

As she walked through to the detective department, she was glad to see Constable Horace Wiley's desk empty. Except for two men at their desks, the CID was relatively empty and hushed. She made her way toward Jasper's office, slowing as she approached the threshold. He was seated at his desk, poring over a case file, with a stack of other reports at his elbow. She rapped her knuckles on the wood frame, and he glanced up.

"Leo?" He stood, and she noticed smudges of exhaustion under his eyes. His tousled hair and rumpled clothing added to his weary appearance. Somehow, the bedraggled look only made him more handsome. It hit her with a wallop as she entered his office. How was it possible that just looking at Jasper could steal her breath?

"Close the door." The order surprised her, as did the sober tone in which he said it.

Leo did as he requested, though with some trepidation. "Do you want this door shut because you're going to shout at me?"

He came around the desk. "That isn't why."

"It isn't?"

"No," he said, not slowing as he neared. "I want the door shut because I am going to kiss you."

Jasper pulled her into his arms and pressed his lips to hers. Leo melted against him in stunned mystification. She hadn't expected a kiss so soon after their argument and certainly not here, in his office, where anyone could walk in at any moment.

He lifted his mouth from hers but kept her close against him. "I don't want to be at odds, Leo."

She closed her eyes as his forehead rested against hers. "Neither do I."

"I'm sorry for my attitude last night," he said. "It isn't your fault that you crossed paths with Andrew."

He stood tall again and loosened his embrace, putting an inch of space between them. Leo worried someone might open the door to his office, but not enough to part from him entirely.

"I couldn't sleep," she admitted. "I worried all night about what might have happened. Did you speak to your cousin?"

"I did. I also found Cillian Carter."

Despite her desire only a second ago to remain in

Jasper's arms, Leo jerked back. "You did? Was Tabitha with him?"

Jasper, his countenance grim, answered, "No. Cillian was alone. And he was dead."

"Oh, no. Oh, God." Her legs unexpectedly feeling wobbly, she went to the chair in front of his desk and sat.

"His throat had been cut, and he'd been tossed into the Thames. The state of his body suggests he had been in the water for days. Possibly the whole of the week he's been missing," Jasper explained.

Concern for Tabitha mounted. If Cillian had been murdered, there was a high probability that Mr. Pierce's wife had also suffered the same fate.

"Where was Cillian when you saw him?" Leo asked.

"The cellar at the Golden Harp." Jasper came to lean against his desk, in front of her, and crossed his arms. "Andrew was there. We spoke briefly. Sean, Brian, and Rory were due to arrive, so I left."

"Does he have any idea who killed his nephew?"

"He's convinced Desmond Pierce is involved, even though I explained that Desmond had hired a private inquiry agency to find his wife. And that he hadn't seemed to know with whom she'd run off. Until I told him," he added with a shrug.

An uneasy notion wormed its way through Leo. "Does Andrew suspect Tabitha?"

"He knows it would take formidable strength to overpower Cillian and slash his throat. She might know something, but I doubt she did the deed herself. Still, he plans to find her and ask."

If Tabitha was still alive and he did find her, he wouldn't ask nicely, Leo was sure of that.

She peered up at Jasper. "Did he charge you with finding her?"

He shook his head. "My attempts to find Cillian were unimpressive, thankfully."

"So then, why didn't Andrew allow his older brothers to come upon you in the cellar?" Leo asked. "Expose you right then and there?"

The idea of it made her ill, but it would have been a believable move for Jasper's cousin to have made.

"I wondered the same," Jasper said with a pensive frown. She stood and rested her hands on his forearms, crossed over his chest.

"While I'm relieved Andrew hasn't commanded your help, I'm worried for Tabitha. If she is still alive and the Carters suspect her, she's in danger."

Jasper covered her hand with his, his coarse palm reassuring. "I agree, though I can't help her if I don't know where to look. She might be anywhere."

"I may have a lead," Leo began, thinking of something Detective Palmer had said the previous night. "Mr. Pierce told Detective Palmer that his wife's routine was steady. She worked at Mary Hobson's bakery every day excepting Sundays."

"Has Palmer been to the bakery?" Jasper asked.

"I imagine he has," Leo replied. "However, it may be worth finding in the London Directory and taking another trip there. Someone Tabitha worked with might have stayed quiet when Detective Palmer was asking about her, though they could be led to say something now, if they knew her lover has been found murdered."

Jasper's lips curved into a roguish grin. "Do you have any plans this morning?"

"None that I cannot see to later," she replied. "*After* we pay the bakery a visit."

Jasper pushed off the desk and collected his coat and hat. "I have a lead in the Lawlor case too. I hope you weren't looking forward to a lazy Sunday."

Leo brightened as she followed him out of his office. "Is it to do with Victoria Herrington's maid?" With last night's furor surrounding the Golden Harp and Andrew Carter, she hadn't asked Jasper about his interview with the former lady's maid.

"It is. I'll tell you about it on our way to Spitalfields."

They took the train to Liverpool Street Station, and along the way, Jasper imparted what he'd learned from the maid, Isabelle Chandler.

"It was the same con, by the same two men," he said as they rumbled along the tracks, the scent of machine oil permeating the closed-up air in the car. "Only this time Sebastian Lawlor, whoever he truly was, saw the entire scheme through and walked away with his wife's fortune. Though it wasn't as impressive as I thought it would be, given Mrs. Herrington's grandfather's former success in the sugar trade."

Sergeant Warnock had looked through the probate records at Somerset House for the Herrington settlement and reported that the fortune had diminished significantly after the death of Victoria's father. Mr. Blake had been swimming in debt, and during probate, his debtors had been repaid with the bulk of Victoria's inheritance. She had been able to maintain the family home and staff, but in truth, she'd been living frugally compared to what the Blake family had previously been accustomed to.

"What if Sebastian Lawlor planned to cut Mr. Gray out of the deal this time around?" Leo suggested. "So, he took what he thought might see him through and tried to flee."

"And the false doctor found him and killed him for it," Jasper said. "It is possible."

They sat close, shoulder to shoulder, in the packed rail car and kept their voices low to avoid interest from their neighbors.

"Did Miss Chandler have an idea on where we might find Henry Gray?" Leo asked.

"No, but she named the other Herrington staff, including the housekeeper, a Mrs. Michaels. She's employed at a house in Marylebone now. I thought we would call on her too."

Housekeepers always knew more about their employers than maids did. As it was a Sunday, it was likely her half day, and she might be free to speak with them.

Once at Liverpool Street Station, they took a cab to Hanbury Street, the location the London Directory had listed for the bakery. Hobson's, as it was called, occupied a street corner, where a short line of customers stood outside the bakery doors. Though antiquated, Sunday closing laws made it strictly illegal to bake or sell bread commercially on the Sabbath; however, smaller shops often opened for a few hours, defying these regulations. Certain shops, Leo supposed, received protection against police interference too. From the Angels, for instance.

The yeasty and malted scents of freshly baked bread

wafting from the shop as its door opened and shut made Leo's stomach grumble; she never did get a bite to eat the night before, and the toasted bread she'd had for breakfast hadn't done much to fill her.

"Have there been any leads from the sketches that ran in newspapers and the *Police Gazette*?" she asked as they joined the line of customers. "Or the pubs in the area of Creed Lane where Mr. Lawlor may have last eaten?"

"None," he answered. "Drake also took the sketches to some chemists around Mayfair to see if either man could be remembered as having purchased laudanum or arsenic." Jasper shook his head firmly at what the result had been.

"The doctor must have gotten the substances somewhere," Leo said, peering into the bakery window.

It was a pocket-sized shop, only able to hold two customers at a time. When they finally stepped inside, Leo shivered at the sudden warmth. A woman stood at the counter, taking orders and payment, while behind her in a kitchen open to view, a man and a young boy minded the racks of bread and the large stone hearth, where more loaves were baking. The woman eyed them without a smile, even though she'd given one to the lady in line before them. Leo and Jasper were unfamiliar, and Jasper did have the distinct look of a police officer.

"Good morning," Leo began quietly, cautious of the person behind them in the shop. "Are you Mrs. Hobson?"

"Aye, that's right. Do ye want somethin'?"

"We'd like to ask about a woman who works here, Tabitha Pierce."

Mrs. Hobson, who appeared to be about forty years old, visibly went on her guard. "What 'bout 'er?"

"She hasn't been seen in several days," Jasper said. "We believe she might be in some danger, and we'd like to find her."

Mrs. Hobson glanced toward the back of the shop, where the man—tall, barrel-chested, and ruddy-cheeked —was filling a basket with rolls. She faced forward and, leaning against the flour-dusted counter, said low and harshly, "Order two currant buns."

"Excuse me?" Jasper asked as the man turned a curious glare toward the front of the shop.

"Just order 'em, *quick*," she pleaded through gritted teeth, her glare no longer suspicious, but frightened.

Leo cleared her throat. "Two currant buns, please."

The woman left the counter for a stand of racks and baskets, and the man in the kitchen turned back to his work. Leo crossed a glance with Jasper, intrigued by Mrs. Hobson's furtive actions. She returned a moment later, shoving a paper-wrapped bundle across the counter. "That'll be a penny."

Frowning, Jasper reached into his pocket for the coin and paid. The woman jutted her chin, as if to order them to move aside. Leo took the wrapped bundle, and as the next customer in line was assisted, she and Jasper made their way from the shop, bewildered. Once outside, the package warmed Leo's hand against the chilled morning air.

"What was that about?" Jasper muttered. "We didn't come all this way to buy two currant buns. I'm going back in."

Leo grasped his elbow. "You'll draw too much attention to yourself."

He sighed but stood back as the door opened, and one

customer exchanged for the next. Leo's stomach complained again, and she opened the brown-paper wrapping. "We may as well eat."

But when she looked down at the contents of the bundle, she saw they'd been given one currant bun, not two. The purpose behind it became clear just as the door to the bakery opened again.

"Oh good, I've caught ye!" Mrs. Hobson said loudly before the door shut behind her. She held in her hand another wrapped package—the second currant bun she'd intentionally forgotten to give them.

Lowering her voice, she said, "I've got a minute before me 'usband gets 'spicious. Yer a copper, ain't ye?" she asked Jasper.

"Inspector Reid from Scotland Yard," he admitted.

"Why're ye askin' 'bout Tabitha?"

"We merely wish to speak to her," Leo answered. "Have you seen her recently?"

Mrs. Hobson sighed. "She 'asn't been in fer over a week. It ain't like 'er. Tabitha's worked fer me two years now. When she didn't show fer a few days, I went 'round to 'er place."

"She wasn't at home?" Leo asked.

Mary Hobson shook her head. "Desmond said she were abed, feelin' poorly, but 'e were actin' odd. A few days later, a bloke came 'round, askin' 'bout Tabitha. Wantin' to know if I'd seen 'er. I told 'im to shove off. When I went to Desmond again, 'e told me to mind me own business."

Leo peered through the bakery window. The young boy who had been helping Mary's husband was serving at the counter.

"Ye think Tabitha's in danger?" Mrs. Hobson asked Jasper, seeming to recall what he'd said in the bakery.

"We think she is hiding," Jasper answered. "Do you have any idea where she might be?"

The woman shook her head. "I knew she'd get 'erself into trouble, stupid girl."

"Why do you say that?" Leo asked.

"Because she were steppin' out with another man. An East Rip, 'e was too. She weren't careful 'bout it. People were talkin'." Anguish pulled at Mrs. Hobson's brow. "And 'er, with a baby on the way too."

Leo stared at the woman, her ears suddenly chiming. "Baby?"

"Tabitha is with child?" Jasper asked, sounding just as shocked as Leo felt.

Mrs. Hobson nodded. "About four months gone, she told me. She were sure the father were the other 'un."

Leo's concern for Tabitha ratcheted even higher.

"Mrs. Hobson," Jasper said. "The man Tabitha was seeing has been found dead. That is why we think she is in danger. Can you think of anywhere she would go to feel safe?"

The older woman pinched her lips in distress. "The church, maybe. St. Emmanuel's. She didn't 'ave many friends; Desmond wouldn't allow it. But 'e did let 'er go to church."

Mrs. Hobson backed up. "I been out 'ere too long. I 'ope ye find 'er. Poor girl." She dashed into the shop, and Leo dropped her shoulders, disappointed they hadn't received more of a lead.

"Andrew said nothing about a baby," Jasper said. "I doubt he knows."

"Perhaps the Carters won't harm Tabitha if they think she is carrying Cillian's child," Leo suggested. Jasper scowled.

"I don't believe the Carters care about that sort of thing."

He would know best. Jasper once confessed to Leo that his mother had been several months with child when his Uncle Robert, one of the late Patrick Carter's brothers, had beaten her to death. Jasper didn't speak often of his mother; however, he had revealed that when his father, another of Patrick's brothers, had died, he and his mother were taken in by Robert and his wife, Myra. Later on, his mother had gotten with child. Leo could be wrong, and Jasper had never said as much, but she presumed Robert had been the baby's father.

It must have been awful for Jasper as a boy to see his mother treated in such a way and not be able to do anything to help her. Perhaps that was one reason why he was so protective of Leo now.

She handed him his currant bun. "Come. St. Emmanuel's can't be too far from here. We could speak to the reverend."

"I suppose it's something," he agreed.

After asking a woman standing in the bakery line for directions, they arrived at the church within minutes. Its Portland stone exterior and stained glass windows needed a scrubbing, and as they came upon parishioners leaving the morning sermon, Leo observed that the congregation was mostly poor and working-class.

She entered the church with some hope of finding Mrs. Pierce, especially when she spied a woman kneeling in prayer in a back pew. A faded blue scarf covered the woman's head and obscured her profile. As Leo moved closer toward her, however, the floor beneath her feet groaned loudly. The sound cracked through the hushed church.

The woman turned at the noise. It wasn't Tabitha, but instead an older woman, her chapped face lined with age.

"Careful, miss." A man's voice echoed from the front of the nave. A tall reverend in a white cassock came toward her and Jasper. "That glass is in need of repair."

Leo looked down to see she stood on a strange portion of glass floor. Underneath appeared to be a chamber of sorts. It held a white marble coffin decorated with a gold cross and other ornamentation. Quickly, she moved off the glass, rejoining Jasper.

"Reverend Julius Hawthorne is entombed in our crypt," the reverend said as he reached them. "He was first to lead the parishioners of St. Emmanuel's at its inception in 1789. We are collecting to reinforce the glass, if you care to make a donation."

Beside her, Jasper barely stifled a groan, but Leo opened her purse and withdrew a shilling. It might encourage the reverend to discuss Tabitha Pierce. He accepted the coin, but when Jasper asked if Mrs. Pierce had been seen at church in the last week, he shook his head.

"She has not been here for nearly a fortnight," he said, then looking between Jasper and Leo, he inquired, "How is she known to you?"

Jasper held up his warrant card. "Inspector Reid from Scotland Yard. We believe Mrs. Pierce may know something about a crime, and it has put her in a fair amount of danger. I'd like to speak to her and get at the truth, but she seems to have disappeared."

"I see. That is quite serious." The reverend clasped his hands together before him, as if in prayer. "I wish I could help, Inspector. But as I said, she hasn't been in church for some time."

A startling *clang* made the three of them swivel and stare—a robed altar boy had been clearing a table at the reverend's pulpit and now chased after an ornate chalice he'd dropped. It clattered down a few steps toward the front pews before he managed to scoop it up. When he stood, his cheeks were red as beets, making his straw-blond hair appear even more radiant.

The reverend raised a hand as if to indicate to the boy he wasn't in any sort of trouble, then, with a tight look of stifled exasperation, turned back to Leo and Jasper. "If you will excuse me. I will keep Mrs. Pierce in my prayers."

"We're going to need more than prayers," Jasper said under his breath as they turned to leave, a shilling poorer and at another dead end.

Chapter Sixteen

Their next stop after leaving St. Emmanuel's unfolded with little more success.

Leo and Jasper arrived at the address in Marylebone, where Victoria Herrington's former housekeeper now worked, just in time. Mrs. Michaels had been tying the ribbons on her bonnet, about to set out on her half day to visit relatives in Bromley, when they turned up at the servant's entrance. The older woman expressed annoyance at being delayed, especially as it was to answer questions about her former employer—whom she had not particularly liked.

"I'm not saying I was happy when she died," Mrs. Michaels said after the three of them had settled at the servants' table in the unoccupied kitchen. "I've never wished ill on anybody. But my former mistress was very odd and very difficult. Honestly, after that business with her stolen brooch, I was always on edge, fearful she might point to me as a thief next time something went missing."

Leo didn't understand her meaning and directed a

quizzical glance at Jasper, who explained, "A friend of Mrs. Herrington's stole a brooch in retaliation for a perceived slight, and Mrs. Herrington accused a maid of the theft." He then said to the housekeeper, "Miss Chandler reported that when your mistress learned the truth, she apologized profusely."

Mrs. Michaels harrumphed, unimpressed. "What use is an apology when your name's been tainted? In service, the accusation alone can ruin a person's prospects."

Leo trusted the housekeeper was correct. "How did Mrs. Herrington learn it was her friend and not the maid?" she asked.

"She hired a private detective. He questioned all of us, but it wasn't until the brooch turned up at a pawnbroker's shop that he traced it back to Mrs. Herrington's friend."

"A detective," Leo echoed, thinking of how Mrs. Lawlor's mother had hired Mr. Castelan. "Do you recall his name?"

Mrs. Michaels sighed impatiently. "Bentley, I think. Detective Bentley."

"And how long was this before Mrs. Herrington married?" Jasper asked.

Meeting his eyes briefly, Leo knew he was thinking the same thing: Augusta and Victoria had both worked with private detectives before their marriages.

"Maybe a year? Why do you ask?"

"Just being thorough," Jasper answered, then went on to pepper her with more questions, including Miss Chandler's suspicions about Mr. Herrington.

"It was an odd business," Mrs. Michaels agreed, "but there was nothing nefarious in it that I could see." The housekeeper tapped her foot impatiently and lifted the miniature fob watch strung on her necklace. She was too eager to be on her way to truly give them her full attention, Leo sensed.

She and Jasper rose from their chairs, preparing to leave. "Miss Chandler mentioned a maid, Marion," Jasper said as the housekeeper jumped to her feet. "She couldn't recall her surname. Can you?"

Mrs. Michaels answered as she walked them hastily toward the exit. "Of course I do; I hired her, didn't I? Marion Clark. She quit her position before Mr. Herrington sold the house and dismissed the staff. I gave her a letter of character to take with her to her next position, but I've no idea where she went."

Leo thanked her for her time as they stepped outside. Without acknowledgement, Mrs. Michaels bustled past them toward the pavements.

"I am suddenly reminded of how fortunate I am to have the housekeeper I do," Jasper said softly as they followed Mrs. Michaels. "Remind me to be more appreciative of Mrs. Zhao."

"You are already appreciative of her," Leo replied. "And she is more than a housekeeper."

Mrs. Zhao was family.

"It is odd, isn't it?" Leo went on, taking Jasper's arm when he offered it. "Both Mrs. Lawlor and Mrs. Herrington had interactions with private investigators before they were tricked into marriage."

"One was for a dishonest suitor, the other for a theft," Jasper said. "The two don't seem to have anything in common. But I can have PC Mills go through our listing for private inquiry agents to find this Bentley fellow. Follow it up, just in case."

They hailed a cab, and Jasper was giving the driver instructions to take them to Scotland Yard when Leo had another idea. "Can you take us to Hill Street in Mayfair, instead?" she called up to the driver.

He nodded, and Jasper climbed into the cab, his expression fixed with doubt. "We've already had two disappointing interviews today. Are we aiming for three?"

"I know Mrs. Lawlor hasn't been cooperative," Leo replied. "But now that there is confirmation that Sebastian Lawlor and Rupert Herrington were one and the same man, she should be informed. She was lucky to come out of her ordeal alive. Victoria Herrington wasn't. Maybe Mrs. Lawlor will now feel some inclination to help us find Mr. Gray."

Jasper didn't look convinced but sat back on the bench without debate. As they started across town, he reached for Leo's hand.

"I sent a wire to the constabulary station in Isleworth this morning, inquiring into the convalescent home your uncle mentioned."

A mix of dread and anticipation buzzed around Leo's stomach. She felt curiously ill with the feeling every time she thought of placing her aunt at Chesterton Hall.

"I'm sure I'll hear something in the next day or two," Jasper went on. "I'm sorry it's come to this. I imagine it won't be easy to send Flora there, even if its reputation stands up to scrutiny."

Leo looked out at the street, at a loss for words. It wouldn't be easy, but her aunt needed more care—more than Claude and Mrs. Zhao were able to provide.

"Will Claude go with her?" Jasper asked after a moment.

Leo had been purposefully avoiding that same question. She hadn't wanted to consider it yet.

She rested her head against Jasper's shoulder. "I believe he will."

In her heart, she knew her uncle would never live separately from his wife. He loved Flora too much to leave her somewhere far away, alone. Leo was more than able to live independently and did not need Claude the same way she once had. However, that didn't mean she was ready for him to move away.

Jasper, seeming to understand her forlorn thoughts, raised their joined hands and kissed her gloved fingers. "You won't be alone here, Leo."

She knew as much; nonetheless, it was comforting to hear Jasper declare it.

When they arrived in Mayfair, they were both taken aback to be greeted pleasantly by Augusta Lawlor. Hastings showed them into the front parlor, and at once, Leo thought she knew why Augusta had experienced a change of heart.

The woman sat regally in her chair by the fire, no longer tearful or wrapped in blankets. Her eyes were clear, her chin held high, and a healthy coloring had flushed out her previously ghostly pale skin. She had evidently started to heal from the drugging haze of laudanum and the continual dosing with arsenic.

"Inspector, Miss Spencer. Do have a seat. Tea, Hastings."

As Leo took to the sofa, the same spot in which she'd sat the other day, she remarked, "You're looking well, Mrs. Lawlor."

Following a sigh, Augusta replied, "That is gracious of

you, but I must apologize for my behavior the last time you both were here. I was unforgivably rude."

"There is no need," Leo assured her. "You'd been through quite an ordeal."

It was not so strange that Augusta had not been willing to consider her husband had acted maliciously against her. Now, however, Leo suspected a change of heart in her.

"These last few days, I've started to feel more like myself again. Better than I have in months." Augusta held her hands clasped together, her brow furrowed in dejection. "I see now that you were correct. Both of you were. I believe Sebastian was intentionally making me ill."

Jasper remained standing by the hearth. "I'm sorry to bring you more distressing news, Mrs. Lawlor, but it appears you were not his only victim. Another woman, Victoria Herrington, was married two years ago to the man you knew as Sebastian Lawlor. He was Rupert Herrington then. You and Mrs. Herrington were similar in many ways, most specifically in that you were both heiresses, without any remaining family."

The older woman closed her eyes, as if against a blow, but maintained her composure. "What happened to her?"

"She fell ill, as you did. Unfortunately, the illness claimed her life," Jasper revealed.

The only fissure in Augusta's poise was a trembling of her hand as she gripped the arm of her chair.

"He inherited everything and disappeared shortly afterward," Jasper concluded. "The difference between you and Mrs. Herrington is obvious, in that you are still alive. But also different is the fact that she died of prolonged arsenic poisoning rather than an attempted laudanum overdose."

"And her husband claimed her fortune, while Mr. Lawlor took only the contents of the safe and a fraction of your wealth from the bank," Leo added. "It seems he rushed to see his plan through and fled, even knowing he would not receive the full financial benefit of your death."

Augusta's emotional trembling had ceased. She frowned. "He had been acting strange for a few weeks. He said some issue at the shop, a late shipment, was making him tense, but I did wonder if it was something more than that."

"Had he received any visitors here during that time?" Jasper asked. "Anyone you didn't recognize?"

She shook her head. "Only Mr. Gray. As I was ill, we weren't receiving any visitors."

Leo crossed a glance with Jasper. He nodded.

"Mrs. Lawlor," she began, "we've discovered Mr. Gray is not who he claimed to be. He and your husband were partners in this scheme. We have not found him or discovered his true name, but is there anything at all you can remember from that last time Mr. Gray visited here?"

Augusta's rigid posture slipped. "That should not surprise me so. He was, after all, the only person from Sebastian's life that I ever met." She sat back in her chair. "I heard them arguing. They were in Sebastian's room, which attaches to my own. I didn't hear them clearly, but Sebastian was quite upset. It was his voice that was raised, not the doctor's. Afterward, Sebastian claimed he was just angry that the doctor could do nothing for my illness." With an arch of her brow, she added, "Of course, now I know that was a lie."

"When was this?" Jasper asked.

"About two weeks before I…well, before I nearly died."

So, the two cohorts were in an argument shortly before Sebastian set his new plan in motion.

The door to the parlor opened, and a maid entered with a tea tray. Leo looked twice at the maid's face as she placed the tray on the table and poured for them. Once the maid left, Leo turned to Augusta.

"I questioned your maids a few days ago, but I don't recall that young woman. Was she absent?"

"Mrs. Vincent hired Enid only yesterday. One of the other maids quit her post without warning."

"Which maid was this?" Leo asked.

"Marianna," Augusta answered. "All the commotion and scandal must have affected her. Mrs. Vincent said she took her things and left without a goodbye. The girl didn't even ask for a letter of character."

Jasper cocked his head. "Marianna?"

Leo recalled her: slim, blonde, pretty. She'd been nervous to be interviewed, the lace trim of her mobcap shaking. Her hands had been white knuckled as she clutched them in her lap.

"How long had she been a maid here?" Jasper asked Augusta.

"I can't be sure," she answered. "Is it important?"

"Seven months," Leo said, recalling the detail from her interview with her. "Why do you ask?"

"Miss Chandler told me the maid *Marion* was hired just six or seven months before Mrs. Herrington's death. She came on staff shortly before Rupert Herrington entered the picture," he explained.

Marion. Marianna. The two names sounded markedly similar.

Excitement—and the possibility of a real lead—shivered along Leo's legs. She got to her feet. "Mrs. Lawlor, am I correct that you met your husband about six months ago?"

She nodded, her attention jumping between Leo and Jasper. "This is coincidental, surely."

"Perhaps," Leo replied. But she wasn't inclined to let the matter settle without looking further into it. "Do you have any information on Marianna? Her address? Any letter of character from her last position?"

As this information wasn't something the lady of the house would possess, Augusta summoned her housekeeper, Mrs. Vincent. She arrived promptly.

"I would never take on a maid who did not have a glowing letter of character," Mrs. Vincent said with some indignance. "The previous housekeeper she worked under wrote she was diligent and quiet. A bit docile, but that isn't something one shuns in a maid."

"Do you recall this housekeeper's name?" Jasper asked, animated now that they might have found a new suspect. "Or which household it was?"

"Mrs. Doris Michaels oversaw the household. I've no acquaintance with Mrs. Michaels, but she wrote of her mistress's sudden passing. Marianna required a new position because of it."

Jasper met Leo's astonished stare and grinned.

"The letter of character said her name was *Marianna*?" Leo asked, confused. "Marianna Clark? Not *Marion*?"

Mrs. Vincent blinked and canted her head. "Why, yes, the letter did name her as Marion Clark. She explained

Mrs. Michaels was always getting her name wrong. The two are close enough, I suppose. But how could you have known that?"

Leo turned to Jasper. "Marianna, or Marion, is part of the scheme as well," she said while Augusta and Mrs. Vincent wore matching looks of bewilderment. "She is the one who overheard Mr. Lawlor giving a cab driver directions to Paddington Station."

"Or so she claimed," Jasper said.

He was correct. Marianna might have given Leo and Jasper a false lead. "She could have been redirecting us. Sending us in the entirely wrong direction."

"And giving Sebastian time to disappear." Jasper inhaled deeply, his excitement turning to visible frustration.

"Someone caught up to him, however," Leo reminded him.

The stab wounds to his chest could have been inflicted by a woman, but Leo recalled Marianna as slight and willowy. Based on what Connor had said about the bruising around the wounds, each puncture had been made with great force.

"Inspector, are you saying my maid is involved in my attempted murder?" Augusta asked.

"All I am certain of is that I need to find her, and quickly. Mrs. Vincent," he said, turning to the housekeeper. "Do you have an address for her?"

She nodded and left in a hurry. Jasper and Leo thanked Augusta for her time and promised to keep her informed.

In the foyer, as Hastings brought them their outer trappings, Leo lowered her voice. "The wedding bands in Sebastian Lawlor's pocket."

"What about them?"

"Marianna's hands. She was clutching them during her interview. I didn't notice it at the time, but now..." Now, the precise image of those clutched hands slid into place, in front of Leo's eyes, as clearly as if she was there again in the salmon-colored dining room. "She was fidgeting with her left fingers during my interview with her. Right where a wedding band would have rested on her ring finger, had she been wearing one."

"They were married?" Jasper asked. "The maid and Sebastian?"

Leo lifted her shoulders. "Anything is possible at this point."

The housekeeper arrived with the address for Marianna, and though Jasper took it, Leo presumed it would be like everything else so far: false. They took their leave, stepping outside into the newly darkened street.

"We will require a sketch of Marianna. I can picture her perfectly, but I can't draw to save my life," Leo said.

"We'll go to the Yard and summon Mr. Gibbons," Jasper said.

"He is becoming quite indispensable, isn't he?"

Jasper allowed a rare grin. Although lately, to Leo's pleasure, they seemed to come less infrequently. "If we can find this maid, we'll find Gray."

And they would have the murderer.

Chapter Seventeen

As Jasper entered the busy lobby at Scotland Yard on Monday morning, the sight of Superintendent Monroe instantly curdled the breakfast Mrs. Zhao had prepared and all but forced Jasper to eat.

He'd skipped dinner the night before, too wrung out from his day tramping across London with Leo. When his housekeeper warned that she was finished cooking for him unless he ate his breakfast, Jasper gave in. But as Monroe, who was speaking to another officer, noted Jasper's arrival, he lamented clearing his plate.

A shoulder knocked into Jasper's arm in the busy lobby, and he looked down to see a red-cheeked young messenger boy attempting to scoot by.

"S-sorry, sir," the boy stammered as he pulled a tweed cap lower over his head of bright blond hair. He scampered out the door.

"Reid," Constable Woodhouse called from the front desk. He held up a note. "Just delivered for you."

Jasper took the note a moment before the superintendent broke away from the other officer and approached.

"Ah, Reid, good to see you." Monroe clapped him on the shoulder. "I hear you're making headway with the Lawlor case. A new suspect?"

The previous evening, after visiting the address Mrs. Vincent had for Marianna and learning it was, indeed, false, Jasper had summoned Mr. Gibbons. The sketch artist had sat with Leo in Jasper's office for nearly an hour while she described in minute detail the features belonging to the young maid Marianna—or Marion. The completed sketch had gone straight to the printing office at the Yard, where the lithographer made copies for distribution to Fleet Street before midnight, in time for the morning editions.

"A young woman," Jasper said to the superintendent. "With any hope, someone will recognize her and bring us a name."

"Before the Home Secretary's dinner, preferably," Monroe said. "You are still attending, I hope?"

The flare of discomfort and annoyance he'd felt the other afternoon after leaving Verrey's returned. Jasper clenched his jaw as he nodded.

"Good, my Rose is looking forward to that dance, Reid." The superintendent gave him another pat on the arm before carrying on down the narrow hall. There was no mistaking Monroe's tone: Jasper was expected to dance with Rose, and that was that.

As he watched Monroe retreat, his stomach beginning to unclench, he took a glance toward Constable Woodhouse.

"Isn't Rose the name of the super's daughter?" he asked.

Jasper suppressed a groan. The last thing he wanted was a rumor to fly around about this.

"There was a miscommunication," he told Woodhouse. "I am not dancing with anyone."

The constable raised a quizzical brow, but Jasper didn't linger to discuss it further. He went to the detective department, his irritation simmering. He'd hoped Monroe would not press on with the idea of matching him with Rose, especially after Jasper reminded him that he was, in fact, courting Leonora Spencer.

There was no choice; he would not attend the dinner, and the next time the superintendent alluded to his daughter, Jasper would just need to be blunter.

At the entrance to the detective department, Jasper's heels dragged to a stop. Seated in one of the chairs near Constable Wiley's desk was Miss Nivedita Brooks. She saw Jasper and shot to her feet.

"Inspector Reid," she said, her manner tense.

"This woman says she wants to see you," Constable Wiley announced from his chair.

He knew perfectly well who Miss Brooks was, and his sneer was not unlike others Leo's friend would receive here. Her former beau, PC John Lloyd, had attempted to place a bomb housed in a suitcase at Scotland Yard. The bomb had detonated, killing him and wounding many others, including Leo. It didn't matter that Lloyd had been coerced, he was still viewed as a traitor. Many officers saw Miss Brooks as suspicious, or even potentially complicit in the Yard bombing that occurred in May.

She eyed Wiley with annoyance but turned her attention toward Jasper. "I need to see you, Inspector," she said. Clutched in her hand was a rolled-up newspaper.

He tucked the note Woodhouse had given him into his coat pocket and led Miss Brooks to his office. There, she placed the newspaper, *The Morning Chronicle*, on his desk. It was folded open to the page on which the three suspect sketches had been printed.

"I saw the sketches this morning while my father was reading the paper at the breakfast table," Miss Brooks said. "You're looking for this woman?"

She let her pointer finger rest on the sketch of Marianna. The short column of text underneath the portraits said Scotland Yard was pursuing information regarding a crime and to contact Inspector Reid at the CID with any information.

"I am," Jasper replied. "Do you know her?"

"No, but I've seen her," Miss Brooks answered. "At Mr. Castelan's."

Jasper had started to hang his coat and hat on the coat stand but now stopped. His pulse picked up its pace. "When was this?"

"Right when I started there. I only saw her once or twice, but I recall her because I was hoping for another woman to work with."

"But you didn't work with her?"

Miss Brooks shook her head, her hands balled into tense fists. "No. I didn't see her again after those first two times when she came to speak to Mr. Castelan in his office. Mr. Hutchins, one of the clerks there, said she once worked for Mr. Castelan but hadn't been around for months. They'd used her in the past as a watcher."

A spy then, like Miss Brooks.

"Do you remember her name?" Jasper presumed it was some form of Mary, but Miss Brooks shook her head, again not knowing.

"Is she in trouble?" Miss Brooks asked. "If one of Mr. Castelan's employees is arrested, it will look bad for the whole agency."

"That is something for him to worry about, Miss Brooks, not you," Jasper said as he put on his coat and hat again. "What about these two men? Do you recognize them?" He tapped the sketches of Sebastian Lawlor and Henry Gray, neither labeled with their false names, only a request to contact Scotland Yard if someone recognized them.

"I haven't seen them before," she said with certainty. But that didn't mean they weren't connected to Castelan's agency. Miss Brooks had been employed there for less than two months, after all.

Jasper noticed her maid's uniform of a dark cotton dress and white pinafore behind the panels of her cloak. "Is that uniform for an assignment?"

"Unfortunately," she sighed, plucking at the pinafore. "I've been placed in a household to discover a man's perfidy. It's what Mr. Castelan's agency specializes in."

Jasper would not ask if Miss Brooks was expected to lure this man into an indecent situation, only to then be "caught"—proving the wife's claim. He had no say over what Leo's friend chose to do for work.

"What about thefts?" Jasper asked.

"Those types of cases are common too," she said. "I wouldn't mind being assigned to one."

Jasper reached for the newspaper. "May I?" She nodded, giving him permission to take it.

"Miss Brooks," he said as he walked her to his office door. "Are there any detectives at Castelan's named Bentley?"

She considered it a moment. "None that I've met. Though there is someone named Benson."

Mrs. Michaels had said Bentley was the name of the detective, but she'd been put out with their visit and in a rush. It had also been a few years since the housekeeper's interaction with him. She may have misremembered his name.

"And how long has Benson been at the agency?" he asked next.

"Years, I think. Why?"

Jasper held out an arm for her to exit his office. "Just a thought I had about something. Thank you for coming in. It's been helpful," he said. "Can I give you a lift? My sergeant and I are going to visit Castelan, if you're on your way there."

But as Miss Brooks was setting out in another direction, Jasper bid her a good morning. He caught Warnock as the sergeant was arriving for the day, and they hired a cab to take them to High Holborn. Along the way, Jasper explained to Warnock about the maid, Marianna, and her connection to both the Herrington and Lawlor cases, as well as what Miss Brooks had imparted to him.

There was a drop of silence in the cab then, and that was when Jasper remembered the note Constable Woodhouse had passed to him. Belatedly, he took the small square from his coat pocket. *Inspector Reed* was written in slanted cursive on the front of it. The misspelling of his name wasn't uncommon, but the folding of a piece of paper into rectangles to enclose a note wasn't something he regularly saw, especially since proper envelopes were so readily available. A drop of hardened yellow wax sealed the tucked flaps; he split the seal and took out the folded paper within.

Stop looking for me. I am safe. Please. -T

He refolded the note, the thin, brittle paper nearly crumpling in his hands. Somehow, Tabitha Pierce had learned that he'd been looking for her.

"Sir," Warnock said, interrupting his thoughts. Jasper tucked the note and makeshift envelope into his pocket again.

"I don't mean to speak out of turn," Warnock went on. "But I…I saw you, sir, the other morning. Outside Charing Cross Station."

The muscles along Jasper's spine went taut. He'd worried the spot Andrew had chosen to meet was too close to Scotland Yard.

"And?" he said, beckoning the sergeant to go on.

"You were getting out of a carriage, sir. I recognized the hired muscle that let you out. He'd come into the station with Mr. Carter, the husband of the woman who was poisoned at Striker's Wharf last winter."

Jasper kept his expression neutral, though his nerves jumped. Stephen Warnock was a sharp tack. He had a good memory if he recalled one of Andrew's nameless hired thugs from nine months ago. He also seemed to understand this was a conversation to have privately, away from the CID.

"I've taken on a private inquiry," Jasper answered. To

deny it would be to invite more curiosity. More prying too. "Mr. Carter has asked for discretion."

Jasper liked Warnock. The lad was bright and ambitious while still careful to follow orders. But he hadn't truly seen just how clever the detective sergeant was until right then.

Warnock nodded. "Of course. I won't say a word to anyone. I just wanted to be sure all was well. Especially since it's the East Rips, sir."

Jasper thanked him for his concern but assured him all was well. A glint of doubt lingered in the sergeant's expression as he turned to look out the window. And why wouldn't there be? Anyone working for, or with, the East Rips should be held in suspicion. It left a greasy sensation in Jasper's stomach, which didn't abate even after they'd arrived at Castelan's agency.

The offices had a distinct upper-class feel, which would attract more well-to-do patrons than a shabbier office might. Stepping inside, Jasper was surprised to find a busy enterprise, with several men at work—including Silas Palmer. The former E Division officer glimpsed Jasper from his desk, and his expression instantly went truculent.

"Detective Inspector Jasper Reid," Palmer said, without rising from his chair. "Have you come to give me an earful about Miss Spencer?"

"I'm not here for you, Palmer," he replied, happy to wipe the hostile sneer from the man's lips. "I need to speak to Castelan."

A smooth voice came from the back of the front office. "Come to hire us for our services, Inspector?"

A man in suspenders and shirtsleeves had emerged

from his office. In the process of shaving, he stood within the threshold with a straight razor in one hand, a towel over his shoulder, and soap lathered over one half of his face.

Jasper was trained not to make impulsive presumptions about people, but the smug twist of the man's mouth instantly marked him as arrogant. Castelan's interest in acquiring Leo as one of his investigators might have influenced Jasper's opinion, but as he walked toward the agency's owner, he perceived a wily cunning to the man. Castelan knew they were not there to contract with his agency; the teasing remark was meant to goad.

"I've come to discuss one of your employees." Jasper extended to him the copy of the *Morning Chronicle*, folded to display the sketches. "The woman shown here."

Castelan took the paper. His amusement disappeared.

"Come in," he said gravely, reentering his office and going straight to the mirrored stand in the corner of the room. The setup was much like what Jasper kept in his own office.

"Her name is Mary Keating," Castelan said as he tossed the paper onto a chair and set about finishing his shave. "And she is no longer one of my employees."

He skimmed the straight razor over his soapy jaw line and cheek, exposing reddened, chapped skin. The tips of his ears were also red, and Jasper wondered if he was upset to have one of his past employees pictured in a widely circulated daily.

"When did she stop working for you?" Jasper asked.

Castelan finished his shave and toweled off the remaining soap. He went to a silver coffee urn on a sideboard and poured himself a steaming cup. With a gesture, he offered coffee to his guests, but Jasper and Warnock each declined.

"She ceased working for my agency over a year ago," he finally answered. "As did Samuel Edwards, the man shown in the illustration to the right of Mary's."

A jolt fired along Jasper's spine. He reclaimed the newspaper Castelan had left in a chair. The illustration to Mary's right was that of Sebastian Lawlor. "This man is Samuel Edwards? Are you certain?"

"Completely," Castelan said, sipping his coffee with one hand in his pocket, as if unperturbed. "What is this about, Inspector Reid? They are no longer my employees, so if they have done something, I have no part in it. And I do not want my agency's name attached to them."

As Miss Brooks had stated, having employees—even former ones—wanted for a crime would reflect poorly on the agency as a whole. It seemed that was the first thing Castelan had thought of.

"Tell me what you know of them. How long were they employed here? What were their roles?" Jasper asked.

Castelan's cheek twitched—the only sign that he was vexed. But then, he went to his desk chair and sat. "Miss Keating was one of my first lady investigators when I opened the agency four years ago. Samuel came on shortly afterward as a private detective. I assigned them cases, as I do all my employees. They followed targets, collected information, posed undercover, and they were very good at their jobs. My agency's success rate is the envy of the private sector, Inspector. I believe Scotland Yard is aware of that."

There were scores of private inquiry agencies in London, but only one or two that the Metropolitan Police

Force deigned acceptable to contract with when caseloads piled up, and not enough detectives were available. Castelan's wasn't one of them. But Jasper would not waste time explaining that an agency best known for investigating infidelity disputes for divorce settlements would not be of much use to the Yard.

"Why did they depart your agency?" Jasper asked instead.

"Miss Keating was the sort who came and went. Valuable in certain situations, but I did have other ladies who were more eager to prove themselves. Eventually, she stopped coming around for assignments. I figured she'd moved on."

"But she was here recently," Jasper said.

"I'd like to know how you came by that information," Castelan said, but he didn't press. "You're correct. She was here…oh, maybe a month or two ago?"

"What did she want?"

"A job. She said she was working as a maid and was bored to tears. Wanted out," he answered.

"You didn't hire her?" Jasper asked.

"There was nothing for her, especially since I'd just hired Miss Brooks. Whom, I believe, you may know through Miss Spencer?" He arched a brow, and Jasper was certain he'd just figured out that his newest employee had been speaking to the police.

"What about Samuel Edwards?" Warnock piped up, lifting his pencil from his notepad. "When and why did he leave the agency?"

"Him, I sacked, two years ago."

Two years ago, Edwards had been about to start posing as Rupert Herrington, Jasper calculated.

"The reason?" he asked.

"Honestly?" Castelan sat back in his chair and crossed his legs. "I didn't trust him. My accountant found that he had been siphoning off the top of his assignments. My detectives have expenses when they are on a case, which I provide for. Samuel would require more than others, and he consistently did not give proof of where or how he spent the funds."

The deceitful behavior fell in line with what Jasper knew of the man so far.

He placed the newspaper on the desk before Castelan and tapped the illustration of Mr. Gray. "What about him? Do you recognize him?"

Castelan took a cursory glance but was already shaking his head. "No. He isn't one of mine." He drummed his fingers on his thigh. "I've given you many answers, Inspector. Now, I would like one from you in return. What is this about? What are Miss Keating and Mr. Edwards accused of doing?"

If he and Warnock left without giving some explanation, Castelan would likely only put one of his men on the hunt for the truth. Jasper didn't have the patience to deal with a private detective nosing about.

"A deception scheme," he answered. "One that left a woman dead and another nearly so."

Castelan uncrossed his legs and sat forward. "This is the case Miss Spencer came to me about. The woman she found alive in a casket in the funeral director's back room. Augusta Lawlor?"

"Yes. Mary Keating was employed as a maid for the Lawlors, and Samuel Edwards was posing as the husband, Sebastian." Jasper wasn't inclined to give too many details to Castelan but did reveal the outcome. "Edwards is dead. He was murdered. It's likely this other man, the one you do not recognize, is his associate. And killer."

Castelan took a moment to absorb the news. He then whistled in awe. "I knew Edwards was a rogue, but this…" He sighed and stood from his chair. "I never would have suspected the man was violent."

"I'll need your files on Mary Keating and Edwards. Addresses too," Jasper said.

Castelan shouted, "Hutchins!" When the man appeared, he requested the files to be pulled.

"And for another one of your detectives, if you don't mind. Benson," Jasper added.

"Benson?" Castelan repeated. "What does he have to do with anything?"

"I'm not sure yet," Jasper admitted. "Does he work for you still?"

Castelan crossed his arms. "Yes. Why?"

"It has to do with a lead I'm following," he answered. It was best to be vague when he did not yet know how Benson connected to Victoria Herrington—or if he did at all.

Reluctantly, Castelan nodded, and Hutchins darted away on his task.

"One last thing," Jasper said, thinking of the wedding bands found in Edwards's ticket pocket. "Were Samuel and Mary romantically involved?"

Some speculative amusement returned to Castelan's expression. "Involved? Why do you ask?"

"Answer the question, please," Jasper replied.

Castelan guttered a sound of exasperation before answering, "I don't encourage my detectives to pursue romantic liaisons here at the office, but I also do not police them. If they were involved, it was no business of mine."

Hutchins returned swiftly with the addresses for Samuel Edwards, Mary Keating, and Lars Benson.

"The files include past assignments for the agency, wages, and addresses, Inspector," Hutchins said. "Lars should be in later today if you'd like to speak to him then. He's out on assignment."

"I'll come back in, thank you," Jasper said, then left Castelan's office.

It was reasonable to assume Samuel Edwards and Mary Keating had quit their lodgings before going to live in the Lawlor household. However, the addresses might still house family members or neighbors who remembered them.

"Edwards's address in Clerkenwell is closest to us now," Warnock said as they passed Silas Palmer, who was still openly scowling at Jasper. "Should we try there first before going to Miss Keating's?"

Her listed address was in the opposite direction, across the river in Southwark, and it would take some time to get there.

"Good thinking," Jasper said, and they started on their way.

During the quarter mile or so to Edwards's old address, tremors of impatience bit at Jasper. Samuel Edwards was dead; there was nothing he could tell them about Henry Gray. Mary, on the other hand, might still be alive and able to provide them with information on the fake doctor.

Still, he and Warnock proceeded with the hope that if

Samuel's family resided there, or former neighbors, they might recall some valuable information. That hope vanished when they spoke to the landlady. She recalled Edwards from a year back. He hadn't had any family that she knew of, and he would often be late paying his weekly rent. She recalled him stepping out with a woman. When shown the illustration in the paper of Mary Keating, she shrugged and said it might have been her.

They took a cab to Mary's address next. It was nearing midday, and as they drew closer to the river, traffic slowed a good deal. However, at last, they reached Broadwall and Stamford Streets, stopping outside a building of apartments. The building was worn, the air inside dank with the scent of mold and rotting wood. The stairs were soft underfoot as they climbed to the second level, and the shrill wailing of a baby came from some apartment nearby.

"I don't much like my landlady's cooking," Warnock said as they came upon Number 12, Mary's last known rooms. "But at least the place smells nice. And there aren't any babies to keep me awake at—"

Jasper held up a hand to signal the sergeant to be quiet. The door to Number 12 was open an inch. With Warnock now on alert, Jasper rapped his knuckles on the doorframe.

"Hello? Miss Keating?" he called out. "This is the Metropolitan Police. We'd like a word."

The baby ceased its wails, and in the sudden silence, a soft moan of pain sounded from within Number 12.

Jasper punted open the door the rest of the way, and in the one-room apartment, near a kitchen sink, a woman lay sprawled on the floor. Blood—vivid and fresh—soaked into the rug underneath her. She moaned again.

"Warnock, quickly, summon a carriage." The sergeant darted away on his task, and Jasper went to the woman.

"I'm Inspector Reid from Scotland Yard," he told her as he knelt at her side. She clutched her abdomen, where blood oozed. She'd been stabbed. Her coloring was pale, her face pinched in anguish, but there was no question as to who she was.

He had found Mary Keating.

Chapter Eighteen

Leo woke Monday morning to the sound of screams. Startled into a sitting position, her mind fogged by slumber, she'd recognized that the anguished cries of pain were coming from Flora.

Now, several hours later, Leo and Claude sat inside a small hospital room at St. Thomas's where Flora lay sleeping. Her aunt had risen from bed earlier than usual and, with Claude still sound asleep, had left their room and gone to the staircase. A normal occurrence for any able-bodied person, to be sure. However, Flora fumbled her footing somewhere on the steps. She fell, landing in a heap at the foot of the stairs. Claude and Leo had rushed to her in a panic, and they had instantly known from the odd angle of her leg that it was broken.

Once at St. Thomas's, the doctor administered a draught of laudanum to calm her. Leo half-wondered if it would have been beneficial to treat her uncle with a few drops of the tincture too.

"It wasn't your fault," Leo told him yet again. And again, he refused to give himself grace.

"I should have been awake to assist her down the steps," he said, his shoulders slumped and his white hair disheveled. There had been little time for either Claude or Leo to dress properly before rushing Flora to the hospital; he had forgotten his suspenders, and Leo still wore her hair loose around her shoulders.

The doctor had set Flora's leg—the break in her femur had been relatively clean, he reported, and fortunately, her hip was not involved. That, he said, would have been a far graver injury for a woman of her advanced age. Afterward, he'd taken Claude and Leo aside and said the very thing they had been trying to outpace.

"I believe Mrs. Feldman will require round-the-clock nursing care, and not just until her leg heals. Incidents like these are quite common in patients with her condition. Cognitive decline affects the whole body, I am afraid, not just the mind."

The doctor had left them to contemplate, and for some time now, they had been sitting quietly in uncomfortable chairs set against the hospital room wall.

"Jasper will hear back soon if Chesterton Hall passes muster," Leo offered. "He wired the local constabulary yesterday. I'm sure the home has a fine reputation, Uncle."

Even to her own ears, her attempt to keep a light and positive tone sounded forced.

"It is time," Claude said with dismal sigh. "I will make the arrangements."

"After the holiday," she urged. "We can let her leg heal a little and enjoy Christmas together."

The truth was, Christmas with her aunt and uncle had

never been a warm, cozy affair. Flora's chill toward her niece did not thaw any time of year, not even then. It had always been the Christmas Eve dinner held at the Inspector's home that Leo had looked forward to. He would have a wrapped gift or two under the small Christmas tree for Leo to open on that evening.

This would be her first Christmas Eve without him, she realized. And come January, she would be alone at the house on Duke Street.

"I know you will be going with her," Leo confessed, with an unexpected hitch in her voice.

Her uncle shifted in his chair, and in her peripheral vision, she saw him peering at her. Leo met his eyes. The clear blue irises gleamed with emotion.

"I know she has never been motherly toward you," Claude began. Leo shook her head, as if to stop him from making any excuse. But he persisted. "Life, long ago, injured her. I believe, irreparably. There was…a child."

Leo stared at him, stunned.

"A little boy," he went on. "We named him David, after my father. He was the most beautiful creature I had ever seen." Here, her uncle's voice cracked. He continued after a moment. "There was a fever. Flora grew ill, but she recovered. David did not. He was six months old."

Leo closed her eyes to an overwhelming surge of sympathy for her aunt and uncle.

"Why did you never say?" she asked.

"Any mention of our son would send Flora into a despair so consuming that I feared I would lose her. So, I learned not to speak of him."

And then, when her sister, niece and nephew were killed, Flora had suffered another excruciating blow.

"She closed off her heart to you. Too fearful to love another child and possibly go through what she had with David," Claude said. "There was a flaw in that thinking, however. By closing off her heart to you, she never allowed herself the chance to know what it feels like to be loved by a child."

Claude reached for her hand. It was warm and coarse and comforting. "It is, I have long believed, the best feeling a person can experience. I have you to thank for that, my dear."

Leo could not keep the tears from slipping down her cheeks. Even if the lump in her throat had not been constricting her ability to speak, she did not know what she could say to such a heartfelt revelation. Claude, bashful as usual, smiled and patted her hand.

"I don't know about you, but I could use a spot of tea," he said, then started to rise. Leo got to her feet first.

"I'll go. You stay with Aunt Flora." She kissed his forehead before leaving the room.

Leo sniffled and wiped the corners of her eyes as she turned down the corridor, heading toward the refreshment room located on the ground floor. She had taken only a few strides when she saw a tall, broad-shouldered figure that she knew at once.

"Jasper?"

He stood farther down in the corridor, in the open doorway to another hospital room. Jasper turned and then, with a look of concern, strode toward her.

"Leo? Why are you here?"

"Aunt Flora fell down the—" Blood smeared on Jasper's cuffs and on his collar silenced her. "My God, what has happened?"

He peered at his cuffs, as if only seeing the stains just now. "I'll tell you in a moment but finish what you were saying. Flora fell?"

"She has a broken femur, but she'll heal," she replied impatiently. "Whose blood is that?"

"Not mine," he assured her, which put her at ease. A little, at least. "I found Marianna, the maid. She'd been stabbed and left for dead, but she's still alive. Barely."

Jasper explained how Dita had recognized the woman in the sketch in the *Morning Chronicle* as a former employee of Mr. Castelan's agency, and when Jasper and Warnock visited Mr. Castelan, they'd learned her name—Mary Keating.

In addition to that, Sebastian Lawlor's real name was Samuel Edwards, a former private detective for Mr. Castelan. They'd obtained addresses for both Mary and Samuel, visiting the nearer location first—Samuel's—before crossing town to Mary's. When they arrived, they found Mary had been severely wounded.

"The attack happened within minutes of our arrival," Jasper told Leo.

Misgiving soured her stomach. "Right after you were at the agency, asking about her?"

"I know. It is too much of a coincidence."

"Who at Mr. Castelan's knew you were going there?" Leo asked.

"Castelan, of course, and his clerk, Hutchins, who pulled their files." Jasper crossed his arms as if trying to rein in his agitation. "And Silas Palmer was listening in."

"Detective Palmer? But why would he try to silence Mary?"

Jasper stated what should have immediately been

obvious to her: "If he is Mr. Gray, he would have every reason to try."

Leo pictured Silas Palmer in her mind but couldn't reconcile him with the illustration of the doctor that Mr. Gibbons had sketched. Then again, Henry Gray had a full beard and mustache. A pair of spectacles, and a head of shoulder-length hair that fell across his forehead. All of which could easily be applied as a disguise.

"But he doesn't possess Mr. Gray's nose," she said, recalling Detective Palmer's rather handsome aquiline nose. In contrast, Mr. Gray's was bulbous.

"I've sent Warnock, PC Drake, and PC Mills to Castelan's agency to question the men there," Jasper said. "I want to know everyone's movements after Warnock and I left."

Leo wished to know as well, but in truth, at a busy office like Mr. Castelan's, it wouldn't be odd to have men coming and going at all times. Someone leaving the office right after Jasper and Warnock had wouldn't necessarily point to guilt.

"What is Mary's condition?" she asked.

"She was stabbed twice, once in the abdomen and again in the chest," he answered, moving back to the open door. Leo followed. Inside the hospital room, a woman lay in bed, her eyes closed, her coloring significantly pale. "The doctor isn't sure if she will pull through. But if she wakes, she will be able to name her attacker."

It was something her attacker would not be pleased to learn. As if reading her mind, Jasper said, "I'm staying until Price arrives with a few more constables to guard her door."

In the bed, Mary's stillness was broken by the flex of

her hand and the flutter of her eyelashes. Leo stepped forward into the room. "She might be waking."

Jasper went swiftly to the woman's bedside. "Miss Keating?" His kept his voice low and gentle.

Mary's eyelids opened, though barely, and then shuttered again. She moaned and rolled her head on the pillow.

"Miss Keating, you are safe now," Leo said, hoping the woman was conscious enough to comprehend. "You're at St. Thomas's, and your wounds have been tended to."

Mary's pale, parched lips parted, and an unintelligible rasp emerged. Jasper lowered himself to one knee next to the bed and leaned forward. "I'm Inspector Reid of Scotland Yard, Miss Keating. I found you in your rooms, wounded. Can you tell me who attacked you?"

Her eyes were still shut, but her brow tensed, and her lips moved again. It took another few moments until sound scraped up her throat. "P…Pa," she said hoarsely.

Pa?

"Palmer?" Jasper asked.

Mary's tensed brow smoothed, and she didn't respond. She appeared to no longer be conscious, though she was still breathing.

"Do you think she meant Silas Palmer?" Leo asked.

Jasper got to his feet. "He was listening in when Warnock and I decided to visit Samuel Edwards's address first. He knew he would have time to get to her before we could."

Leo felt ill thinking of the time she'd spent with Detective Palmer at the Golden Harp and that he could be the false Mr. Gray.

"I need to bring him in," Jasper said moving away from

Mary's side. He then drew to a stop, grimacing. Leo knew why.

"Constable Price will be here momentarily, I'm sure. If you'll only stop in Room 8 down the hall and tell my uncle where I am, I can stay with Mary until he arrives," Leo said. She rested her hand on his arm. "You need to find Detective Palmer before he disappears."

If Silas Palmer had been at the agency when Warnock and the other constables arrived, and if he found out Mary was not yet dead, he might take the opportunity to run.

Jasper hesitated only another moment. "All right. I'll ask for a warder to come stand outside this door until the other constables arrive. Just to be safe."

"It will be fine, Jasper. Go."

He covered her hand with his, then nodded before exiting the room into the corridor.

Leo turned back to Mary, whose coloring had marginally improved since she roused to consciousness. The wounds she'd sustained could still kill her, however, especially if infection set in.

Leo pulled a chair to the bedside and settled into it, prepared to speak to Mary, should she wake again. *Pa* was hardly a firm indication that Palmer was her assailant. Should Mary not live and be able to more aptly name her attacker, Leo doubted any charges against Silas Palmer would hold up in court.

"Mary?" Leo thought perhaps the sound of a voice might stir her awake. She took the woman's cold hand, lying flat on the blanket, into her own. "Mary, we need your help."

Leo gave her hand a light squeeze. Should she live,

Mary would be arrested for her involvement in a scheme that had left one woman dead and another, nearly so. There was no telling just yet to what extent she had participated in the murder of Victoria Herrington and the attempt on Augusta Lawlor's life, but Leo imagined the young woman might currently be wondering if fighting to live would be worth it.

The tapping of footfalls out in the corridor signaled someone's approach. Leo presumed it was the warder Jasper had promised, but when she turned in her chair, she saw Mr. Castelan.

"Miss Spencer, I didn't expect to see you." The private detective lingered in the doorway, his bowler hat clasped in his hands. "I came as soon as I heard about Miss Keating. How is she?"

Mr. Castelan had evidently not passed Jasper in the corridor. If he had, Jasper would have informed him of Mary's condition, and of Leo's presence. But then, Jasper had been concerned Mary's attacker would return to finish the job. He wouldn't have allowed Mr. Castelan—one of the men who'd known of Jasper's intent to visit Mary—to come in here alone.

A strange qualm filled her.

"She is alive," Leo replied. "And lucky to be so. Inspector Reid found her at a critical moment."

Mr. Castelan came into the room, closing the door behind him all but for an inch. "As I have heard. Does the inspector have any leads?"

"He is looking for Silas Palmer," she said warily.

Mr. Castelan tucked his chin. "Palmer? You cannot be serious."

"I'm afraid I am," she replied. "When did you last see him?"

He sighed. "Last I knew, he was at the office."

"Was he questioned?" Leo asked.

"Questioned by whom?" he replied, his light gray eyes narrowed in confusion.

A realization struck her: He did not know Sergeant Warnock and Constables Mills and Price had been sent to his agency to interview the staff. Had Mr. Castelan left before they had arrived?

But then...how else would he have learned Mary was here after being wounded?

Leo's hand, still clasping Mary's, felt a weak squeeze. While Mary's eyes were still shut, she no longer had the softened jaw or mouth of a person who was asleep.

Keeping Mary's hand in hers, Leo peered over her shoulder at the private detective. "How did you hear of the attack?"

The private detective smiled coyly. "I have my contacts at the Yard, remember?"

"I remember," she replied cautiously.

Mr. Castelan came to the foot of the hospital bed. "I spoke to a doctor on the way here. He says her chances of survival are slim."

"I'm not so certain of that," Leo said. "She was conscious a few moments ago."

"Oh? That is optimistic. Did she say anything?"

Mary's fingers, enclosed in Leo's hand, flexed again. It wasn't a twitch, but an intentional squeeze. She was awake but pretending to be unconscious...and judging by a quick spasm of her chin, she was frightened.

Pa. That was all Mary had rasped, and Jasper had taken

it for *Palmer*. But now, Leo wondered if it had been the start of someone else's name.

"No," Leo answered, a thread of misgiving pulling taut along her spine. "Nothing coherent."

"That is unfortunate." Mr. Castelan sounded sincere. But the question of whose name Mary had been trying to say had already sent Leo's memory on a quest. She knew exactly what she needed and fetched an image of Mr. Castelan's office. It was meticulous in detail, right down to the paper clutter on his desk, the pattern of the Oriental rug on the floor, the blunt, squared-off shape of his fingernails as he gestured her toward the button-tufted black leather chairs in front of a coal brazier.

But what she wanted to scrutinize hung on the wall behind his desk, in a mahogany wood frame. The certificate of his membership in the League of London Private Detectives, issued in the year 1879—to Mr. Paul Castelan.

Mary had not meant to say Palmer.

She'd meant to say *Paul*.

Chapter Nineteen

"You appear rather wan all of a sudden, Miss Spencer." The private detective settled a hand on the wrought iron frame at the foot of the bed. "Perhaps you should find some tea and allow me to sit with Miss Keating for a spell?"

"That isn't necessary." Leo's throat cinched tight around her response, and her mind spun in search of a solution. "I'm happy to stay with her until Inspector Reid returns. Which will be shortly. I expect him at any moment."

Jasper's impending return was a lie, of course, but she hoped it would unnerve Mr. Castelan enough to convince him to leave. However, he only narrowed his gaze on her, an inquisitive frown forming.

"You may be waiting for some time. I believe I just saw the inspector on his way out."

Leo peered at Mr. Castelan. Their gazes locked and held. Unspoken awareness settled between them, at once transparent and incontestable.

He knew what she had deciphered. There was no more use in pretending.

"You were waiting for Inspector Reid to leave, weren't you?" Leo asked. "Your contacts at Scotland Yard told you nothing. You know what happened to Mary because you are the one who attacked her."

He did not flinch or scoff at the accusation but remained utterly still. His solicitous expression glazed over and hardened into something predatory.

"You were in a rush at her apartment," Leo went on, her pulse beginning to strum in her neck. "Inspector Reid and Sergeant Warnock were on their way, and you couldn't allow Mary to be questioned."

On the hospital bed, Mary's limbs rustled under the blanket, catching Mr. Castelan's hawkish eyes. Leo still held her hand, not taking her attention off the danger in the room.

"You planned to be much more thorough here," she said.

"Why would I wish to harm Miss Keating?" he asked, though far too placidly. He was only toying with Leo.

"*You* are Mr. Henry Gray, aren't you?" Now she understood the cause for the reddened skin on his clean-shaven face. "Your face isn't chapped because of the cold, dry air as I'd presumed, but from the adhesive you used to keep a false beard, mustache, and even a prosthetic nose in place."

Mr. Castelan continued to stare at her, his composure steady even if his eyes flashed.

"And your father and grandfather," she went on, recalling something more that he had said at their first meeting. "You come from a family of surgeons. It's how you knew to be facetious with your false name for a doctor."

"You have a strong memory," he commented, stepping back from the bed.

"You have no idea." Leo released Mary's hand, and the woman instantly tried to sit up. She didn't get far and only groaned in pain. Leo, however, got to her feet, nearly overturning the chair in the process.

Mr. Castelan, who stood between her and the partially open door, remained docile. She measured at least three strides between them. Now that she knew exactly what he had done, those three strides were perilously close.

"You and Samuel Edwards partnered to trick wealthy spinsters with no family into marriage. Mr. Edwards would lace their food or drink with arsenic and then, when the women began to fall ill, you swooped in as Mr. Gray and convinced them—and their servants—that they were dying of some incurable disease. With Victoria Herrington, it worked," Leo said. "As her widower, Mr. Edwards collected the inheritance due to him. A fortune, which the two of you then split. Or perhaps the three of you," she said, thinking of Mary.

Mr. Castelan released a dismal laugh. "It was hardly a fortune."

The subtle, but clear admission changed things instantly. He was finished pretending. And he had no plans of letting Leo leave this room so that she could repeat what she'd discovered about him.

"Is that why you enacted the scheme again? This time with Augusta Lawlor?" she asked, wanting to keep him talking. Jasper was supposed to send a warder to Mary's room; he might be nearly here. "You'd investigated a suitor for her a few years before. You knew of her wealth. And you probably knew her last living relative had died."

Mr. Castelan formed a cold smile. "I underestimated your abilities, Miss Spencer. It seems all of Scotland Yard has."

As he spoke, her peripheral vision roved the room for something—anything—that might be used as a weapon for protection. On the bedside table, there was an empty metal kidney bowl. But that was all. She was sorely outmatched.

"I do not want your compliments," she said. "What I want are answers."

"I don't see the point. You won't have the opportunity to share them with anyone."

His intent, and his sheer lack of remorse, chilled her.

"You have made things more difficult for me, Miss Spencer, but the mess is nothing I cannot manage," he continued.

Resolved as she was on keeping him locked in a stare, Leo had failed to see his hand reach into his coat pocket. There was a glint of metal—a blade. Her heart lurched into her throat.

Mary Keating struggled to sit up and wailed stridently, *"No!"*

Mr. Castelan lunged forward, and Leo reached for the paltry kidney bowl.

"Stop where you are, Castelan."

Jasper's commanding voice resonated through the room as he kicked the door open fully and came in, his Webley drawn and aimed. The private detective stumbled to a halt. His face contorted with thwarted fury and desperation. He tried to slip the knife back into his pocket.

"Toss the blade onto the floor," Jasper ordered.

For several seconds, Leo could not read Mr. Castelan's stony grimace…whether he intended to do as instructed, or if he planned to resist.

"Do not make the mistake of thinking I won't shoot you in the back," Jasper growled after an interminable stretch of seconds. "After what you've done, it would give me great pleasure. Drop the knife."

The private detective opened his hands, and the knife —a small slip joint blade—clattered onto the tile floor. Mr. Castelan raised his arms in defeat.

Jasper came forward, his revolver still raised and kicked the blade aside. "Claude, fetch a warder. Constables should be here any moment. Meet them in the lobby and direct them here."

Her uncle's name caused Leo's heart to lurch yet again. She spied him standing within the open doorway, and as Jasper holstered his weapon and grasped Mr. Castelan's hands behind his back, Claude's expression fixed into one she had never seen him wear: loathing. He directed it at Mr. Castelan's back.

Claude's gaze softened as he met her eyes briefly. He then left with his orders.

"Are you harmed, Leo?" Jasper asked, assessing her as he locked the private detective's wrists into a pair of handcuffs.

She shook her head. "His name is *Paul*," she told Jasper, still quivering though her pulse had started to regulate. "Mary wasn't trying to say Palmer."

Jasper spared a glance toward the hospital bed. The

woman lying in it whimpered. She'd gone slack, her face leeched of all color. "I stopped to tell Claude where you were and decided to walk him here. I overheard your conversation at the door."

Leo exhaled shakily. It had been simple luck that had brought Jasper back here in time.

"Paul Castelan, I'm arresting you for conspiracy to kill Victoria Herrington and Augusta Lawlor, the murder of Samuel Edwards, and the attempted murder of Mary Keating." He forced Mr. Castelan's bound wrists up toward the center of his back at a painful angle. The private detective grunted and swore. "And if there is a charge I can bring against you for pulling a deadly weapon on Miss Spencer, I will gladly add it to the list."

Chapter Twenty

Despite the late hour, the detective department at Scotland Yard was a hub of activity.

When at long last Jasper arrived, he was met with congratulatory nods and grins from some of his fellow officers. He'd spent the last few hours at St. Thomas's, while constables had escorted Castelan to the Yard for booking, and Sergeant Warnock had secured a warrant for the search of the suspect's home and offices. Judging by Jasper's reception as he made his way to his office, word of the arrest had spread throughout the Yard.

He accepted a few comments lauding Castelan's capture but was in no mood to field questions. The hours he'd spent questioning Mary Keating had been a lesson in patience. Once the doctors had assessed her, to be certain her sutured wounds had not torn during the incident in her hospital room, Jasper had been given permission to question her. Coaxing her to speak, however, had all but drained his tolerance. She'd needed stretches of rest between intermittent bouts of sobbing, confession, and pleas for forgiveness.

Relief coursed through him now when Sergeant Warnock stood from his desk to greet him.

"Paul Castelan is in the interview room," the sergeant said. "How is Miss Spencer?"

"Unharmed," Jasper answered, though he still felt a flash of cold sweat when he considered how different the outcome could have been, had he not returned when he did.

As he'd promised Leo he would, Jasper had stopped to inform Claude where his niece had gone. After a short discussion in Flora's hospital room about her fall, Jasper had decided to walk Leo's uncle to Mary Keating's room. Coming upon the nearly closed door, he'd held up a hand to silence Claude. Leo's voice and that of Castelan's had come through the small opening.

He and Claude had listened at the door as Leo laid out the private detective's deeds, and Castelan had responded in turn. Trepidation seeped in as he'd listened, knowing that the man planned to silence Leo. It had taken everything in him not to barge in before Castelan could admit to anything. At Mary Keating's rasping cry of alarm, Jasper had yielded, and without a second to spare.

Jasper removed his coat and hat and draped them over Warnock's chair as the sergeant picked up an evidence box from his desk. "Found some interesting things in the suspect's home. The coroner's report you requested is inside as well."

Jasper glimpsed the contents of the box and instantly understood his sergeant's sly, prideful grin. "Let's see what he has to say for himself."

He and Warnock started for the interview room but were intercepted by Chief Inspector Coughlan and Superintendent Monroe. The beginnings of Jasper's improved mood instantly evaporated.

"Reid," Monroe called merrily. "I hear you've made an arrest in the Lawlor case."

"I did," he replied, then with a glance toward Chief Coughlan, added, "With some help from Miss Spencer."

The chief looked distinctly uncomfortable at the superintendent's questioning glare. "Miss Spencer?"

Chief Coughlan coughed. "She was consulting."

Monroe reserved comment though he didn't appear happy. "A private inquiry agent is behind it all?" he asked instead.

"Bloody frauds, the lot of them," Chief Coughlan snarled.

"Not all of them, Dermot," the superintendent corrected. "But the majority, to be sure. Mind if I sit in on the interview, Reid?"

There was no need for him to ask permission. If he wished to observe the interview, he had every authority to do so. Jasper forced a nod, though he would have much rather questioned Paul Castelan without the superintendent looking on.

He, Warnock, and Monroe entered the interview room, and thankfully, as Jasper locked eyes with Paul Castelan, Monroe's presence ceased to bother him. He had a job to do, and he was confident in his ability to see it through.

"You took your time," the disgraced private detective said, his fingers drumming the table. The motion caused the rings on the iron chain strung between his wrists to clink. "My solicitor and I have been waiting."

The man seated next to Castelan grimaced. Jasper wasn't certain his displeasure was aimed at him, or at his client.

"I wouldn't be in any rush if I were you, Castelan," he replied. "The only place you're going to from here is Newgate."

"You have no evidence against me," he said with an arrogant smirk that boiled Jasper's blood. "Whatever you think you heard being said between myself and Miss Spencer is circumstantial."

Tamping down a scowl, Jasper gestured for Sergeant Warnock to come forward with the evidence box. The sergeant placed it on the table and took from within a pair of wire spectacles, a prosthetic nose cast of India rubber, a hairpiece, and faux beard and mustache, laying out the lot, one by one, on the table in front of Castelan and his solicitor.

"These were found in a bean crock in Mr. Castelan's larder," Warnock announced.

Superintendent Monroe whistled. "I believe you would greatly resemble the man from the sketch of Mr. Henry Gray, were you to put these items on."

Castelan hitched his chin and averted his eyes from the articles of disguise. "Obviously, they have been deposited in my home to incriminate me. I have never seen those things in my life."

Jasper picked up the flexible, bulbous nose cast of India rubber. The underside of the edges showed remnants of adhesive paste. In the hospital room, Jasper had overheard Leo mentioning the irritated skin on

Castelan's face, a result of applying the paste. He'd noted it himself while Castelan had been shaving.

"There are a number of costumiers in London, though not many specialize in facial prosthetics," Jasper said. "How difficult do you think it will be to find the one who made this for you?"

Neither Castelan nor his solicitor replied. Jasper pulled out a chair and sat.

"I heard your confession to Miss Spencer, and I have a full, detailed confession from Mary Keating. You're an intelligent man, Castelan. The game is up, and you know it."

Castelan scoffed. "Mary would say anything to save herself."

"Perhaps. But what of the two individuals at her address on Stamford Street who told my constables they saw a man enter, then leave, the building in a rush shortly before my sergeant and I arrived and found her wounded? I am confident the witnesses, given the chance, will recognize you as that man."

The solicitor touched Castelan's arm, an indication for his client to remain silent.

"Your agency's records are being collected as we speak, Mr. Castelan. I believe they will verify what Mary Keating and your detective, Lars Benson, have already stated—that Victoria Herrington, *née* Blake, hired your agency to investigate a missing brooch in April of 1882. Benson investigated, and from his report, you discovered much about Victoria's wealth and her lack of family. You designed a way to get your hands on her fortune without getting your own hands dirty. You placed Mary within Victoria's household as a maid, and then, when Mary knew her mistress's schedule, you arranged for Samuel Edwards to meet her at Regent's Park as Rupert Herrington."

Castelan's smug arrogance fell off, but still, he did not speak.

Jasper sat forward, bracing his elbows on the table. "The bounty wasn't what you thought it would be. We have the probate records. We know the settlement turned out to be disappointing. Not only that, but Samuel and Mary disagreed that you should take half of the spoils, leaving them with a quarter each. They had been the ones doing all the work and taking all the risks."

The private detective remained stoic and silent, while his solicitor looked increasingly uncomfortable.

"Then came the second marriage scheme involving Augusta Hart. They agreed to it, but as time went on, Samuel and Mary wanted more of an equal split. Mary came to your offices, petitioning for more money. You denied her at first. But on her second visit, you made Mary a different offer: Instead of splitting the reward three ways, you two would cut Samuel out entirely. And permanently. Sebastian Lawlor, you suggested, would be so overwhelmed with grief, he would take his own life."

"This is all unfounded gossip from a woman who is desperate to avoid execution," the solicitor barked. "It will never hold up in court without proof."

He was correct. There was no proof Paul Castelan made any such offer to Mary. Just her confession. Much of it, however, would be supported by evidence.

"Tell me," Jasper said, "did you know Mary and Samuel married shortly before they undertook this second scheme?"

At this, Castelan's chin hitched. He had not known about the marriage, just as Mary had stated earlier at St. Thomas's.

"They didn't tell you, worrying that you would not trust them to properly act the parts of Sebastian Lawlor and the maid, Marianna, without attracting suspicion."

Instead, they'd tucked away their meager savings and wedding bands in a safe deposit box, keeping the memento of their marriage to themselves.

"Mary, of course, told her husband about your idea to eliminate him," Jasper continued. "Together, they formulated an alternative plan. They would conclude the scheme early. Samuel would flee the house, and Mary would join him three days later, as soon as her departure from the Lawlor household would not be deemed too suspicious. They would then leave London and start fresh elsewhere, with the small fortune Samuel had withdrawn from the Lawlor bank account."

Mary had laid out the details of their plan in full.

On the first day, Samuel would let a room at a hotel on Ludgate Hill. He would shave to alter his appearance and purchase different clothing for himself at an unassuming secondhand shop. On the second day, he would go to Threadneedle Street. There, he'd access his safe deposit box at Prescott & Company Bank, which Mary explained Samuel had originally opened on the recommendation of Paul Castelan.

On the third day, Mary would quit her position at the Lawlor household and return to the rooms she had secretly continued to lease while employed as a maid—rooms where she and Samuel would meet from time to time during the months he was married to Augusta. There, she would wait for her husband.

But Mr. Castelan had already found Samuel.

"You anticipated Samuel would visit Prescott & Company to retrieve his possessions. So, you waited for him to exit the bank after emptying his safe deposit box. When he did, you followed him. He made it to Creed Lane before you had the opportunity to corner, and then kill, him."

"I did no such thing," Castelan said calmly. Predictably too.

"The folding knife you were brandishing at Miss Spencer at St. Thomas's proves you did." Jasper withdrew the slip joint blade from the evidence box and opened it.

"Do you see this?" Jasper pointed to where the base of the blade hinged open and locked into place. A brass plate covered the flat top of the wooden handle, which cradled the blade. "You stabbed Samuel Edwards with such force that he was bruised by this plate. The coroner and Miss Spencer noticed a pattern to the bruising. Four round marks, each one three millimeters in size." Jasper tapped the four small studs that pinioned the brass plate in place, then produced the coroner's report for Samuel Edwards. "You can look for yourself, of course. You'll see they are a match."

"Anyone in the city might own a similar blade," the solicitor sputtered.

"You are welcome to take your chances making that argument to the judge and jury." Jasper sat back in his chair, waiting for Castelan to react. The man was conniving and calculating, and surely searching for how to achieve the best possible outcome, given the circumstances and mounting evidence against him.

He turned to his solicitor, and the two men leaned their heads together. After a moment spent whispering back and forth in each other's ears, they faced Jasper again.

"My client agrees to cooperate on the condition that you advocate on his behalf for a partial verdict, reducing the charges to a non-capital offense," the solicitor stated.

Jasper had expected nothing less. No man wanted to hang, and Castelan was savvy enough to weasel his way out of an ultimate punishment.

He glanced over his shoulder at Superintendent Monroe. The man was scowling, as if being in the same room with someone as low as Castelan was able to taint him. He gave a single nod.

"Very well," Jasper said. "What have you to say for yourself?"

After a moment, Castelan raised his chained hands, palms out. "Samuel came at me first. I was simply defending myself."

"Is that so?" Jasper asked, his doubt plain.

"And I did not directly kill Victoria Herrington. Nor did I attempt to take Augusta Lawlor's life. I brought them the laudanum, of course, but Samuel took care of the arsenic and administered both substances to them. I did not physically poison either woman. I merely selected them as potential brides. Samuel did the rest."

His solicitor put a hand on his arm, as if to stop him. But Castelan shrugged it off.

"Samuel Edwards ran the entire scheme. It was his idea," he went on. "He knew the kind of money it takes to operate a business such as mine, and he wanted a partnership. Castelan *and Edwards* Private Inquiries."

"It's easy to rest all the blame at the feet of a dead man, isn't it?" Jasper said.

Castelan shrugged. "It is the truth."

"Even if a jury does believe you," Jasper said, "you will need to answer for why you attacked Mary Keating."

She'd told Castelan that she'd given up the rooms, but earlier, when Jasper had asked the private detective if Samuel and Mary were romantically involved, he must have put together the possibility that she had been lying. His two employees would need somewhere to meet if they were plotting together.

"I went to warn her that you were on your way to speak to her," Castelan said. "That you knew everything. She accused me of selling her out and flew into a raging panic."

"So, she tried to kill you first, just as Samuel did?" Jasper said, his disbelief bordering on amusement. "What about Leonora Spencer? What is your excuse for lunging at her with a knife?"

Jasper's voice had climbed as he spoke, his fury climbing along with it. Had Superintendent Monroe not been present, Jasper would have reached across the table and taken hold of the man by his collar. The private detective made no reply and continued to gloat, as if he knew exactly what Jasper wished to do but couldn't.

"Where is the money Samuel stole from Mrs. Lawlor?" Jasper tried next.

"I cannot say," Castelan replied. "I never saw it."

"If you want the superintendent to advocate for a

lesser punishment, I suggest you start telling the truth," Jasper growled. "The money. Where is it?"

Castelan held his jaw firm for nearly a minute. It was practically visible, the way the man's mind sifted through all the possible ways to extricate himself. Finally, he relented. "My office, in a wall safe."

Jasper exhaled, relieved. Recognizing that the police would crack his safe and find the money anyway, the private detective had decided to capitulate.

"You admit to selecting Victoria Blake and Augusta Hart for this scheme. Why?" he asked next. "Because they were wealthy spinsters? Alone, with no family?"

Castelan frowned, his expression suggesting the answer should be obvious. "They would never have married anyway. Never had children to pass along their fortunes."

"And because of that, they were expendable?" Jasper pressed.

Castelan merely shrugged again and, with cruel indifference, said, "They simply did not matter. No one would miss them."

Jasper pushed to his feet. With a confession and enough evidence to secure a conviction, he was finished here.

"Well, Castelan, you're either going to prison for the rest of your life, or you'll hang. Either way, I suspect you won't be missed, either." He turned to Warnock. "Arrange for his transfer to Newgate."

Jasper stormed from the interview room feeling less than satisfied. Paul Castelan had claimed little responsibility and felt even less remorse for what he'd done. There was no question that he'd organized both schemes and that Samuel Edwards and Mary Keating—while still culpable for murder—had been his underlings. A plea of self-defense when charged with Samuel Edwards's murder would be weak, and Jasper hoped he would not be granted clemency by a judge. But it was now out of his hands.

"Well done, Reid," Superintendent Monroe said as he followed Jasper from the interview room. "He may not hang, but he certainly won't know what freedom tastes like for the rest of his life."

"Thank you, sir. If possible, I would like Mary Keating to be shown some leniency for her confession too. If she lives," he tacked on, as there was still a possibility she would die from her wounds. She was by no means innocent, but in the end, she had at least cooperated with the police.

"I'll see to it that she avoids the noose, at the very least," Monroe said. Then, with a clap to Jasper's shoulder—something that was becoming more and more irritating—added, "The Home Secretary will be pleased with this outcome. It's good publicity for the department. And for you. Rose and I will see you at the dinner Saturday evening?"

It might have been fatigue, or perhaps frustration with Castelan's unrepentant arrogance, but as Jasper searched for a response, he found his well of tolerance for the superintendent's designs utterly drained.

Just then, Leo Spencer entered the detective department. Her lively hazel eyes found him from across the room and brightened even more as she started walking in his direction. No doubt, she'd come to learn what had transpired with Castelan.

"I plan to attend," Jasper replied to the superintendent, his resolve strengthening. "And Miss Spencer will be accompanying me."

Monroe's open expression shuttered, and a frown of disappointment swept away whatever good sentiment he'd exited the interview room with.

"I see," he replied curtly.

"I'm glad you do. Good evening, Superintendent," Jasper said, just as curtly. Without hesitation or a backward glance, he strode forward to greet Leo.

He felt a jaunt in his step, reveling in Monroe's look of disappointment and feeling a thrill of the unknown. Monroe could retaliate, but Jasper would not worry about that yet. He'd done what he needed to do, and it had felt good.

Leo peered at the retreating superintendent's back. "He didn't look very happy. Is it about Mr. Castelan? Did the questioning not go well?"

She followed Jasper toward Warnock's desk, where he'd left his coat and hat.

"Everything went well. He confessed, and he'll be on his way to Newgate shortly," Jasper replied, and to move past the topic of Superintendent Monroe, he added, "I wasn't sure if you'd be able to come. How is Flora?"

Leo and her aunt and uncle had left the hospital while he'd been interviewing Mary Keating. Two warders had gone with them to help transport Flora, whose leg was confined to a cast for the time being. Before departing, Leo said that she would try to make it to the Yard later.

"Mrs. Zhao arrived a short while ago," Leo said. "She sat with Flora while Claude and I arranged the sitting room into a temporary bedroom. It was quite a lot of work, but thankfully, the laudanum the doctors gave Flora kept her calm. She was sleeping when I left." Displaying her usual lack of patience, Leo immediately asked, "What more did you learn from Mr. Castelan?"

Jasper took his coat and hat from Warnock's chair. "I'll tell you everything while we eat."

"We are eating?"

He put on his coat. "Christ, I hope so. I'm starved."

Reaching into his coat pocket for his gloves, his fingers grasped paper instead. The note from Tabitha Pierce. He'd completely forgotten about it in the disorder with Castelan and Mary Keating.

"I should tell you about this," he said, giving Leo the note. "It came in earlier this afternoon for me."

Faint lines creased the space between her brows as she read the brief message. "How did she know you were looking for her?"

"Someone must have heard me while I was in Spitalfields, asking after her." It was the only thing he could think of at least. He'd presented himself as Inspector Reid both at the bakery and at St. Emmanuel's.

Leo's fingers rubbed the sheet of thin paper. It had been torn at one edge, Jasper noted now, as if ripped from a book. She turned it this way and that, peering at it.

"This has been taken from a Bible, I think. Or a hymnal."

Jasper hadn't inspected it closely earlier, but now, he did. "Are you certain?"

He'd been forced to attend Sunday services as a boy at Cheltenham, but he'd hardly ever opened a Bible to follow along.

"We have Bibles in the lobby at the morgue for families

in need of them," Leo said. "It's the thin texture of the paper. Do you see? It's nearly translucent, like onion skin."

Parishioners had been exiting St. Emmanuel's when he and Leo had arrived. There had only been one parishioner, an old woman in a pew; the reverend; and then at the pulpit, the altar boy.

"The boy," Jasper murmured. He saw it now. The messenger boy who had bumped into Jasper's arm in the Yard's lobby. His flaming red ears and cheeks, and straw-blond hair under a tweed cap.

"The altar boy who dropped the chalice at the church," Jasper said to Leo. "He delivered this note."

Tabitha Pierce was at St. Emmanuel's.

"We need to go there. Now," Leo said. "Before the Carters find her."

"I will go," he said. "You've been in enough danger for one day."

She cut in front of him as he started for the door and placed both hands on his chest. "I am coming with you, Jasper Reid. It is high time you accept that I will determine for myself what is too dangerous."

Jasper grated out a curse under his breath, loving the pressure of her hands on his chest and yet also frustrated by her stubbornness. Frustrated…and undeniably awed.

He gestured toward the door. "After you. You bloody, obstinate woman."

Chapter Twenty-One

The cabbie whickered to his horse and slowed the cab as it entered the narrow streets of Spitalfields. Leo was grateful Jasper hadn't wasted time arguing against her accompanying him to the church, but he'd been mostly silent as they drove from Scotland Yard to the East End. His searching eyes had been locked on the window and the streets they were traversing. He had not moved to hold her hand, either, despite their closeness on the single, forward-facing seat.

"Why are you so quiet?" Leo asked. "Are you angry?"

"No. Sorry," he answered, twisting again to peer out the window. "I thought a carriage was following us at first, but I haven't seen it in a bit."

The cab didn't have a back window to peer through, though Leo still twisted to look through the side opening. There were other cabs and carriages, and plenty of pedestrians, but nothing that stood out as suspicious.

"It's nothing. I'm being overcautious," Jasper said. At

last, he settled his hand on hers. "Warnock saw me getting out of Andrew's carriage the other morning at Charing Cross Station."

Alarm itched through Leo's veins. "What did you tell him?"

"That I'd taken on a private inquiry. It was a half-truth. An excuse." He tightened his fingers around hers. "Those are things I despise. I'm not that man, Leo."

"I know you are not." A fervent rush of compassion for him flooded her chest. She only wanted to fix what was wrong. But what could she do? She'd lain awake so many nights, pondering how to sever Jasper's ties with Andrew Carter. No ideas had come... except one: to leave London. But now was not a good time to bring that up. They needed to concentrate on Tabitha Pierce.

A church spire came into view.

"There it is," Jasper said and rapped on the cab's roof. The hansom came to a stop.

"Wait here," he told the cabbie as he and Leo stepped out onto the pavement. The driver shifted uneasily.

"You've got five minutes, guv," he replied.

Leo understood his hesitation. The cabbie had a pocketful of fares; he would soon become a target for thieves if he sat around for any length of time.

The church looked different at night. Cloaked by the darkness, it appeared less tired and worn. Faint light shone cozily through the few stained glass windows facing the street. A pregnant woman, alone and frightened, could easily view a place like it as a sanctuary.

Jasper led them to the arched doors leading into the church, and Leo wasn't surprised when he opened one without meeting resistance. A house of the Lord was supposed to be unlocked and open for all, at all hours. Though it was late in the evening, she expected they would find at least one or two parishioners. But as they entered the nave, their footsteps echoing into the arched rafters above, the place appeared empty.

Several prayer candles on a stand in a back corner were lit, and ahead, at the altar, a few lanterns flickered. The only other light seemed to be coming from the strange section of glass floor Leo had trodden upon the day before.

She went toward it and, stepping along the perimeter of glass, looked down onto the large marble coffin of the first reverend, Julius Hawthorne. The coffin's cap was decorated with an ornate gold cross.

Jasper joined her. "The light." His soft voice bounced through the nave.

Leo saw it too. Light glimmered dully over the side of the coffin and danced along the gold cross. The source was coming from somewhere else within the crypt, out of view.

"Someone is down there," Leo whispered. She peered into the corners of the nave behind them, searching for a door that could lead below. A slim panel of arched wood neighbored the stand of prayer candles.

She started for it, but Jasper took her arm and held her back before she could twist the small brass knob.

"I will descend first," he said.

She assented. He was, after all, the one carrying a weapon. He opened the door, and as Leo had hoped, it led to a narrow stairwell leading down. Muted light shone over steep, twisting stone steps. Unholstering his Webley, Jasper started to descend. Leo stayed close on his heels.

They entered a low-ceilinged crypt, much like the one under the morgue, where old coroner's files, abandoned personal belongings, and storage from the former church were all deposited in a state of disarray. Dank, musty air greeted them. The glass floor above the coffin let in some light, but there was another light source deeper within the crypt, behind arched pilasters.

"Tabitha?" Leo called out, breaking the silence.

The scuffing of shoes on the stone floor came, followed by the extinguishing of the light.

"It is all right to come out, Tabitha. We mean you no harm," Leo said. She took a few strides into the crypt, made brighter only by the filtered light coming through the glass floor above.

Jasper stayed at her side, his Webley lowered. "Mrs. Pierce, I'm Inspector Reid from Scotland Yard, and this is Miss Spencer. I received your message. You asked me to stop looking for you, but I could not, not when I know you to be in danger."

"We know Cillian Carter was murdered," Leo said. "And we know there are dangerous men looking for you. Men who believe you are responsible or at least involved."

The scuffing of shoe soles came again. Then, a timid voice emanated from the dark. "I'm not. I swear, I never would've hurt Cillian."

Leo pinpointed the woman's location in the crypt, though she could not see her. "Then, why are you hiding?"

"Because I saw it happen," Tabitha answered, sounding frazzled. "I saw him killed."

It was just as Leo had thought possible. Unfortunately, hiding also made her appear guilty.

The shadows ahead shifted, and from the direction in which Tabitha had been speaking, two figures took shape. One figure was the tall, berobed reverend to whom Leo and Jasper had spoken the day before. The other was a slender, short woman. Tabitha Pierce appeared as frazzled as she'd sounded as she and the reverend came forward.

"Please," the reverend said, his hands pressed together as if in prayer. "You don't understand the danger Mrs. Pierce is in. I am arranging for her to be taken from the city to somewhere much safer."

"You needn't leave London, Mrs. Pierce. Cillian's father and uncles only want to find the person who murdered him," Leo said. "If you know who that is, and you tell Inspector Reid, he will assure the Carters you weren't involved."

Tabitha shook her head, her brows pulled taut. "Assure them? But they already know it wasn't me. They're looking for me because it was them. *They* killed him. I saw it."

An electric jolt fired up Leo's spine, and her startled eyes clashed with Jasper's.

"Are you certain?" he asked.

"I know what I saw," Tabitha said. "Cillian and me, we were on our way to the Golden Harp when two men came up to us. I'd seen them before with his uncle, Brian, and Cillian didn't seem worried. But then..."

Tabitha's voice cracked, and she paused to take a breath.

"They just…they attacked him. Cillian shouted for me to run. I didn't want to leave him, but I knew I couldn't do a thing to help. So, I did. I ran, and I'll never forgive myself for it."

"You did what you had to," the reverend said to her, resting his hand on her shoulder. "For yourself and your baby."

"Were these men alone?" Jasper asked.

Tabitha shook her head. "I didn't get far before I heard Cillian shout again. This time, he said a name. It was Brian."

"Brian Carter was there?" he asked.

"I looked back and saw him. His uncle. I'd seen him at the Golden Harp a few times. Cillian introduced us." Her voice broke again.

"What did Brian do?" Leo asked.

A thin wail rose from Tabitha's throat. "He drew a knife…across his throat. He killed him. He murdered my Cillian."

As Tabitha wept softly, Leo touched Jasper's arm. "Andrew doesn't know, does he?"

"He never would have asked me to find Cillian if he did." Jasper swore under his breath and swept off his hat. "Why would Brian kill his own nephew?"

"I don't know, but if he finds Tabitha now, he will certainly kill her." Leo turned to the woman. "You must come with us."

She shook her head. "No. Reverend Thorpe says I'm safe here."

"The arrangements are made," the reverend said. "She is leaving before dawn. There is a parish near Birmingham that will give her sanctuary. They will care for her and her child when the babe is born."

Dawn was still several hours away. Leo couldn't shake the urgency for Tabitha to leave, and quickly.

"If we figured out where you've been hiding," Jasper said, "so could Brian before the night is over."

"Yes, he certainly could."

The new voice resounded through the crypt, and Jasper took Leo by the arm. He swung her behind him while raising his revolver. His broad back nearly obscured three men as they emerged from the narrow stairwell, one after another. Tabitha Pierce cried out in panic.

"It's him," she moaned. "Cillian's uncle."

Brian Carter. *Damn.*

He looked nothing like Andrew, who'd been handsome and intense in a charming, if predatory, way. Brian was much older, probably in his mid-forties, with a pronounced brow, blunt nose, and thick torso. The man to his right was familiar: Leo had seen him behind the bar at the Golden Harp. He and the other man flanking Brian gripped knives, the blades long and glinting in the filtered light. Brian, however, held a gun.

"Drop your weapon, Carter," Jasper ordered, but the criminal only chuckled.

"How am I to kill you without it?"

"This is the Lord's house," Reverend Thorpe chastised even as Tabitha wailed. Leo glanced over her shoulder and saw her huddling behind the reverend.

Brian Carter ignored the reverend's rebuke and smiled at Leo. "Too bad you joined that detective agency, Miss Spencer," Brian said. "Oh, aye, I know who you are, love. Imagine my surprise when you started sticking your nose into this business. The lucky little Spencer. Not so lucky now, though, are you?"

Leo began to sweat as the air in the crypt seemed to grow thin.

"You've been following her," Jasper growled. He'd thought a carriage had been tailing them, Leo recalled, and he'd been correct.

"I've been hearing about her detective skills. I was right to put my money on her finding Cillian's whore before those other hacks could," Brian said.

Leo cursed herself for not noticing that someone had been shadowing her. After she and Detective Palmer had gone to the Golden Harp, she presumed.

"Why did you kill your nephew?" Jasper asked.

"Cillian was a muck-up," the man replied casually as though no gun was trained on him. "Gambling and whoring I can let slide, but fraternizing with the Angels? Taking one of their wives for himself? He was bound to start a war. One we don't need."

Jasper had explained to Leo that the Angels and the East Rips were holding a tenuous peace. Cillian's actions could have led to a break down in their accord, but to kill him seemed an extraordinary measure.

"You betrayed your own brother. Your own family," Leo said, dread pooling in her stomach. Jasper's Webley had perhaps six shots. But Brian's weapon was equally deadly. The question was who would strike whom first.

"Cillian was a weak link. He needed taking out before he became too much of a liability," Brian retorted.

"He was a young man who trusted his uncle," Jasper said, his voice rising. "He didn't deserve what you did to him."

"Our family's legacy, every single East Rip, depended on it. Allow a pathetic, inadequate boy to take them over once Sean was dead? Bow down to *him*? Not while I still draw breath."

As Brian explained his decision to murder his nephew, Leo glanced toward the other end of the crypt. There had to be another way out, another set of stairs. If there was, it was draped in shadows.

Shadows that, to Leo's astonishment, suddenly seemed to move.

"You won't be drawing breath much longer once Sean finds out what you've done," Jasper said.

Brian laughed. "And who's gonna tell him? I'm tying up loose ends here. In more than one way, I suppose, with you, Miss Spencer."

"Lower your gun, brother."

The smooth voice stemmed from the back of the crypt, where Leo had seen movement.

Brian's arm came up in a flash, swinging out toward the voice. Jasper recoiled, shoving Leo back as he, too, swiveled.

A beat of silence passed. The world hung on a precipice. And then, an explosion of gunfire filled the crypt. Leo's ears rang from the blasts, and from Tabitha's shrill screams as she, Leo, and the reverend scurried to the far end of the marble coffin. Crouching, Leo turned—and realized Jasper hadn't followed.

"Jasper!" She peered around the coffin's corner. Her heart leapt when she saw him leaning against the broadside of the coffin. It then crashed—one of his hands gripped his abdomen while his other aimed the Webley toward several swarming figures in the diffused light of the crypt.

"Stay back, Leo!" His strained command barely rose

above the report of a gun and the clamor of men shouting and fighting.

Ignoring Jasper's order, she crawled toward him. Panic fluttered in her chest as he dropped to a crouch alongside the coffin, and she saw blood on the hand gripping his right flank.

A man scampered toward them out of the shadows, a knife raised—the bartender from the Golden Harp. Jasper fired his Webley, and the bartender staggered back. Another gunshot rang out, striking the man, though it hadn't come from Jasper's weapon. The bartender fell to the crypt floor.

And then, blessed silence came.

All Leo could hear were her own clipped breaths and Tabitha's whimpering behind the coffin. Leo's nostrils burned with the acrid chemical odor of spent gunpowder. Her eyes watered from the smoke-filled crypt, but through it, she could see three figures lying on the floor. One of them belonged to Brian Carter. He squirmed and moaned, still alive but wounded.

"You're out of bullets, Inspector."

That voice.

Leo pressed closer to Jasper, now seated against the coffin, as Andrew Carter stepped into the light.

"I might have one left," Jasper replied, his voice labored. Andrew chuffed a laugh at his bravado.

"Where are you shot?" Leo asked Jasper, more concerned for him than she was about Andrew approaching them.

"My side. I don't think it's bad," he told her.

"We'll let a doctor decide that," she retorted. She

looked up at Andrew, anxious as to what he intended to do now.

Like usual, his two hulking men were with him. One nudged the body of the bartender with his foot, as if to make sure he was dead. The other was rifling through the pockets of Brian's second cohort, lying prone and motionless on the crypt floor.

"How did you know we were here?" Jasper asked as Leo gripped his arm and helped him to stand.

"I didn't." Andrew turned his attention toward his wounded brother. He sauntered over to him. "I was following Brian. He was watching the detectives Desmond Pierce hired. You said they'd lead you to Tabitha, didn't you, brother? You said you'd bring her to us."

On the floor, Brian writhed and groaned, his teeth clenched in pain.

"But you were hiding something. I could see it in your eyes, Bri, even if Sean and Rory couldn't," Andrew said with deadly calm. "Now, I know what it was."

He'd overheard his brother's confession. Knew Brian had been the one to spill their nephew's blood and toss him into the Thames.

"Get him up," Andrew ordered. His two hired men hauled Brian to his feet, wrenching an anguished cry from the older Carter's throat.

"Just do it, coward." Brian spit a gob of blood as he gargled a cough. "Kill me."

Leo eyed the blood dribbling from his mouth. A bullet had either pierced his lungs, and they were now filling with blood, or his abdomen had been struck. Either way, his wound was likely fatal.

Jasper was not coughing up blood and seemed to be in minimal pain, but those things didn't put her at much ease.

"I think I'll let Sean have that pleasure," Andrew replied to his brother. He jutted his chin to his men. "Get this turncoat into the carriage."

They moved, lugging Brian to the stairs, his legs limp and toes dragging behind him.

Andrew holstered his gun. His eyes caught on Tabitha and the reverend, who had both found the courage to stand and peer over the end of the marble coffin.

"I'll make sure Sean knows the woman had nothing to do with it," Andrew said. "So long as she keeps quiet. You too, Reverend. You should all go before the coppers come. The gunfire will have drawn attention."

Tabitha exchanged a look with Reverend Thorpe. He nodded, and in a flash of motion, she ran for the stairs.

"As for you, Jamey," Andrew said, an eyebrow hitched, "I think you ought to let Miss Spencer take you to a doctor." He turned and followed Tabitha from the crypt.

Leo let out a long breath, her legs quivering. "Let me see your wound."

He lifted his coat, and Leo winced at the blood darkening the right side of his waistcoat. He covered it again. "There isn't time for you to take a closer look. Trust me, it's a minor wound. You have to leave."

She reeled back. "You are staying?"

"It's a crime scene. Men have been killed. I cannot just leave."

He was right, of course. But there were two dead men sprawled on the crypt floor. Jasper would have to give an account as to what happened. Anything having to do with the Carters would only lead to more questions and trouble.

"What will you tell the police when they arrive?"

Jasper slipped his arm from around her shoulder and stood on his own. "I'll figure it out. But you need to go. Explaining why you are here will only complicate things."

Reverend Thorpe had gripped the small cross strung around his neck and now knelt next to one of the dead men, praying.

Jasper led Leo up the narrow stairs, but instead of moving toward the front doors, he directed her to a side entrance. It emptied into a narrow alley. Police whistles shrilled in the distance.

"Minor wound or not, you've been shot," Leo said. "You need to see a doctor."

"I'm certain the bullet grazed my side, nothing more," Jasper replied.

His stoicism infuriated her. "There are vital organs along the right flank, Jasper. Your kidney. Your large intestine. Your liver and gallbladder."

"Christ, not my gallbladder," he muttered sarcastically. "I've grown rather attached to that one."

"The gallbladder is important," she shot back, unamused. "Even flesh wounds can become infected if not properly treated. You have no idea how many people die from sepsis related to infected wounds."

"I am not going to develop sepsis, and I am not going to die. But on the off chance…" He grasped her wrist. "You should kiss me before I expire."

Her next argument dissolved on her tongue as he tugged her to him and crushed his lips to hers. She gave in to his kiss, allowing it to melt her agitation.

Just then, a police whistle, closer than before, pierced the air.

Jasper pushed her from the doorway into the alley. “Find a cab. Go to Charles Street. I’ll join you there as soon as I’m able. Please, Leo.”

She hated to leave him, but he was right. “I’ll wait for you there.”

With that, Jasper stepped back inside and closed the door behind him.

Chapter Twenty-Two

Leo's frantic worry dissolved as she traveled back to Charles Street. All evidence pointed toward Jasper's wound being superficial. Men who were seriously wounded or dying did not kiss feverishly or make humorous quips as he had while shuttling her out of St. Emmanuel's. But she did continue to stew over what explanation he would give the Metropolitan Police constables when they arrived at the church. Deep down, she'd known Jasper would not leave the scene. He had a duty as a police officer, and he took it seriously. It was one of the reasons she loved him.

The windows of Number 23 Charles Street were dark when her hansom pulled up. Mrs. Zhao was still with Claude and Flora, it would seem. Most likely, the housekeeper would not leave until Leo returned to Duke Street.

Using the key the Inspector had given her many years ago, which she kept in her handbag, she let herself in. She set about bringing the house to life, lighting gas sconces, stoking the coal braziers in the study and in Jasper's bedroom, and adding wood to the cottage range in the kitchen.

His home, so much larger than her own, was drafty and difficult to keep warm, but she tried to prepare it as Mrs. Zhao might have. An hour passed. Then another. Leo had made herself a few cups of tea and had tried to read the newspapers in Jasper's study, but she was too restless and found herself in the kitchen, wondering how miffed Mrs. Zhao would be if she were to attempt cooking something.

Thankfully, she heard the front door open before she could try.

"Leo?"

The sound of Jasper's voice accelerated her walk toward the foyer into a run. In the front hall, she found him shrugging out of his coat, his waistcoat darkened with even more blood than before.

"Have you seen a doctor yet?" she asked.

He tossed the coat onto the newel post. "There wasn't a chance. Mrs. Zhao keeps her kit in the kitchen. Top cupboard, next to the range," he told her, then started up the stairs.

"Where are you going?"

"My room," he answered. Then, with a playful smirk lifting the corner of his mouth, "I believe you know where that is."

Heat gathered under Leo's skin as she returned to the kitchen. She noticed a tremor in her fingers as she took the kit down from the cupboard. Flexing her hands, she chastised herself for being so easily flustered. It wasn't like her at all. Nor was the warmed honey consistency of her legs as she made her way up to Jasper's bedroom.

Composing herself, she entered the room—and promptly lost her breath.

He sat on the edge of his bed, and he wasn't wearing a shirt. Peering at his wound, dabbing the deeply gashed skin with a kerchief, Jasper was too distracted to see her gazing at his muscled chest and abdomen in stupefaction. This wasn't the first time she'd seen him stripped to the waist. However, those earlier instances had been prior to their declarations of love, and especially of their longing for one another.

Leo collected her wits and marched into the room, thankful she'd thought to prepare it earlier. Jasper lifted his head and removed the kerchief. The bullet had carved into the flesh of his waist, just above his hip, and as he'd insisted earlier in the crypt, it was merely a graze. An angry, bloody one, though the blood had dried.

"Are you now satisfied that I'm not dying?" he asked.

"Very well, I am satisfied." She hoped he didn't hear how affected she was by the sight of him half dressed. Bypassing him, she set the tin box that held Mrs. Zhao's collection of salves and bandages on the foot of the bed before moving toward his dresser and a decanter of whisky there. She poured them both a finger; it would serve her well to calm her frazzled nerves before tending to his wound.

Leo turned to bring him the whisky and found that he had leaned back, settling against the headboard and pillows. Even with the bloody gash marring his right side, he looked devilishly appealing. His sooty green eyes followed her progress toward the bed.

"I nearly died, and that is the sad pour of whisky I am to receive?" he asked wryly.

Leo stuck out her tongue, splashed half the whisky from one cut crystal glass into the other—and then handed him the less full glass. She sipped from the fuller one as she went to retrieve the tin.

Jasper laughed. "Minx. I suppose I deserved that."

"You did. Now, tell me what happened after I left the church."

As she set about cleaning his wound, he explained how he'd handled the scene at St. Emmanuel's—interspersed with winces and muffled groans when her treatment was too rough.

"I told the constables from H Division the truth—or at least enough of it," he said. "A private inquiry had led me to the church. Reverend Thorpe confirmed that I'd been caught in an altercation between several men and defended myself. The others involved scattered, and I stayed behind to assist the police."

As Leo listened, she located several gaps in his account that would raise questions from his superiors at Scotland Yard. He must have known what she was thinking; he covered her hand with his as she dabbed a wet cloth to clear dried blood from his torso.

"Sergeant Warnock knows Andrew hired me. I cannot keep that secret, not any longer." He exhaled heavily. "I hope to contain it, but if I am questioned, I will be honest."

It would be on his conscience forever if he lied, she knew.

"You should have sutures," she said, after a moment. He lifted his hand from hers.

"Just bandage me. I'll be fine."

Though she disagreed, Leo did as he asked. Once she'd

applied the salve Jasper indicated as Mrs. Zhao's favorite for open wounds, then wrapped his waist with the roll of cotton linen, he took her hand. Jasper brought her knuckles to his lips.

"Thank you," he murmured. "I much prefer your ministrations to Mrs. Zhao's."

Leo chuckled. "I should hope so."

His eyes, glittering with humor, grew serious. "What if the next time Andrew approaches me, it is for something I cannot consent to?"

Being tasked with finding Cillian had at least been legal. Otherwise, Jasper would have rejected the order... and who knew what the East Rip would have done?

"It concerns me too," Leo said softly.

Jasper shifted to sit up straighter. "I know I once told you that no Carter was going to keep me from my life in London."

"Or from me," she said, remembering the moment vividly. He'd just met her at the Harrow train station, after spending four months in Liverpool. She'd started to worry Jasper would not come back to London, the distance from Andrew a layer of protection. As much as she'd missed him while he was away, a large part of her had been grateful Jasper was out of the criminal's reach.

He pulled her hand toward him and flattened her palm against the smooth, warm skin of his stomach. The feel of his bare skin ignited a fluttering in her neck.

"Or from you," he echoed softly.

She heard a caveat on its way. "But?"

Jasper hesitated, his stomach expanding as he took a deep breath. "I think we should consider leaving London."

Leo flinched. The thought had crossed her mind

several times, but she hadn't known that he, too, was considering it. By his grimace, he didn't truly want to.

"It is a lot to think about," he added quickly. "I don't know where we would go or what we would do, and I know your life is here. Your work. Your home—"

"You are my home, Jasper." She adjusted her seat on the bed, pressing closer to him. "I don't want to leave London, but I do want you free of Andrew and the other Carters. I'm only relieved that you haven't suggested leaving the city without me."

"I know it's selfish," he said, his hand cupping hers tighter, "but I'm not giving you up."

Leo leaned forward, until she was bracing her forearm against his chest. "I wouldn't allow you to."

Jasper nudged her forearm aside, removing the barrier between them, and pulled her flush against him. Leo reveled in the hard planes of his chest and abdomen against her softer curves. As she kissed him, her arms wrapped around his neck, her fingers raking into his hair, Leo determined that she could spend hours like this, luxuriating in his kisses, consuming the spice of whisky on his tongue.

However, as his hands—had they always been so large? his palms, so warm?—coasted to the small of her back, to her hips, and then lower to the seat of her skirts, the keen ache of desire came rushing in. Jasper felt it too; he shifted on the bed, trying to press her closer to him.

Leo gasped for a breath of air as she broke from his lips, and at her resistance, Jasper went utterly still. He kept his arms locked around her but pulled back to look into her eyes.

"Forgive me," he said, his breathing ragged. His hand returned to a prim spot on her back. "I was overzealous."

"No. You were perfectly zealous," she replied, with a light laugh and hot cheeks. She again braced herself against his chest with her forearms. The barrier gave her room to sort her muddled thoughts. "We should probably…not be here. In your bedroom. Together."

Jasper formed a sly grin. "Are you worried I won't remain a gentleman?"

Leo blushed. "Not at all. It's only that if we were to…" Her tongue suddenly fell useless. It wasn't like her to stumble over words, even when they were forthright.

Jasper's sly grin stretched wider. He whispered, "Become lovers?"

She grew hot under his steady gaze. "Yes. That. I worry you might feel beholden to propose marriage."

Abruptly, he sat up, which forced her back, into a fully seated position. He was no longer smiling. "*Beholden?*"

"Obligated," she explained.

"I know what beholden means, Leo," he said, then cocked his head. "Have I given you the impression that I don't wish to marry you?"

"I…" She blinked. "Well, no."

He'd confessed love, though not the specific intent to ask for her hand.

Jasper, with unvarnished confusion, added, "We are courting, are we not?"

"We are. But courtships can end," she pointed out, remembering well the moment she'd learned that he'd called off his courtship with Constance Hayes. The release of a tight coil deep in her chest had been liberating. She now knew it had been envy giving way.

"Yes, they can." Jasper reached for Leo's hand. "But not this one. Leo, I have every intention of making you my wife."

A torrent of pleasure coursed through her, nearly drowning in its ferocity, and she forgot how to breathe.

His eyes searched hers. "If you would have me."

A smile trembled to her lips. "Jasper, are you proposing marriage? *Right now*?"

He matched her grin and kissed her fingertips. "That is exactly what I am doing. Will you marry me, Leonora Spencer?"

A spring of tears pricked the corners of her eyes, blurring his handsome face. In the months since she'd come to realize the irritation she felt for Jasper Reid, the provoking exasperation, and the ceaseless, frustrating thoughts of him, was, in fact, love and attraction, Leo had allowed herself to muse, just a little, on what this moment might feel like. The reality was better than anything she could have imagined.

Overcome, she was unable to blink back the tears before a few slipped down her cheeks. "I can think of nothing more wonderful than calling you my husband."

Jasper grinned, his pride like a beam of pure starlight. He dragged her closer, but this time, he lifted her over him and laid her on the bed. Turning onto his uninjured side, he braced himself on an elbow and brushed a lock of hair from her face.

"It may be greedy, but I would very much like to hear you say *yes*," he said.

Leo laughed. "*Yes*, I will marry you, Jasper Reid."

Several minutes later, after indulging in his kisses and grazing hands, Jasper rested his forehead against hers.

"Stay with me tonight." At Leo's mild flinch—she didn't know if it was nervousness or anticipation—he reassured her of his intentions. "Just sleep next to me. Let me hold you. I'm practically an invalid anyhow," he said with a glance toward his bandaged side. He then winked at her. "Not to worry, however. I'll make a miraculous recovery as soon as I am your husband."

Leo let the tension out of her shoulders and legs, and sank deeper into the pillows, delighting in the comfort of his arms surrounding her. She didn't have to try to fix this moment into her memory. It would preserve itself, in all its glittering perfection.

Chapter Twenty-Three

Early the following morning, while the streets were still lit by guttering gaslights, Jasper led Leo out the back door of his house. They strolled toward Trafalgar Square, arm in arm, each of them quiet and contemplative.

His side ached, the pull of skin around the deep gouge carved by Brian Carter's bullet more painful than he'd admitted to Leo the night before. Sutures would have been best, as she'd suggested, but no earthly power would have been able to drag him from his bedroom after Leo had come in, intending to see to his wound.

The soothing sounds of her breaths as she'd slept next to him, in his arms, and the perfect pressure of her body against his, had assuaged the pain of his bandaged side better than any salve could have, that was for certain. Nothing untoward had happened, as he'd promised her, and yet he couldn't help but anticipate bringing Leo into his bed properly. Now that they were engaged to marry, that moment was closer than ever.

"I'll be fine from here," she said, attempting to stop at the intersection of Charing Cross Road.

"I will walk with you to Duke Street," Jasper said. The night brume lingered, and the streets could be just as dangerous in the early morning hours as they were at midnight.

Astonishingly, Leo didn't argue. She only fell back into step with him.

"Will you always be this compliant as my wife?" he asked in good humor.

"Absolutely not," she replied.

For that, Jasper was grateful. He didn't want her to change at all, even if their circumstances might. The idea of leaving London and Scotland Yard put a boulder in his gut, but the events of last night, in the crypt at St. Emmanuel's, presented a heavier burden. He would be made to explain his actions there to Chief Inspector Coughlan. When the department learned he'd accepted a private inquiry from Andrew Carter, it would not reflect well on him or the Yard.

"How will you explain your absence overnight to Claude?" Jasper asked after they'd walked a little further.

With a burst of pleasure, he thought of how soon no excuses would be necessary. She would be his wife, and they would spend every night together.

"I'll tell him the truth. My uncle can handle a little impropriety. Besides, he trusts me. *And* you," she added.

As they came upon the entrance to Duke Street, he loosened his arm from hers. "Tell Mrs. Zhao there is no need for her to rush home. I'm going into the Yard early to write up my report for last night."

Leo rose to the tips of her toes and kissed him; the

kind of chaste kiss husbands and wives gave each other in greeting or before departing. Jasper looked forward to those kisses too.

"I will come by later," he said. "I should pay a call on Flora—and probably ask Claude for permission to marry you."

Leo's soft laughter drifted through the quiet as she started away, glancing over her shoulder a few times. He waited in place until she'd reached her door and gone inside.

The fog had begun to lift, and the increasingly blue dawn brought out pedestrians, carts, and carriages, all starting the business of the coming day. He considered going straight to the Yard before the detective department filled. But he'd refused Leo when she'd risen from slumber, her first words a request to check his wound and change his bandage. Instead, he'd nuzzled her neck and distracted her from the task. As much as he hated to admit it, he did need to check his wound. A bath wouldn't be amiss, either.

Arriving home, he went around to the back door again, expecting to find it locked, as he'd left it. But it wasn't. Instead, the door was ajar by an inch.

Cautiously, Jasper stepped into the short, tiled vestibule at the back of the house, which led into the kitchen. He keenly felt the absence of his revolver and cursed himself for leaving it behind while walking Leo home. It wasn't like him to let down his guard.

He strode slowly toward the kitchen, where lamplight sputtered. He had not lit a lamp before leaving; whoever had picked the lock was at least not lying in wait to ambush him. When he came fully into the kitchen, he found Andrew Carter seated at the table, a cup of tea in front of him.

"Helped myself," he said, taking the porcelain handle and bringing the cup up for a sip. "Didn't think you'd mind."

"Make yourself at home," Jasper said with marked sarcasm. He swept a look around the rest of the kitchen. The two men his cousin usually traveled with weren't present.

"I'm alone," Andrew said.

"What do you want?" Jasper hadn't thought he'd see his cousin so soon after last night.

He remained standing, refusing to take the chair across from Andrew, as if to break bread together.

"Brian's dead," he announced. "He was practically a goner anyway by the time I hauled him in front of Sean and told him what he'd done."

"You didn't come here to tell me that," Jasper said, growing impatient. This man was a blight.

Andrew set down his teacup. "Sean was already suspicious of everyone and everything, but he's gone half-mad now that he knows his own brother betrayed him. Killed his only son." Andrew tapped his temple. "He's not in a good way."

"Tell me why I should care," Jasper replied. From what Jasper could recall of his eldest cousin, Sean had always been a fiend. Violent, coarse, unpredictable. That he'd come unhinged after such a betrayal by his own brother didn't seem far-fetched at all.

"Sean's now on a mission to find out who else has deceived him," Andrew said.

Like his long-dead cousin, James. But then, Jasper

hitched his chin, and a deeper understanding tolled through him. It wasn't just *Jasper* Sean would see as a traitor.

"You've kept me a secret," Jasper said.

"You see my predicament," Andrew said with a solemn nod. "If Sean finds out, he'll consider *me* a turncoat."

If Andrew exposed Jasper's true identity to the other Carters now, he would be putting his own life at risk. Sean might learn for how long Andrew had known the truth—six months. Jasper would certainly tell him—with his dying breath, if need be. Andrew's two hired men, and the one he called Muncie, might even fold under the scrutiny of the East Rips' leader.

That his youngest cousin had come here alone struck him again, this time ominously. Jasper approached the table and braced against it with his fists. "Where are your men, Andrew?"

He held Jasper's glare, his ice-blue eyes tranquil. Andrew didn't answer. He didn't need to. If they had posed any threat to Andrew, they were likely already dead.

That left Jasper.

"You came here to clean up your mess," he said. *Christ.* If he got out of this alive, he would never again take off his Webley.

"I've come to make you an offer," Andrew replied. "I think you'll take it."

Jasper stayed vigilant, ready to move at any flinch of Andrew's hand or body. "I'm listening."

"We part ways and forget each other exists."

Jasper restrained his burgeoning hope, unwilling to let down his defenses. "Why not just kill me?"

Sean would have no chance of finding out about Andrew's betrayal then.

But it seemed Andrew was already one step ahead of Jasper.

"Because if I did, your Miss Spencer would know it was me," he replied. "She'd make trouble, and I can't have any noise reaching Sean, inspiring any doubt."

Jasper went cold. Then hot. "And you wouldn't just kill her?"

"Believe it or not, Jamey, I'm not a complete villain," Andrew answered. "I don't kill women."

"No, you just threaten to pluck out their eyes with a knife."

Andrew grinned at the reminder of that interaction. Jasper's mind whirled. His cousin, however, waited patiently for an answer.

"You will stay away from Miss Spencer, and from me," Jasper said, parsing out the terms of the proposal. "For good."

Andrew stood up from the chair. "Don't make me regret this, Jamey. I don't want to have to *discover* you all over again."

Jasper said nothing as Andrew picked up his hat from the table and slipped it on. Then, the East Rip strode out through the back door without another word. As soon as he was gone, Jasper's legs nearly buckled. He sat on the edge of the table, trying to grasp what had just happened.

Andrew would not *discover* Jasper again. If he did, he ran the risk of Sean learning it wasn't the first time, and that Andrew had betrayed him by keeping it a secret—and by planning to extort Jasper for his own benefit.

The betrayal would not be as grievous as Brian's had

been, but it would still be deceit. Andrew was cunning; he would protect himself, even if it meant losing out on having an associate to lean on within the Metropolitan Police Force.

The shuffling of feet in the short vestibule to the back door brought Jasper to his legs again. But it was only Mrs. Zhao, her carpetbag, which she took on overnight visits to her sister's home in Limehouse, clutched in the crook of her elbow. She threw a glance over her shoulder.

"Who was that man?" she asked.

"Leo was supposed to tell you there was no rush to come home," Jasper said.

Mrs. Zhao raised a brow and dropped her bag on the table. "She said you'd been shot. I wanted to check your wound to see if it had festered before you left for work for the day."

As it was with Leo, there wasn't any use arguing with his housekeeper when she had her mind set.

"You didn't answer me," Mrs. Zhao said as she fetched her kit from the cupboard, which Leo had returned that morning. "Who was that man I just passed at our back door?"

Jasper shrugged out of his jacket and started on the buttons of his waistcoat, finally allowing himself to breathe. "With any hope, he is someone we'll never see again."

THANK YOU FOR READING HAZARD OF THE PURSUIT, BOOK 6 IN THE SPENCER & REID MYSTERIES.

Please leave a rating and review on Amazon to help other readers discover the series.

Keep up with me and the Spencer & Reid Mysteries by joining my newsletter.

You can pre-order Leo and Jasper's next book, proof of violence, coming in August 2026.

Also by Cara Devlin

The Spencer & Reid Mysteries

SHADOW AT THE MORGUE

METHOD OF REVENGE

COURIER OF DEATH

CLOAKED IN DECEPTION

TEARS FOR THE FORSAKEN

HAZARD OF THE PURSUIT

PROOF OF VIOLENCE

The Bow Street Duchess Mysteries

MURDER AT THE SEVEN DIALS

DEATH AT FOURNIER DOWNS

SILENCE OF DECEIT

PENANCE FOR THE DEAD

FATAL BY DESIGN

NATURE OF THE CRIME

TAKEN TO THE GRAVE

THE LADY'S LAST MISTAKE (A Bow Street Duchess Romance)

The Sage Canyon Series

A HEART WORTH HEALING

A CURE IN THE WILD

A LAND OF FIERCE MERCY

THE DARING TIMES OF FERN ADAIR

A Romantic Historical Fiction Novel

THE TROUBLE WE KEEP

A Second Chance Western Romance

About the Author

Cara is the author of the bestselling Bow Street Duchess Mystery series. She loves to write romantic historical fiction and mystery, especially when the romance is a slow burn and the mystery is multi-layered and twisty. She lives in rural New England with her husband and their three daughters. Cara is currently at work on the rest of the Spencer & Reid Mysteries.

www.ingramcontent.com/pod-product-compliance
Lightning Source LLC
LaVergne TN
LVHW100520110826
845146LV00002B/714

* 9 7 9 8 9 9 2 3 0 5 7 5 3 *